Tangling a Web of Deceit

by

Laura Freeman

Cover Art by *The Wild Rose Press, Inc.*

The Wild Rose Press, Inc.
PO Box 708
Adams Basin, NY 14410-0708
Visit us at www.thewildrosepress.com

Publishing History
First Edition, 2024
Trade Paperback ISBN 978-1-5092-5397-5
Digital ISBN 978-1-5092-5398-2

Published in the United States of America

Dedication

To my lunch book buddies: Dorothy, Ellin, Jaime, and Stephanie. Thank you for all your support.

Praise

Chapter One

Emily heard the *squish* beneath her foot before the foul odor rose in a pungent cloud from the freshly crushed pile of soft dog poop. She froze on the limestone towpath and fought her gag reflex. She'd worked in a morgue. She could handle the smell of processed dog food, but what had this creature eaten? The pile looked like thick mustard. Was that normal?

She moved to the grass and scraped her running shoe back and forth in rapid jerks to remove the excrement. Each stroke heated the remaining goop and emitted new scents.

"What happened, Emily?" Her former boyfriend, Charles, turned and jogged in place on the pathway. "Did you get a cramp? I told you to warm up. How could you forget everything I taught you about running?" He wrinkled his nose. "What is that smell?"

She pointed at the towpath. "I stepped in that yellow blob."

He gagged and made a face that threatened a larger mess. "Why would you do that?"

Did he think she had done it on purpose? Sarcasm dripped from her excuse. "Because I hate running, and I thought this would be a great way to avoid it."

"If you hate running, why did you agree to come today?"

Emily had been asking herself that same question

for the last mile. Charles was competitive. He liked to win. No, he had to win. His masculine pride demanded he was better than all others. For the last mile he'd bragged about his new job, how much money he was going to make, and how all his dreams were coming true but one. He'd asked her on the run because he expected her to reconsider and renew their relationship after his grandiose sales pitch.

She expected to compete in sports, for jobs, and in life, but she wanted her romances to be a partnership, not a contest. She didn't miss his badgering, his questioning of every decision, or how he compared everything she did to his own accomplishments. Then there was the sex. Who rated a sexual performance? He had sucked all the fun out of the relationship. Why had she agreed to join him? She offered a lame but honest excuse. "Because you asked me, and I didn't have a good reason for saying no."

"If you didn't want to come, you could have lied and made up an excuse. You have to set boundaries, Emily, or people will walk all over you," he lectured.

Which was why she had broken off the relationship with him. She knew her own shortcomings. She was a people pleaser, which meant she agreed to whatever crazy idea someone suggested. To a point. Even though she had relegated Charles to friend-only status, he had made it clear during the run he still harbored hope for more. Accepting his invitation to jog had been a mistake. "Why don't you run ahead and catch me on the return lap?"

"Are you sure?"

She waved at him to move along. "Get out of here."

He joined the group of runners without even a

sympathetic backward glance. She'd made the right decision, but she led a cursed life. No one else had stepped in the pile of dog doodoo. She had scraped the sole of her shoe clean, but the smell persisted. She raised her foot. The soft yellow paste had filled the open spaces in her tread. "Yuck."

Nausea threatened, and she blew out a few short breaths to control the involuntary reaction. She'd interned at the county medical examiner's office her final semester at college and had learned not to throw up at the plethora of smells while watching the doctor perform an autopsy. Although her degree was in criminal justice, she had taken lab courses in chemistry and forensics because her dream job was to be a forensic investigator. She had taken the Medicolegal Death Investigators exam last week and was waiting for the results. Others didn't understand her fascination with forensic science, but she enjoyed finding the clues that solved a crime.

Scraping her new shoe until the tread wore down was not an option. She needed to dig into the crevices and extract the foul mess or wash it away. The national parks had converted the limestone towpaths used by mules to tug the flat boats through the shallow waters of the canal into hike and bike trails.

Built across the state of Ohio in the nineteenth century to transport products and passengers to Lake Erie or the Ohio River, much of the canal had been destroyed in 1913 because of flooding. This section of the canal remnant resembled a wide ditch, which had filled with muddy water from heavy rains last night.

Emily checked for poison ivy before plopping down on the ground and pulling her shoe free. Using a small twig, she scraped the grooves of the tread clean and then carefully rinsed the rubber sole in the water to remove the remaining goop. She waved the sneaker one more time through the water and sniffed. The worst of the smell was gone. She shook her footwear to rid it of any water and set it aside to dry as she studied her surroundings.

Few people outside Ohio knew that between the crowded metal buildings of Cleveland and Akron was a green necklace, a wooded parkland that surrounded the Cuyahoga River and historic canal. Birds chirped their spring mating calls, squirrels dashed up and down the bark of the trees, and new leaves sprouted on overhead branches.

Charles and the other runners came early to beat the crowds. Running had kept her warm, but the sweat on her body was evaporating, and her shorts and tank top weren't enough to battle the chilly morning air of May. She tugged her shoe on, tied the laces, and stood, ready to jog.

Did an object in the water wave at her? She stared at the smooth surface shimmering beneath the sunlight and squinted at something poking out of the water. It didn't look like leaves or an animal. It looked like human fingers.

Emily removed the small backpack where water, car keys, mace, and her phone were stored. She took a photo. She tapped on the edit icon for a closer view. They looked like fingers on the digital display.

She stared at the flesh poking above the still water, analyzing her find. Four fingers and a thumb painted with red nail polish had to be attached to a body. She'd never discovered a dead person before. She fought a growing panic as she rushed to the towpath and searched for someone to help. Nobody was in sight. She was on her own. *Remain calm and think.*

She returned and faced the evidence as the hand beckoned to her for help. She did what everyone was trained to do. She dialed 911.

"What is your emergency?"

"I think I found a body in the canal."

Silence. "What sort of body?"

"A dead body, but all I can see are fingers sticking out of the water."

"All you see are fingers?"

"Yes, but I'm pretty sure they're attached to something. I know it sounds like a prank, but I worked for the medical examiner's office, and I think you should send someone to investigate."

More silence. "What is your location?"

"I'm on the towpath just north of the Ida Road park entrance."

"I'm going to send a patrol car to the parking lot. Can you mark your location and walk to the entrance to meet the officer?"

"Yes, I can do that."

"Don't touch the fingers."

That was the last thing Emily planned. She arranged two pieces of wood into an X just like on a treasure map. What else could she do to help? Her former employer would know. She called the medical examiner's office.

The secretary answered. "This is the Summit County Medical Examiner's Office. Sharon speaking. How may I help you?"

"Sharon? Hi. This is Emily Stevenson. Remember me? I interned last semester."

"You were the student who didn't faint during the

autopsy, right?"

"I was a bit light-headed but stayed upright." It had been a moment of pride when the other intern collapsed in a heap.

"Are you calling about the forensic investigator position? We're accepting resumes."

"I sent one in, but that's not why I'm calling. You're not going to believe this, but while I was running, I stepped into dog poop. That's not important." She focused. "I think I found a body in the canal."

"You're not sure?"

"Right now, it's just a hand poking out of the water, but I called 911. They're sending a police officer. Should I do something in the meantime?"

"Let me talk to the medical examiner and see if she wants you to do anything."

Emily jogged in place to stay warm.

The doctor came on the line. "Emily? What can you see?"

"Just fingers poking above the water. I took a photo with my phone."

"Can you take some more photographs and send them to me? Do you have our email?"

"Yes. I'll send them now." She zoomed in and sent the photos. "Do you see them?"

"They look like fingers. You know what it's like on a Saturday. We're busy, so I could use your help. Are there any broken plants or footprints in the area of the body?"

She looked around. "Nothing looks disturbed. I don't see any footprints, and it rained last night. The body could have been dumped elsewhere and floated down."

"We'll let the police figure that part out."

"Will you send out a van?"

"The last vehicle in our fleet went out to pick up a victim at a shooting ten minutes ago. I'll notify the fire department to dispatch a paramedic team to collect the body. Can you document the extraction for us? The police don't always remember to take photos."

As an intern, she'd assisted in documenting crime scenes but never alone. This was an opportunity to prove herself. "No problem. I'll send the photos to you when I'm done."

"I'll have Sharon notify the paramedics you'll be on the scene."

She made sure the call was disconnected before letting out a squeal of excitement. The doctor wanted her to take photos. She allowed herself a few minutes of celebration before accepting reality. She was pragmatic, and her resume was one in a pile of potential candidates.

Her wet shoe squished as she ran down the towpath and turned off at the Ida Road entrance. She waited at the information kiosk at the edge of the parking lot. A park ranger pulled into his designated spot. The dispatcher must have notified the park officials about her find. They worked with local law enforcement whenever crimes occurred in the park. She waved after he stepped out of his truck.

He grabbed his wide-brimmed hat that matched an olive-green uniform and headed her way. "Are you the person who called about a possible body in the canal?"

"Yes, sir. I'm Emily Stevenson."

"Ranger Motts." He tapped a finger to his name tag and looked around. "Where is it?"

She pointed in a northern direction. "Down the

towpath. I marked the spot."

He nodded as if approving her action. "We better wait for the police." He rose on his toes and fell back onto his heels several times. "Do you come to the park often?"

"I come all the time. I joined some friends to jog this morning. They ran ahead after I stepped in dog poop." *Brilliant conversation, Em.*

He pointed to the kiosk. "We provide plastic bags to clean up after their dogs, but we can't force owners to use them."

"I'm sure most do. This dog must have been ill." She lowered her voice and cupped her hand as if sharing a secret. "You do not want to know about it."

He had a confused expression. "Why not?"

Her explanation was interrupted by a black-and-white police car screeching to a sudden halt along the curb instead of pulling into a parking space.

"Hot dog," Emily criticized under her breath.

The police officer stepped out. He wore a long-sleeved shirt tucked into a heavy leather belt with a gun on his right hip and handcuffs next to it that reflected the morning sunlight. He was young, tall, and swaggered toward them. His dark curly hair framed pale-blue eyes, but he wasn't a pretty boy. His nose had a scar along the narrow ridge and might have been broken at some time. It gave his delicate features a rugged quality.

Her heart did a little flip-flop, but she quelched any emotions. No one found romance over a dead body. Besides, Charles had shaken her confidence about judging the opposite sex. He had seemed perfect before he tried to sculpt her into something she didn't want to resemble.

Chapter Two

Officer Travis O'Toole had started his Saturday shift trying to keep a couple from killing each other after an argument about who forgot to pay the car insurance on their recently totaled car. Wedded bliss. It made him appreciate the single life.

He welcomed the call about a possible body in the canal. There was an opening in the detective bureau division, and he had applied. This could be a chance to prove himself.

Darrow Falls was a small town on the edge of the park. They depended on visitors to stay at their hotels and eat at their restaurants. In return, the police responded to crimes committed in the park.

A ranger was waiting by the kiosk where the parking lot and trailhead merged. A young woman in shorts and a tank top stood next to him. She hopped from one foot to the other and rubbed her arms to stay warm. Her long legs curved in and out in graceful lines that continued upward to a small waist and swelled into well-shaped breasts.

As a cop, Travis needed to behave in a professional manner, but as a man, he could appreciate a well-toned figure. He liked the athletic type, but it had been a long time since he had a girlfriend to share his life. Women didn't mind dating a cop, but they didn't want a serious relationship. He needed to concentrate on the ranger.

"Officer Travis O'Toole." He extended his hand.

"Ranger Motts."

"Dispatch said you found a possible floater."

"This young lady reported it." Motts stepped aside and nodded toward the woman.

Her blond hair was braided along her scalp and down her back, but wisps had escaped and framed a face that he wouldn't forget anytime soon. Her eyes were a mixture of colors labeled as hazel with no sign of tears. She appeared too calm for someone who had found a body. She shivered, and a mile of goose bumps decorated her exposed legs. The sun was warming the cool air but hadn't reached a comfortable temperature for bare skin.

He went to his car and brought back a blanket. "It's chilly. You can wrap this around you to stay warm."

She draped it over her shoulders and grasped it in front. "Thank you."

He removed a small spiral notebook from a side pocket in his cargo pants and flipped to a clean page. "Can you tell me what happened?"

"I was running and stepped in dog crap." She lifted her shoe, but the sole was clean. She frowned. "I cleaned it off in the canal. When I was done, I saw fingers above the surface of the water." She raised her hand and posed her fingers. "I called 911 and marked the spot like the dispatcher told me." She had her phone in her hand.

He wrote down the quick burst of facts she had shared. "What's your name?"

"Emily Stevenson."

"Do you have any ID?"

She pulled off her backpack and searched the contents.

"Were you running alone?"

She paused to look at him. "Oh no. I was with a group of friends from college. We were celebrating graduation, and one of them thought running through the park would be a great way to spend time together before everyone went their separate ways. We were just north of here when my shoe met fecal matter. I told the others to run ahead. I'll catch up with them when they return." She removed her wallet and handed him her driver's license.

He wrote down her address and added her birth date. She was twenty-two. He had three years on her. "Phone number?"

Emily recited the numbers. "You can verify my information in the fingerprint database."

He studied her innocent face. "You're in our system?"

"I didn't commit a crime." The corners of her mouth turned up as if she was teasing him. "I interned at the medical examiner's office. I had to pass a background check. Like teachers and cops."

Her words took time to register. "You worked with dead people?"

Her smile darkened to a frown, and the chill wasn't from the air. "I helped figure out how they died. I majored in criminology."

He had majored in criminology. "You want to be a cop?"

"No, I want to solve crimes using facts and science."

She wasn't so attractive anymore. "I'm a cop. I solve crimes."

"Are you a detective?"

Her skepticism made him mad. "And you found a body while running?" He looked around. "Is this a hoax?"

"I resent that comment." She tilted her chin, and her tone of voice had attitude. "I take my career seriously. I would never call in a false report knowingly. But I did see fingers above the water. They had to be attached to a body."

"Now you admit you didn't see the body."

"No, but the fingers weren't floating on top of the water," she defended. "They were attached to a hand, which had to logically be attached to an arm, which had to ultimately be attached to a body. Would you prefer that I ignored it instead?"

Travis felt dizzy. They were having a spat over whether or not a dead body existed. "Can you show me where you saw these fingers?"

She spun on her heels and trotted down the path with the blanket billowing like a cape. "Follow me."

He easily came alongside her. "I'm sorry if I hurt your feelings."

"I don't bruise easily." She let out a deep breath. "I can understand why you would be skeptical. It's not every day someone finds a body in the canal."

"This would be my first."

She flashed a smile. "I'll be gentle."

Her words sent his heartbeat into overdrive. If she became an investigator for the medical examiner, their paths could cross in the future. *Please, let them collide.* "I don't mind rough as long as the hands are gentle."

She blushed but didn't read him the riot act. The department had rules about behavior while on duty, and he had no intention of breaking them. They were both flirting. Why not? They were young and single. At least she wore no ring.

He nearly collided with Emily when she abruptly stopped. She turned off the towpath into an open area along the edge of the stagnant water. Two twigs had been crossed on the ground.

"X marks the spot. Hey, didn't Stevenson write *Treasure Island*?"

Her smile was accompanied by a soft laugh. "Yes, but no relation."

Travis walked to the edge of the bank. A log broke the surface near the far side, but he couldn't see any evidence of a hand poking above the surface, let alone an entire body. "Where did you see these fingers?"

"I don't see anything but some old leaves floating on the water." Ranger Motts had trotted behind them and looked at Emily with disbelief. "Perhaps you mistook a leaf for a hand."

Travis gave her a reassuring smile. He liked to give people the benefit of doubt before coming to a conclusion. Besides, he didn't like the smirk on the ranger's face. He had two older sisters. They would have twisted his ear if he looked at them in that condescending way.

Emily searched her phone and showed them the picture she had taken. "What does this look like?"

Travis studied the display. She was right. It looked like human fingers. He glanced at the swamp and turned to Motts. "How deep is it?"

"Normally only a couple of feet, but it's been raining on and off for the last three days, so the water is high. It could be close to four feet in the middle. Then there's the mud. You could sink a foot before hitting the clay bottom."

"Clay?"

"It's why the canal holds water. The builders lined it with clay."

Travis sighed as he considered his options. "I suppose you don't have waders in your truck?"

"Try this." Emily picked up a long thin tree branch that was on the ground. "You might be able to hook something and drag it to shore."

"Whoa!" Motts waved his hands and grabbed the branch. "No disturbing nature."

She frowned. "It's a branch."

"People think they can collect specimens. Pretty soon the woods are stripped bare." He placed the branch back where she had picked it up off the ground.

Travis kicked the twigs marking an X on the ground before Motts saw them.

Emily mouthed, "Thank you."

He turned to the ranger. "Do you have a rake or something to snag the body?"

"I have a pole with a hook on it in my truck," Motts said.

"That should work."

"I'll go get it." He hesitated. "Don't touch anything until I return."

Emily watched him head back along the towpath. "He seems territorial."

"They don't like it when people dump bodies in the park."

Her mouth dropped open. "Is it a common occurrence?"

"Unfortunately, yes. Skeletal remains were found down the road, and a couple was shot last year sitting on a park bench. Every time someone is attacked or murdered in the park, attendance dwindles."

"This park is free. They only charge for the use of the shelters."

"But it relies on donations. People won't give money if they don't think the park is safe."

She sighed. "I hate the fact that money motivates everything."

"That's what a capitalistic society is all about."

"Are you rich, Officer Travis O'Toole?"

"I'm a cop. What do you think?"

"Poor but proud." She spread the blanket on the ground and sat in the sun with her arms wrapped around her bent knees. She studied her phone and the water as if the fingers would reappear.

Travis wanted to join her, but it was hardly the time for a picnic. If there was a body, he wanted to find it. Other officers had bid for the detective position. This could give him the advantage he needed to be noticed.

Motts returned, carrying a long pole with a grappling hook on the end.

Travis took it. "This is perfect." He reached the pole out as far as he could, dropped it into the water, and pulled.

Nothing.

He dragged the canal with the hook, pulling a few dead leaves from the bottom and stirring up muddy swirls. "Let me see that photo again."

Emily stood and showed him her phone's image. "Maybe it moved."

"Yeah, she swam to deeper waters."

The corners of her mouth lifted slightly. "At least she didn't have to worry about holding her breath."

He cast the pole into the water again. "You have a morbid sense of humor."

"I inherited it."

"You're admitting to a dark side in your DNA?"

"My father runs a funeral home." She shrugged. "The family was expected to help with the business."

Was she kidding? "You embalmed dead people?"

"No." She shook her head. "You need training for that. I placed the flowers around the casket and set up chairs. But attending all those funerals made me curious about the journey. I wanted to know why they ended up dead."

"Ergo, your career choice." He dragged the pole toward them. "I prefer to keep people from being killed."

"And I admire your optimistic goal." She pointed to another spot. "Try over there."

"I heard the call about a possible floater in the canal. Did you find anything?"

Travis recognized the voice of Detective David Crane as he stepped into the opening behind him. *Great.* Crane would help decide who to hire as the new detective. It wouldn't help his case if there was no body. "I need waders. Do you have any, Detective Crane?"

A tremor of a smile broke on Emily's bow-shaped lips. "Crane?"

Travis gave her a warning look. Crane was sensitive about his name. Maybe it was because, with his stilt-like legs and hook nose dominating his long face, he resembled the blue herons who inhabited the park during the summer months.

"Do I look like a fly fisherman? When do I have any free time to stand in a river and trick a fish to bite? I don't even like fish." Crane's voice had a nasal rattle that rose in pitch with each question. He was known for his impatience and lack of humor.

"That would be a no on the waders?" she asked with a smile that would have charmed any man but Crane.

"Who are you?"

She extended her hand. "Emily Stevenson. I found the body."

"What body?" Crane looked up and down the canal. "I don't see anything. I hope you're not wasting my time."

She showed him her phone display. "I don't think she swam or walked away."

Travis cringed. Crane ate officers for breakfast, and Emily was making witty remarks. At least he couldn't fire her. His own employment was questionable.

Crane raised his voice, which was already loud. "How do you know it was a woman?"

She pointed at the photograph. "Looks like red nail polish on the fingers. But it could be a man who likes to look pretty."

Crane reddened and pointed to the same spot where Travis had been casting the pole. "Try over there." He stepped away from Emily who resumed her seat on the police blanket.

She was naïve and courting trouble. An experienced person would have realized Crane did not appreciate jokes while on the job.

Travis repeated the toss and drag motion to the rhythm of Crane's voice as he bragged about his latest drug bust. He had the gang surrounded when a female voice interrupted his story.

"Officer O'Toole. Travis!" Emily stood and pointed at the canal. "Look!"

He had snagged something that bobbed to the surface. A hand with bright-red nail polish broke the surface as if to wave.

Crane jabbed the air with his forefinger and rushed to the edge of the canal waters. "Whoa! What have you got there?"

Travis eased the tension on the pole as a mass of dark hair splayed out on the water's surface.

Crane smacked him on the back. "You caught yourself a live one, O'Toole."

"You mean a dead one," Emily corrected.

Crane stuck his beak in her face. "You trying to get on my bad side, girl?"

She didn't budge. "I'm trying to clarify the facts, sir. The woman is dead."

"And it's my job to determine how she died," he defended.

"Actually, it's the medical examiner's job to determine cause of death. Your job would be to find out who murdered her and why."

Travis made a cutting motion across his neck, but Emily gave him a questioning look. Didn't she understand a simple signal to shut up?

Crane's eyes narrowed, and he jabbed a finger in her direction. "Why aren't you upset about finding a dead body?"

Her chin tilted in defiance. "I am upset. A woman is dead."

"Where are your tears?"

"Like you, I have a job to do. Does a lady doctor faint at the sight of blood? Does a woman soldier run away on the battlefield? Does a female paramedic become hysterical when confronting a mangled body at the scene of an accident?"

He spat and sputtered. "The women I know scream

when they see a dead body."

Her hands went to her hips in a pose of defiance. "I am not one of them."

Emily had guts. She hadn't gone weak-kneed or thrown up at the sight of the corpse bobbing to the surface and now was arguing with Crane and winning. Who was this woman?

Travis tugged on the body, but it snagged on something and stopped just out of arm's reach.

He stared at the water. He didn't want to think about the snapping turtles, water snakes, or the fact a corpse was in the water. He handed the pole to Crane and called to Motts who was on the towpath talking on his phone. "How deep did you say it was?"

"You won't know until you go in." He joined them and stared at the muddy water as an arm and shoulder rolled to the surface. "That's a body."

"There goes your theory about rotting leaves," Emily said.

Motts reddened. "I'm sorry."

She softened her voice. "If it's any consolation, I was hoping it turned out to be a bunch of leaves, too."

He stared at the water. "This is bad for the park."

"Ranger, you're going to have to keep everyone away from this area." Crane pointed to a couple of bird watchers with binoculars who had paused to see what was going on. "It's a crime scene now."

"I'll have to contact my supervisor about this new development." He stepped a few feet away to talk on his cell phone.

"Move along," Crane instructed the ornithologists, who hastily departed. He still intimidated some people.

Emily took photographs of the floating corpse.

"What are you doing?" Crane demanded.

"The medical examiner asked me to document the crime scene."

"Why?"

She paused to face him. "I worked as an investigator for the ME's office the past five months. I called them when I saw the fingers. The doctor told me to take photos."

"Is that so?"

"Yes." Her voice remained sweet in spite of Crane's sarcasm. "You can call her to confirm it."

"I'll do that."

Chapter Three

Emily documented the floating corpse. Unrelated pictures could be deleted, but initially everything needed to be recorded as possible evidence. She looked up to find the two men staring at her. "I'll email these to the coroner's office." She didn't want Crane ordering her out of the area and losing her opportunity to impress the medical examiner.

Travis sat down on the blanket she had abandoned and removed his socks and shoes.

"Maybe I should go in," Crane suggested but made no move as Travis rolled up his pants.

He had muscular legs with a trace of dark hair. Very masculine. Why did she have to be attracted to men? They always disappointed her. One date had berated her for smacking a mosquito sucking blood out of her arm. He loved all creatures to the extreme. She loved animals as long as they didn't bite, suck her blood, or leave poop for her to step in.

Travis stood and removed his gun belt, which he handed to Crane. He unbuttoned his shirt and dropped it on the blanket. Emily automatically shook it out and folded it neatly. He raised a single eyebrow in question.

"I enjoy folding laundry. It's therapeutic. You ought to see me tri-fold a towel."

"Tri-fold?"

"I like large towels. You have to fold them over

twice and then tri-fold them, or they're too big to store."

He gave her that look she was painfully familiar with. She was analytical, too smart for most men, and had never learned to curb her tongue and act stupid. She couldn't help saying something that wounded their male egos. They were intimidated or outright scared. It was one of the things Charles had tried to change. Her tongue was scarred from biting it before any words escaped to offend his delicate sensibilities. When she ultimately made her feelings clear, he had fled in perfect running form. She was doomed to be single.

Travis pulled on the straps to his bulletproof vest. His arms knotted with well-toned muscles as he removed it. "These things don't wash well."

He probably had women begging him to write them a ticket. Cops were popular leads in romances. She was the best friend in a love story. In any story. A sigh escaped her lips. He looked at her as if he could read her thoughts. She tried to think of a cutting remark to put him in his place, but words escaped her. He was too yummy.

"I'll find a clean place on the blanket for it." Emily laid her hand on his bare arm. A thin layer of dark hair covered the hard muscles of his forearm, and she absently stroked the silky texture. Could she borrow him for a night of rapturous enjoyment? She'd wager he knew how to have fun between the sheets and wouldn't want her to fill out a scorecard in the morning.

He handed her the vest, and she placed it on the blanket where his clothes were arranged in a neat row.

"You're very orderly."

"The medical examiner likes items bagged and tagged."

"I bet they liked you."

"I hope so. I applied for a job."

"The paramedics are here," Motts announced from the towpath where he had been ushering spectators along.

Emily joined him. The ambulance beeped in the distance and stopped at the edge of the towpath, which was too narrow for the wide vehicle to back up to their location. Two paramedics unloaded a stretcher.

"I should help direct them." Motts hurried away.

Crane looked at the body floating in the muddy water. "I better tell them to bring a body bag." His long legs gobbled up the distance.

Emily returned to the canal. "I guess you're on your own."

His blue eyes sparkled with mischief. "If I don't make it back, promise to take care of my cat."

She laughed. Like her, he used humor to handle stressful situations. "What's your cat's name?"

"Sly. Short for Sylvester."

"I bet he earns his name."

"You'd win. He likes to pounce when you least suspect it."

She'd like to surprise him with a pounce. Who was sending pheromones into the air? She needed to control her sex drive, which was humming.

Travis pulled a pair of latex gloves out of his pants pocket and snapped them on. He stepped gingerly into the mucky water and sank up to his knees, wetting the folds in his trousers. Black swirls rose to the surface along with decayed leaves stirred up from the bottom.

Emily summed up the experience in one word. "Yuck."

He met her gaze. "It's not so bad." He took another

step and slipped. He waved his arms to regain his balance.

She took a picture. "You'll want this for your next Christmas card."

He chuckled before grimacing with the next step. "Email me a copy."

He followed the pole to where the body had snagged. He tugged on the end near the hook. The corpse in a red sequined blouse bobbed to the surface. "Whoa!" He stepped back as the body settled in the water.

Emily snapped a photo. Doing a task kept her from thinking about the reality of a dead woman floating in the canal. She would process her feelings later. The body was definitely a woman. Long dark hair was tangled in a wet mop of thick tendrils around her head. Her face was turned sideways and just above the surface. It was bloated, but there were traces of makeup smeared across the discolored skin. If she had been attractive, it was hard to tell anymore.

Travis walked backward, using the hook to pull the body with him until he reached the shore.

Crane had returned with two paramedics. They pulled the body up out of the water as Travis pushed and lifted. He slipped as he climbed out of the water.

Emily grabbed the front of his undershirt, but he caught himself from falling.

"You'd have gone in with me," he warned, looking at her hand still gripping the fabric. "And believe me, it was disgusting."

She let go and stepped back.

He leaned forward as he caught his breath and steadied himself on the slight slope of the bank of the canal.

She pointed at his bare foot. "Leech!"

He jumped several times before brushing at his foot with his hand. A wadded brown leaf fragment fell off. He glared at her. "That wasn't a leech."

Had she just reacted like a hysterical female? How embarrassing. She took a deep breath and met his gaze. "It looked like a leech."

He peeled off his latex gloves. "You nearly gave me a heart attack."

"Lucky for you, the medics are here."

"You're incorrigible."

Many had tried to reform her but failed. "I take that as a compliment." She pointed at his bare legs. "You're a pretty good dancer. Was that an Irish jig?"

"I could show you an Irish jig," he whispered in her ear as his lips brushed perilously close to her skin.

She gulped. A man paying attention and playfully flirting in spite of her hopelessly bad behavior felt good.

They turned their attention to the paramedics who were making the initial exam of the body loaded on the stretcher.

She stepped closer and raised her phone. "I need to take photos for the medical examiner."

A paramedic looked up. "Hey, Emily. Sharon told us you would be documenting the scene."

"Mo Wagner." Darrow Falls was so small that running into someone she knew wasn't unusual. Mo had delivered more than one dead body to be examined by the medical examiner or prepared for burial by her father. She was hard to forget. The female paramedic had short spiky pink hair and wore matching lipstick that seemed a little too bright for the job of gathering the dead. But Mo was no-nonsense and tough as nails. She examined the body as Emily sent photographs to the ME's office.

Mo opened the dead woman's mouth with her gloved hand, and muddy water dribbled down the side of her face and into the body bag on the stretcher. She pried open an eye and shone a light into it. "Get a doc on the radio so we don't have to start CPR. This one ain't coming back."

"You sure, Wagner?" the other paramedic asked Mo. He had thick brown hair, thick hands, and a thicker body. He was a cube of three-hundred pounds, slow but strong. The total opposite of his petite partner. "She looks like your type."

"You're the necrophiliac, Bean. Want to give her mouth to mouth?"

Crude, vulgar, and insulting. Emily was not in the midst of polite society. Working with the dead didn't require manners. It took grit. She admired those women who worked in traditional male jobs. It often required thick skins, colorful vocabularies, and a love of the job to gain respect. To survive, they gave as good as they got.

Men tended to describe Emily as a marshmallow because she wasn't driven to win or be the best. She'd pass the ball so the girl who had never scored could kick in the goal. She didn't need the accolades or bragging rights. She wanted the friendship and teamwork.

The men she knew wanted to win even in a romantic relationship. She fell for their flattery, charm, and promises. Then they would tell her what to wear or what books she should read to impress their friends. And like a marshmallow too close to the flame, she would burn to a crisp, disappearing in their smoke. She had yet to learn how to balance being in love with staying true to herself.

"Do you think she was raped?" Crane asked the question as if asking about the weather.

"If she was, the swamp douche washed away any evidence," Mo shot back.

"Her neck and face look bruised," Bean said.

Crane and Travis took a closer look.

Emily focused on the victim's battered body. Bruises darkened her neck, face, and bare arms, but her clothing appeared intact. The low-cut blouse sparkled when the light hit it, and she wore a tight black leather skirt splotched with mud. Emily took several photos. The ME would take more.

"You're going to want to document this." Mo lifted the woman's blouse higher to expose her abdomen. It was black and blue. "Someone used her for a punching bag."

Emily couldn't stop thinking about the woman's last moments. She would have had to be terrified and in excruciating pain. What monster had done this?

"Do you know her?" Travis asked.

Emily shook her head, but when she looked up, Travis was looking at Crane. He said no.

"I thought she might be a pro. It would explain the beating."

"That's a lot of johns to question if she is." Crane rose and stared down the trail where people were waiting behind a barrier or being diverted to the road.

They thought she was a prostitute. What woman would sell her body to strangers? It wasn't her job to find the answers, but she was curious. She had done her part, and the county lab and local police would take over the investigation.

"It's up to the coroner to figure this one out." Mo

looked at her. "You helping on this one?"

"When I called the medical examiner's office, the doctor said everyone was out on cases and asked me to take pictures. But that's it. My internship ended last week."

"That's right. You graduated. Congratulations."

"Now I have to find a job."

"Good luck. If you don't find something right away, we could use your help. A paramedic is great training for dealing with crime scenes."

"I'll keep it in mind."

Mo arranged the woman's arms across her chest.

Emily pointed at her hands. "No rings."

Mo examined her ears. "Pierced, but empty. Maybe someone took her jewelry."

"They took more than that." Emily felt the tug. Who was this woman, and why had someone killed her? Maybe she should become a cop. She looked at Travis. "Are you going to find out who did this?"

He nodded. "We'll get justice for her."

"Let's bag her." Mo pulled the black bag up over the body and zipped it closed.

Travis swiped a towel from the paramedic's bag, sat on the blanket, and wiped his legs and feet clean. He put on his socks and shoes before gathering his other clothing.

"I expect your report to be completed this afternoon," Crane said before following the body.

Emily snatched the blanket from the ground and gave it a good shake before neatly folding it. "Thank you for letting me borrow this."

"Are you warm enough?"

She picked up her backpack. "I'll warm up running.

Am I free to go?"

"I've got your information. Are you sure you're fine? I can take a break, and we can talk."

She debated whether to take him up on his offer. She had compartmentalized her feelings up to now, but someone's life would be overturned when Crane found out who the woman was and informed her family. She had witnessed how wrenching that heartache could be firsthand at all the funerals she had attended.

"I hear it's unhealthy to keep feelings bottled up inside, but some people find it difficult to express emotions," he said.

She was a crier. It was one of the reasons she had fought to keep her tears in check. His words broke the dam. Tears streaked down her cheeks, and her body shook.

"Hey." Travis pulled her into his arms, and she collapsed against his chest. His warm body felt like a comforting blanket.

She took a few quick breaths and stepped back after regaining her composure. She searched her bag for a bottle of water and small towel and concentrated on the task of washing her face. Hopefully, she'd never see him again and be reminded how she cried like a baby instead of being professional at a crime scene.

"Feeling better?" He handed her a card. "My personal email and cell number. I was serious about wanting that pic. And if you change your mind about talking, feel free to call me."

She shoved the card into her backpack to avoid his concerned gaze. "It all hit me at once. I guess I'm not as tough as I pretend." She had turned into a stereotype.

"You're human." He helped her slip on her

backpack. "I usually wait until I'm in the shower to cry."

"You?" Charles never cried. He considered it a sign of weakness. "A big bad cop cries?"

"I have learned that men who don't manage their anger break things. Sometimes those things are people. I meditate, I work out, and I cry to keep from becoming the monsters I arrest."

A shadow passed before his pale eyes. He was telling the truth. Like a marshmallow, she turned all gooey and sweet inside. *Stay away from the flame.* "Thank you for being kind and believing me." She looked at her shorts and tank top. "I need to find my friends and finish my run."

She tossed him a wave and broke into a jog on the towpath toward the parking lot a few miles north where her car was located. She'd never see Officer O'Toole again. A stab of disappointment shot through her. Even though he was a bit cocky, he had a sense of humor and seemed to enjoy her wit. Or was it hopeful thinking? She needed to curb her tongue, but every time she did that, she felt like a hypocrite. Could she speak the truth and also be likeable? Men didn't think so.

She was several yards down the trail when Charles joined her. "You'll never believe what I saw, Emily."

"I doubt it beats what I saw."

Before she could say more, he interrupted, "The paramedics were loading a body into the ambulance. Can you believe it? I must be one of those people who is always in the right place at the right time."

She shook her head. "You're one of the lucky ones, Charles." He never did ask her what she had seen. Typical.

Chapter Four

Travis watched Emily run down the towpath. Her shorts danced as her legs pounded the pathway. The view was as interesting leaving as arriving. She glanced back once, and he waved. She had worked her way under his skin but in a way he liked. She hadn't drooled all over him, but she had folded his clothes and tried to save him from drowning in muck. That meant a woman was interested, right?

He had her phone number. Maybe he'd call to see how she was doing. He made it a point never to become involved while on the job, but Emily deserved to be an exception. Besides, her role in the investigation was over.

He reached the towpath entrance just as Motts opened the barricade, and a group of runners nearly collided with him. The neck turners watched the ambulance depart with the body before they dashed down the path. Was this the group Emily was running with? She'd have a story to tell them.

Crane retrieved a roll of yellow *do not cross* tape from his vehicle and handed it to him. "String this around a few trees to block off the bank."

"Aren't you done?" Motts asked.

"The fire department is sending over the dive team to look for evidence."

"It looks like her jewelry was taken," Travis said.

"It's a good bet he took her purse."

"If you want to be a detective, don't jump to conclusions without gathering all the evidence. I doubt we'll find matching shoes and a handbag, but we have to look."

Was that a funny remark from Crane? He didn't know how to react.

"We're going to have to keep people away from this area," Crane ordered Motts.

"For how long?"

"As long as necessary," Crane said with enough attitude to deter any argument. "I opened up the path, but don't let anyone stop at the site. Keep spectators moving and out of the way of those working the scene. The spot has been compromised enough."

"I thought Emily was extremely helpful," Travis defended.

"Did you see her lack of reaction when you pulled the body out of the water? She's no doctor. How many dead bodies has she seen in her lifetime? She took photographs of it." His voice rose an octave with the last observation.

"For the medical examiner. She did an internship in their office."

"A pretty girl like that shouldn't have to work with corpses."

So much was wrong with Crane's remark, but he kept silent. Crane was a dinosaur when it came to equal opportunities for women.

Crane squinted at him. "Are you working first shift, O'Toole?"

"Yes." He shrugged as he examined his muddy pants. "What a way to start my day."

"I saw your name on the list of detective candidates. I usually ask officers to help on an investigation to see how they handle themselves. Are you interested?"

Had he heard right? Crane was inviting him to work the murder case? "Yes, sir. Are you authorizing my work?"

He scanned his dirty clothes. "Yes, but do you have a clean uniform?"

The heat had ripened the smells on his clothing and skin. "I'd like to go home and shower."

"Go. By the time you report, we should have an ID on the corpse. You can sit in on an interview or two."

He showered and changed in record time, reported to the police station, and waited to be called into Crane's office. The metal desk had a fake woodgrain top, and the chairs were lumpy and stained. He chose the one that looked cleaner than its mate. The wall behind Crane's desk was covered in framed commendations for his work in narcotics, the primary work for the detective bureau. Homicides were rare in a suburban town, but part of the national park was located within its boundaries, and that made body dumps like the one in the canal their jurisdiction.

Crane had a pile of folders in a metal basket and more on his desktop. He tapped on the keys of his computer. "The chief narrowed down the applications for detective to you and Adam Pratt." He looked over the top of the PC. "Since you found the body, I had Pratt go with me to the coroner's office. He threw up."

Pratt was older and had earned his sergeant stripes, but if he had lost his breakfast over a corpse, Travis might have a chance to beat him out for the detective's spot.

"I checked on Emily Stevenson."

Why? "She's a suspect?"

His eyes narrowed. "She said she was taking photographs for the medical examiner."

"She lied?" How could he have been fooled by such a wholesome girl-next-door type?

"No, but always check on the testimony of a witness. Intuition can be faulty, especially with a pretty woman. A man forgets to think with his brain." He chuckled as he selected a folder on his desk and shoved it toward Travis. "They confirmed employment for an internship. They liked her. Said she was spunky. I haven't heard that term in a while."

Spunky. It brought up the wrong image. One with her in his bed. "Then she's not a suspect."

"You planning to date her?"

Travis was caught off guard. Was he that transparent? He hoped Crane wasn't studying him. What if he was interested in Emily? She wasn't a suspect. He had a right to date a woman he found interesting. He flipped through the pages of the file, scanning the contents. All the different reports, including his, had been entered into the computer system and compiled under the assigned case number. Crane had printed the pages and was building a binder of information.

He paused at the medical examiner's report. "Did they identify the woman?"

"Christina Porter, age twenty-nine. Her husband, Ken Porter, reported her missing this morning. He's in the interrogation room."

"He's a suspect?"

"The husband is the default suspect until we rule him out. He's a successful accountant. They were married for nine years and have two children, ages six and eight. He claims he was out of town on business all night." Crane stood. "Let's see if he's lying."

Travis followed Crane down the winding stairs to the interrogation rooms in the basement located next to the jail cells used for short-term sentences. Long-term prisoners went to the county jail. The only prisoner in custody was asleep.

They entered a room with computer monitors interfaced with cameras to record the interviews. "Everything is recorded for trial evidence, so don't pick your nose." Crane hit the record button, and the screen displayed a man in room two attempting to find a comfortable position on a molded plastic chair at a six-foot table. Two more chairs were located across from him. The windowless rooms provided a cold, sterile environment, perfect to intimidate a witness.

"That's Ken Porter."

Ken wore a dark-blue suit and appeared overdressed for a Saturday. He studied his cell phone and glanced around.

"How long has he been waiting?"

"He just came from the morgue where he identified the body. He didn't take it well."

Did he throw up like Pratt? "What do you mean?"

"Cried like a baby," Crane said. "Claimed he loved his wife."

His eyes were puffy, and his pale skin looked blotchy.

"What makes you think he was lying?"

Crane shook his head. "Sometimes a man can love his wife so much he can't see her living with anyone but him. She was dressed for fun when we plucked her out of the canal."

We? Travis had done the plucking. Would he receive any credit for working the case? At least it would be good experience, and he'd find out if working with Crane was worth the detective position.

Crane continued, "He was away all night at a meeting with a female client."

Travis attempted to control his excitement. "Business or pleasure?"

"That's what we have to find out."

"I'm glad I didn't miss this."

"Being a detective isn't like in the movies or television. We're not going to figure out who the killer is in an hour. It requires days of legwork and luck. We don't have many murders in our territory, but we have to show the chief we can solve our own cases, or the local FBI will take over the investigation. I want you to take notes. It's the lies or details that don't match that trip up a person."

Chapter Five

Travis took out his notepad and followed Crane to the sparse interrogation room. He glanced toward the cameras. Did Ken know about them?

"How are you doing, Mr. Porter?" Crane's greeting was friendly, and he shook hands. "This is Officer Travis O'Toole."

Travis followed Crane's example and shook Ken's sweaty palm before sitting down across from him.

Crane removed a photograph from his folder and placed it on the table. It was Christina in better days. She had been an attractive woman with a polished sophisticated look. Her hair was styled in an intricate knot at the nape of her neck, and her makeup was subtle but dramatic around the eyes to attract attention. Her expensive white dress emphasized an intricate emerald necklace and matching earrings above a low-cut neckline. "We're sorry for your loss. What can you tell us about your wife?"

Ken stared at the photo. "Christina was a good wife and mother. Everyone loved her."

Travis wrote down the information on an empty page with Ken's name at the top. He paused, waiting for Crane's next question.

"Did she work outside the home?"

"No, she was devoted to the children."

Crane flipped through a few pages in his folder. "I

have a part-time job listed at the Hair-em Salon. Is that incorrect?"

Ken looked nervous like he'd made a mistake. "That was a hobby. She didn't have to work with me supporting her. She passed time there when the children were in school."

Travis put a star by the name of the salon.

"Did you and your wife have any problems?"

"Problems?" His voice squeaked. "I gave my wife everything she wanted. She had no reason to complain."

Travis put two stars by this comment. The man was digging his grave. What couple didn't have problems?

"Where were you Friday night?"

"I was working." Ken smoothed back his thinning hair before removing his glasses and rubbing his swollen eyes.

Crane waited for more. Most people hated silence and would fill the void with chatter. Ken was no different.

"I had a meeting with an important client. I spent the night there."

"We'll need the name of the hotel."

He wiped his glasses with a handkerchief he'd pulled out of his pants pocket. "It wasn't a hotel. I stayed at my client's apartment. I had to review stacks of personal papers. I'm an accountant. A CPA."

Crane had a legal pad beside his folder. He tapped his pen against the blank page. "I'll need a name and address."

Ken's face reddened, and he coughed into his handkerchief. "I would rather not involve her in this."

"This is a murder investigation, Mr. Porter." Crane raised his voice. "You need an alibi. What is her name?"

Ken twisted the kerchief in his hands. "I don't want my wife…" A slight smile thickened his razor-thin lips. "It doesn't matter anymore, does it?" He took a deep breath. "Talia Shaver."

"The news anchor?" Crane didn't hide his surprise.

How did someone like bookish Ken Porter score with two beautiful women? Or was he trading up? Travis wrote her name and added the address he provided.

"I've done her books for years," Ken said.

Crane snorted.

Ken straightened his shoulders and glared at the detective. "My relationship with Talia was strictly professional."

"But you were spending the night in her home." Crane returned the glare. "Were you intimate?"

Ken stuttered. "I don't think that has any bearing on my wife's murder."

"If you stayed in separate rooms, how can she verify you were there all night? It's not that long a drive from her home to yours. You could have murdered your wife and returned to Ms. Shaver's home before she woke."

"I was only protecting my client's reputation. We were intimate. Sometimes it's lonely being famous." He paused. "I love my wife," he added like an afterthought.

"Did your wife know about your affair with our *local celebrity*?" Crane's tone made it clear he wasn't impressed by her credentials.

"No." Ken waved his hand in dismissal. "She wasn't interested in my work, and I was discreet. Christina was young and innocent when I married her. She didn't understand that men had certain needs outside of marriage."

Crane paused before continuing, "Was she aware

you would be gone all night?"

"She knew my schedule and could contact me by cell phone if there was an emergency. The house has an alarm and motion detectors. There was no sign of a break-in. She would have been safe if she had only stayed home."

It was an odd comment. Travis made a note.

"Do you know where your wife was going Friday night?"

"She sometimes goes out with her friends Lucy Vance and Sue Marino."

Travis needed clarification. "Who are Lucy and Sue?" He looked at Crane to see if he'd overstepped his boundaries, but the detective nodded, which he hoped was approval.

"They're beauticians who work at the Hair-em Salon. Christina worked for Lucy, the owner, before I married her. She had her hair and nails done there every week." Ken waved his hand as if to dismiss them. "They're a bunch of clucking hens when they get together. They wanted her to return to work, but that was foolishness."

"You didn't want your wife to work?" Travis asked.

"She had no need for money, and she knew her primary responsibility was to take care of my children. I indulged her consorting with her old co-workers as long as it didn't interfere with her duties to the children or to our social engagements."

Travis poised his pencil over his notebook. "You had a lot of those?"

"I met with clients on a regular basis. Some are wealthy and influential. Christina was stunning on my arm. You would never know her father was a truck driver and her mother a waitress, but once in a while a diamond emerges from a lump of coal."

Travis forgot to write. How had he reduced a woman to a decoration on his arm?

Crane continued as if the man had said nothing offensive. "We found two cars registered to you in the garage. If your wife didn't drive one of them, who picked her up Friday night?"

"Probably Sue or Lucy. At least she had the good sense to leave the vehicle at home. You don't drive an expensive car to the places they frequented."

Ken was glad the vehicle was safe while his wife's body was in the county morgue. Travis made a note of his comment. The man was cold. He looked at the timeline Crane had created for Christina's whereabouts the night of her disappearance. A local country-western bar was listed as the last place she'd visited. "Did you know she went to the Boot N Scoot?"

Crane scribbled something on his notepad.

Travis glanced at the words. *Good question.*

"Is that where Lucy and Sue dragged her? I warned her to stay away from dumps like that. She at least left her wedding rings at home."

A married woman removed proof of marriage for one reason. "Did she often remove her rings?"

"No, but they were worth ten thousand dollars. The diamond was a full carat, and the wedding band was an heirloom from my family. Three generations. It was irreplaceable."

Unlike a wife? Travis underlined the amount. "Do you know if she wore any other jewelry that night?"

"The medical examiner said no jewelry was found on her body," Ken said. "I assumed she wore none."

41

Crane turned to the next page in his folder. "I have a police report from Friday night that the police responded to a call from your home about a woman causing a disturbance outside."

Ken's expression brightened. "There's your suspect."

"We'll talk to all persons of interest. Then we'll eliminate each one until we have the suspect in custody." Crane showed him a photo. "The responding officer captured this image of your wife. She was wearing a skirt, blouse, and several pieces of jewelry. Do you recognize them?"

Ken studied the photograph. "This looks like the ruby necklace I bought when my daughter was born. How did she get it? I keep everything locked in my safe."

"Did she know the combination?"

"No, and she didn't ask. If we were going out, I gave her pieces to wear. She had a couple of costume pieces she wore every day, but this necklace, earrings, and bracelet are worth six thousand dollars and were secured in the safe."

Crane leaned forward. "Is it possible she found the combination and borrowed a few pieces?"

Ken frowned. "I can check my inventory and see if anything is missing."

"You keep an inventory of her jewelry?" Travis asked.

"I keep records of all my assets," Ken justified. "It's necessary for insurance. Do you think someone robbed her?"

"We haven't discovered the motive yet." Crane slid a card across the table with his name and email address. "We'll need a list of anything missing with a description and value."

Ken picked up the card. "I have photos of each piece and appraisal value. If anything is missing, I'll email the information to you." He wiped his hand through his hair. "I'll need a police report for insurance. I hope she took these pieces off before going out."

Travis was curious. "How much is the jewelry in the safe worth?"

"Around half a million."

Had he heard correctly? "How much?"

"It's an investment," Ken defended. "The stones are real, not synthetic, and many of the pieces have increased in value, especially the older ones I inherited from my family."

Crane turned to the next page. "You reported your wife missing this morning. How did you find out she was gone?"

"The babysitter she hired called me in the morning and told me Christina hadn't returned. I drove home and phoned the police to report her missing. You called and asked me to identify her body. Now you're asking all these questions." He put his glasses on and tightened his tie. "When can I go home? My children need me. I don't want them to hear about their mother's death from strangers."

"We won't keep you any longer than necessary," Crane said. "Do you know of anyone who may have wanted to harm your wife?"

"Christina led a dull life except for the soirees I escorted her to. No one had any reason to harm her."

Crane stood and opened the door. "Thank you for all your help, Mr. Porter. I'll have an officer show you the way out."

Ken paused in the doorway. "Christina was my wife and the mother of my children. I want you to find out who caused her death."

"That's my job." Crane shut the door and turned. "What do you think?"

Travis flipped through the pages of his notes. "Although he said he loved his wife, he talked about her like a possession. He's controlling. He doesn't want her to work. The jewelry is an investment. What is that report of a disturbance about?"

Crane handed him the folder. "Before Christina headed off to the Boot N Scoot, there was a disturbance at her home. A woman accused her of cheating with her husband. She knocked on the door until Christina answered. When the police arrived, she moved to the sidewalk but kept shouting about the affair. Ken thinks she went out Friday night with Lucy and Sue, but according to the complaint report, she left the house with a man."

"Adultery makes a good motive for murder," Travis said.

"I want you to interview the woman on the sidewalk and her cheating husband."

"I should have taken more counseling courses in college."

"If one of them killed her, you won't have to worry about couples therapy."

Chapter Six

Three o'clock came too soon for Emily as she headed for work at the local hospital. It had been the perfect job for a student. Working second shift on weekends allowed her to take a full load of courses during the week and complete her required internship. She had emailed applications for possible employment, but her college loan payments would be due soon. A part-time job didn't pay enough to cover her new expenses.

The dress code for working in the information technology department was casual, allowing her to wear black jeans, a sweatshirt over a tee, and sneakers. She didn't have to waste money on an office wardrobe. She packed a meal to save a few more dollars and headed out the door. Instead of paying the additional costs of living in a dorm or renting an apartment, she lived at home in a remodeled room above a garage built for four vehicles, one of which was a hearse. She had claimed the space from her brother after he graduated from college and found a job in Colorado.

She had told her parents about finding the body in the canal. They'd been shocked but also intrigued. Her father owned a funeral home, and her mother loved reading mystery novels. The obsession with the dead and crime solving was inherited.

She drove out of the suburbs where rows of colonial

and Cape Cod houses were broken by an occasional liquor bar or convenience drugstore.

The interstate highway had bypassed the community and killed Main Street, which was now littered with fast food places, secondhand stores, and fleabag hotels. She drove past the used-car dealership, a drive-through liquor store, and semi-abandoned strip mall before reaching the intersection where the three-story hospital was located.

Emily described her job as babysitting a large computer to those who had no clue about the job of a computer operator in the information technology department. In a temperature-regulated room, she watched the monitors in case the two mainframe computers decided to crash, which was rare. She had other job duties equally exciting. She took the system down for repairs, did nightly backups, and printed reports distributed to the different departments in the hospital.

The elevator by the cafeteria reached the IT department in the basement. She entered a code for the entrance door. The offices along the left side of the hall were for the vice president and department supervisor. An open area with lockers and a table provided a place to eat and store her belongings. Farther back was another area where programmers were assigned a cubicle. At the end of the room was a coded entrance that opened into a staircase, the only other access to the department.

Emily did the combination to her locker and shoved a backpack inside. The bag was a larger version of the one she wore running and had seen wear and tear from her college years. She normally filled it with her textbooks and notes and studied in her free time. What would she do now? School was over, and a new phase of her life was beginning. She was no longer a student. She was an adult. The moniker didn't feel real without a career job.

The computer room had been built opposite the two offices and between the rest area and the entrance. An elevated floor hid the plethora of cables and wires needed to operate the two mainframe computers, three printers, and four monitors. A steep ramp led to the entrance and required a combination to enter. The front and side wall were glass panels, and the remaining two walls were made of concrete block. The room was temperature regulated at sixty-eight degrees with a battery-operated backup in case of a power outage. Critical information about patients and the hospital finances were kept on the mainframes' hard drives.

The job was important enough to have a team of three full-time and three part-time computer operators working shifts to cover twenty-four hours, seven days a week.

Doreen Markem worked part-time third shift and arrived at eleven p.m. Emily was scheduled to leave at eleven thirty. The half hour overlap was for communicating about work, but there was rarely anything to pass along. It was gossip time. Doreen was seeking a divorce, and Emily provided a sympathetic ear.

Doreen had suspected her husband, Roger, had been cheating on her and followed him to the Boot N Scoot bar where he met the other woman. Tina was younger, which didn't sit well with Doreen. She debated seeking marital counseling, but Roger asked for a divorce on Valentine's Day just as they were getting dressed to go to dinner. He told her how Tina was his soul mate, and they were going to start a new life together. Ouch! Roger knew how to throw a wet blanket on an evening slated for romance.

Doreen and Roger had been married for eighteen years with two teenagers. From the tales of their growing misdeeds, she had good reasons to keep them tightly in tow. She edited contracts for an insurance company from home during the day and worked at the hospital on the weekends but needed Roger's child support to make ends meet. He balked at the amount, but she held firm.

She kept her friends at the hospital informed of each new development. It was getting ugly, and Emily felt some guilt in anticipating the next chapter every time she came to work but not enough to mind her own business. Up until she found a body in the canal, Emily's most exciting experience had been winning a photography contest. Doreen had a life even if it was a disaster of a life.

Emily heard the door click open and marked her mystery novel before closing it. The night had been dull, and the stormy look on her co-worker's face meant she had a new experience to share.

Doreen joined her in the common area and shoved her belongings into her locker. She snapped the lock closed. "His cheap slut called the cops on me!"

"What?" Cops were involved in a divorce?

Doreen growled and waved for Emily to follow as they went around an interior wall where a short hallway ran along the glass side of the computer room. Printed reports were sorted on metal shelving, and boxes of paper were stacked on the floor.

Doreen hauled a twenty-pound box of green-striped bar paper up the ramp, entered the code, and dropped the box in front of the door to keep it ajar. She hauled another box into the computer room and plopped it on top of one of the box-shaped printers.

She was a tall woman with skinny arms and legs but a barrel-shaped body. Emily wasn't sure if it was from lifting the heavy boxes or because she was a habitual smoker and her chest had expanded so she could breathe. Her explosive voice had a rattle that would have worried most cigarette addicts. Her short hair was bleached blond, and she always wore full makeup, including blush and eye shadow. Emily was lucky to remember mascara. Who was going to see her in the basement of the hospital?

Emily watched from a safe distance in one of the swivel chairs in front of the long desk supporting the monitors. Doreen preferred no help and no interference. She always maintained the same pattern each night, and Emily told her she was obsessive-compulsive. Doreen didn't argue. She had reasons for her set routine. She loaded new boxes into the printers so they wouldn't run out of paper as they churned out stacks of departmental reports. She could go upstairs for several hours and visit her friends in admission before she had to return to separate and distribute the finished product. Emily heard the initial story about Doreen's life. Admission was entertained with the enhanced and revised version.

When the printers were loaded, Doreen sat next to her at the desk and typed the codes to set up the process for updating the information for the reports.

Emily spun around to face her. "Why did she call the cops on you?"

"She's a lying tramp!"

Emily shook her head. There had to be more to it than that. "What did you do?"

Doreen shrugged her broad shoulders. "I just went over to see her."

"At her house?" Sometimes Doreen lacked good judgment. After all, she'd married Roger. Emily had met him a few times and thought Doreen was better off without him.

"I followed Roger there," Doreen answered matter-of-factly.

"Did he spot you?"

"No, I have an app for tracking my son's car so I would know where he was going. I added Roger's truck to it."

"Is that legal?"

"I paid for it."

Emily wasn't sure how to argue her logic.

"He parked in front of one of those big mansions in the wealthy part of town with lots of windows and a crystal chandelier glowing in the foyer. I know what he sees in her." Doreen rubbed her fingers together to signify money.

"You know they're having an affair," Emily reminded her. "Why cause trouble?"

"He can afford to entertain Miss High Society but can't send me child support?" she demanded. "I want my money!"

Emily couldn't help asking, "What happened?"

"I knocked on the door and demanded to see him. She claimed he wasn't there. The cunning harlot. Does she think I'm stupid?"

Emily didn't tell her what she thought. It would have broken the peace between them. If Doreen was having trouble with child support payments, she should have contacted her lawyer. That's what she's paying him for.

But no, she'd driven over to the *other* woman's house and demanded to see her husband. "Did you see Roger?"

"No, he wasn't even man enough to face me. He owes me money, and I'm going to get it before she sucks him dry."

"If she has money, why would she want his?"

"That type expects a man to pay to impress. All her money goes toward clothes and jewelry. You should have seen the party girl standing on her front porch, decked out for a night on the town. She wore a short skirt and low-cut blouse that clung to her skinny frame. Then there was all her tacky jewelry. The woman has no taste."

That had to be true. She wanted Roger. "What did you do?"

"I refused to go, so she called the police."

Emily was almost afraid to ask. "What did they do?"

"They told me to leave, but I was on the sidewalk," Doreen defended. "That's public property."

"Did they arrest you?"

"They threatened to charge me with disorderly conduct. Me!"

"You're lucky they didn't throw you in jail," Emily warned.

"I'm not the one committing adultery. That's a sin in the church."

"You're getting a divorce."

"It's not official yet," Doreen argued. "And she's married, too. Maybe I should tell him about the affair."

"He doesn't know?"

"He will. She can't hide her affair from her neighbors anymore either." Doreen smirked. "I made sure of that."

Emily was sure a curious audience had witnessed

the confrontation. She also figured there had been more to it, but Doreen had her version and was sticking to it. She refused to give up her man without a fight and made sure everyone knew exactly where she stood.

When Roger wasn't installing carpet, he was hunting, fishing, or drinking. He saw a woman as someone to fetch his beer or supper. He didn't need a wife. He needed a golden retriever.

Doreen quickly marked off her run sheets even though she hadn't printed any reports yet. She used different colored pens to highlight jobs that needed special attention later that night. Once everything was filled out, she straightened the papers and placed her pens parallel to the top.

"Let me get my cigarettes." Doreen headed for her locker. She removed a shiny metal case and a leather coin purse. The cafeteria would be closed, but the snack machines did a hefty business on third shift. "I need a smoke."

Smoking was banned at the hospital, but Doreen said she wasn't ready to kick the habit and considered third-shift employees exempt until someone reported them puffing away in the darkness of the outdoor courtyard.

Emily handed Doreen the pager each computer operator wore during their shift, and she hooked it on her blouse. The single number made it easy for anyone in the hospital to notify an operator for help with phones, computers, or printers. Emily grabbed her coat and backpack so she could go straight to the time clock and then head home at eleven thirty.

Doreen took a side trip up the ramp and kicked the box of paper away from the glass door so it would close and lock. Employees were supposed to take security seriously, but unauthorized personnel came and went all the time during late hours. Doreen sometimes had her kids in the room, and even Roger had visited before their breakup.

Someone buzzed for entrance into the room, and Emily glanced through the narrow window cut in the steel door. It was Travis. She yanked back on the handle.

"What are you doing here?" they both demanded in unison.

"I work here," Emily said.

Chapter Seven

The last person Travis had expected to see in the basement of a hospital was Emily Stevenson. She was staring at him, waiting. He noted the symmetry of her features and slight dimples at the corners of her pouting mouth. Her hair was down and a little messy. His fingers itched to touch the soft curls. Why did this woman affect him in such a primal way?

"Did you forget to ask me something?"

Her voice betrayed worry. He wanted to hold her in his arms, kiss away her fears, and carry her to his cave. Wait. It was the twenty-first century. He lived in a Cape Cod with a huge mortgage. He had to stop romanticizing about Emily and focus on his job. "No, they told me Doreen Markem works here."

"That's me." Doreen stepped forward. Her voice sounded like a barking seal. All thoughts of seduction fled. Poor Emily worked with this woman? Life could be unfair.

The police report had claimed Doreen was screaming and verbally abusive toward Christina Porter Friday night while demanding to see her estranged husband. Her greeting had been intimidating. Her stocky appearance was threatening. She outweighed Christina by more than a hundred pounds.

Doreen narrowed her eyes, and her voice was filled with suspicion. "What do you want with me?"

Travis removed his notebook and pen from his pocket. "I need to ask you a few questions, Ms. Markem."

"Make it quick." She tapped an unlit cigarette on a metal case. "I'm on the clock."

She looked like she was taking a break. "Do you know Christina Porter?"

"I know a Tina Porter. That's the bitch who's been screwing my husband."

He showed her the photograph of Christina. "Are you talking about this woman?"

Emily leaned over to look, but recognition didn't register on her face. "Who is she?"

"I'll get to you in a minute."

Her eyebrows came together in a frown. She looked cute when she was mad.

He presented the photo to Doreen again. "According to the police report, you were harassing Mrs. Porter." He looked at her for confirmation.

Emily made a strangling sound. She looked guilty. If she knew the woman in the canal, why hadn't she said something? Maybe he was interviewing the wrong woman.

"I was polite," Doreen barked. "I wanted to talk to my husband, but she lied to me. She said he wasn't there."

Travis looked at his notebook. "Why did you need to talk to Roger Markem?"

"My husband owes me child support." Doreen raised her chin. "I wanted my money."

"How did you know he was there?"

"His truck was parked on the street."

"You followed him?" He failed to hide his disbelief.

Doreen put a hand on her hip. "Yes."

Emily turned away, but he focused on Doreen. "How did you know what house he entered?"

"I knew her name and address. My husband wouldn't visit anyone else in that neighborhood." Her voice rose in volume with each answer. "I was civil. She had some nerve calling the cops."

"What happened when the police arrived?"

"They warned me to stay away from her, and I left." She tapped her foot, and the sound echoed in the small quarters. "I didn't break any laws!"

Although Travis kept his voice as calm as possible, Doreen was too agitated to dial her emotions down a notch. He paused before continuing. "Did you talk to your husband before leaving the Porters' home?"

"How? He never came to the door. Is she trying to cause more trouble?" Doreen put the cigarette in her mouth and removed it, staring at the unlit end. "As if calling the cops on me isn't enough. If she has a problem with me asking her about my husband, she shouldn't let him hide behind her little leather skirt."

"Leather?" Emily looked from Travis to Doreen. "Was it black?"

He held up his hand. "I'm asking the questions." He turned to Doreen. "What was your husband doing there?"

"He was plying the carpet between her legs, if you know what I mean."

"Doreen." Emily looked distraught. Did she know how much trouble her co-worker was in?

He turned a page in his notebook. "How long has their affair been going on?"

"He confessed in February, but I had my suspicions

before then. We had a good marriage for eighteen years until that homewrecker stole my husband."

The income difference between Roger and Ken was more than a hundred thousand dollars if they were telling the truth about their finances. It was a big step down for Christina Porter's lifestyle. "Did her husband know about the affair?"

Doreen snorted. "I never met him, but Roger and Tina sneaked around. Usually, he didn't go to her house and met her somewhere private. She was stringing my Roger along and taking every dollar that belonged to me and the children. That's why I was there. She was causing marital discord."

His lips twitched, but he controlled any laughter at her description. "What did you do after the police asked you to leave?"

"I went to the store for cigarettes."

Travis scribbled in his notepad. "You didn't follow them?"

"No. I went home and waited for my son to get off work. Then I went to sleep."

"You don't work Friday night?"

"No, I work Saturday and Sunday nights."

"What hours?"

"From eleven at night to seven thirty in the morning just like tonight." Doreen poked her finger toward him. "I work at the hospital two nights a week and work four days editing insurance forms. I can't pay the bills and raise two children if my husband is spending all his money on that gold digger. I have a right to talk to my husband about family matters. And if she wants to accuse me of something, she can say it to my face! Or better yet, I want to file a cross-complaint. She slandered my good name."

"You can't do that."

"There has to be some law she's breaking. What about coming between the sanctity of a husband and wife? They used to stone women like her."

"We don't stone people in this country, and you can't file a complaint because Christina Porter was murdered last night." Travis nodded at Emily. "Your co-worker found her body this morning in the canal."

Doreen turned to Emily. "You killed her?" Her expression turned from shock to bold congratulations. "Thank you, Emily!"

"I didn't kill her!" Emily cried out as Doreen caught her in a bear hug and lifted her off her feet.

Doreen danced around in a circle with Emily clutched in her arms. "The witch is dead!" she sang in triumph.

Emily escaped and stared at Travis. "Are you sure the woman in the canal is the same woman Roger is having an affair with?"

She looked completely innocent. "Like you didn't know?"

She pointed at his pocket where he had returned the photograph. "I never met Christina Porter, and the waterlogged woman in the canal didn't look anything like that picture you shared."

"How could you not know? Didn't Doreen talk about her?" Travis stared into her angelic face, searching for signs of insanity.

Her mouth opened, but no words came out. Doreen was not the type to keep her husband's infidelities a secret. How much did Emily know? Forget about calling her for a date. Even if she wasn't a suspect, she was involved. He buried any feelings of disappointment.

Emily glanced toward Doreen who was texting on her phone. "She complained about Roger and Tina to anyone who would listen. How was I to know Roger's mistress and the floating corpse were the same woman?"

"We need to talk."

Her lip trembled, and her eyes looked watery. "Talk? Am I a suspect?"

He fought the urge to comfort her. "Everyone who knew Christina is a suspect."

She swiped at a stray tear. "You wouldn't have a body without me. I reported it."

Travis nodded toward Doreen. "Maybe you were doing your friend a favor."

"We're co-workers. I wouldn't murder anyone for her."

"It's the thought that counts." Doreen opened the door. "Let's go upstairs to the courtyard. I need a smoke."

Travis waited for Emily to leave next. She looked hurt, and his hand brushed against her back as he escorted her to the elevator.

The hospital was built in a big square around an outdoor courtyard. Patio tables and chairs of black mesh were scattered around the brick surface. Small trees and bushes added to the escape from the sterile building. The temperature had cooled down in the evening as stars twinkled in the clear sky above the outdoor dining area, and Emily put on her coat. The cold didn't seem to bother Doreen, who lit and inhaled her cigarette.

Travis questioned Doreen first, who insisted she hadn't killed Christina but made no secret she hated the woman and blamed her for her failed marriage. He reviewed his notes. "You said you returned home around nine thirty. Did anyone see you come home?"

"My daughter was in her room, and my son came home from work around eleven."

"You left your daughter home alone?"

"She's fourteen." Doreen defended her maternal skills with sarcasm. "She babysits. Everyone was asleep by midnight, including me."

Travis flipped through his notebook. "What was Mrs. Porter wearing when you confronted her at her home?"

"She had her clothes on if that's what you mean." Doreen gave a snort that turned into a coughing fit. It didn't stop her from lighting up a fresh cigarette.

Emily sat upwind of the smoke and scowled at him. Why was she angry? He didn't invent her connection to the suspect. She had to be unlucky to find the woman who had come between her co-worker and husband. Maybe she was lucky in love. He shook any romantic thoughts out of his head. The pretty young woman who could have been his girlfriend was a distraction he couldn't indulge in during this investigation. He stared at his notes. "Was she wearing jeans, a dress, a bathrobe?"

"For that princess? She wore a tight leather skirt, shiny red blouse, and was all painted up." Doreen sneered as she blew out a puff of smoke. "She was not dressed for mother of the year."

"Did you notice if she was wearing nail polish?"

"Tart red!" Doreen tapped her own fingernails on the table. "And I know where she had them done. I used to go to the Hair-em Salon to have my hair and nails done until I found out the slut Roger was humping worked there."

"Are you a customer at the Hair-em?"

Emily yawned before answering. "Oh no." She shook a head full of unruly curls. "I trim my own hair."

She shoved her hands into her pockets, but he had seen her nails. No polish. No makeup except on her eyelashes, which fluttered to stay open. She was tired. She'd had an early start to the day, and the time was pushing midnight.

"You can't believe I had anything to do with that woman's death."

Emily sounded afraid, but it was too early to reassure her of any innocence. "Until Detective Crane rules you out, you're a person of interest. Even if you didn't kill Mrs. Porter, you might know something that might help the investigation."

"I've told you everything I know," Emily said.

"And I appreciate it. I think that will be all for now." Travis closed his notebook.

"It better be all, period." Doreen smashed her cigarette out on the ground and picked up the butt. "I have midnight processing to complete."

"Where can I reach you if I have any further questions?"

"I sleep in Sundays, so don't come knocking on my door until after one." She didn't wait for a reply as she headed for the door to enter the inside hallway of the hospital.

He followed Emily into the corridor and down another hall branching off to an exterior door that opened to the parking lot. "Does Doreen hate her job, or is she always this agitated?"

"You upset her routine and delayed midnight

processing."

"What is that?"

"It's the most important thing about her job. At midnight, the computers update all the financial and medical records for the hospital. New reports are based on that information. You wouldn't want to take the wrong patient to surgery or overcharge someone."

"I guess that explains Doreen's attitude. It must be hard to work with her."

Emily clicked open the lock on her car door. "I usually spend half an hour with her between shifts except for tonight. She's not so bad. When Roger sprang the divorce on her, she was devastated. She loved him, and his betrayal turned her world upside down."

"You might want to be careful."

She turned to him as she opened the car door. "You don't seriously think Doreen killed Christina Porter?"

"My job is to gather information."

Her voice was sympathetic. "You've had a long day."

"Crane assigned me the woman Christina called the police about the night she was killed. I couldn't reach Doreen earlier, but the hospital staff told me she worked third shift, so I came to her place of employment. I didn't know it was your place of employment, too."

"You weren't the only one surprised. I didn't think I'd ever see you again."

"You wanted to see me again?" Did he sound eager?

She ducked into her car. "You have my number."

Travis studied her in the soft glow of the dome light as she sat behind the wheel. "What do you know about Christina Porter?"

She shrugged. "Nothing."

"Doreen never talked about her?"

"She was the main topic of conversation for months. But any woman who wanted Roger for a boyfriend had to be desperate in my opinion."

"You don't like Roger?"

"I've met him a few times and was not impressed. Doreen was blinded by love, but now all she does is complain about him. The honeymoon took eighteen years to be over."

"Do you know why she went to Christina's home?"

Emily leaned against the steering wheel. "Roger owed her money and had been avoiding her. She's had a tough time making ends meet."

"You know Doreen better than me, but it seems she had a good reason to kill Christina Porter. She wanted Roger back. Or at least his paycheck."

"Maybe."

"Maybe she killed him?"

"No, maybe she wanted him back," she defended. "I always thought she was better off without him."

"Why is that?"

"He only thought about himself. His marriage involved three other lives, and he ignored all of them because of a younger woman in a mini-skirt."

"Some women are hard to ignore, Emily." He closed her car door and watched her drive off.

Chapter Eight

Travis discovered detective work meant hours weren't scheduled. He had entered his notes into the police computer system from his interview with Doreen the night before, and he'd talked to everyone on the list Crane had given him but Roger Markem who had been fishing Saturday on Lake Erie. He agreed to come in Sunday afternoon for an interview.

Crane wanted to join him for the talk with Roger and told him to meet first in his office. He knocked on the open door.

Crane looked up from a folder on his desk. "I read your report, but what were your impressions of Doreen Markem?"

She was Emily's friend and co-worker, but he had to be honest. "She's hot tempered and impulsive. She followed her husband to the Porter home and threatened Christina, but it was very public. She had to be an idiot to kill her after the police warned her to leave. She went home, but her children were asleep by midnight. She could have left."

"How strong is her motive for murdering Christina?"

"She had enough rage to kill her, especially since her husband was having an affair with her. She claimed Christina was causing *marital discord*."

Crane snorted but regained his composure. "Did she

have the strength to beat and strangle her?"

Doreen was built like a linebacker. "Yes, but none of her manicured nails were broken, and I didn't see any scratches. Wouldn't Christina have fought back, especially against a woman?"

"She stays on the suspect list," Crane said.

Adam Pratt knocked on the door. "Am I late?"

"No, I want both of you in on the interview with Roger Markem."

Adam was his competition for detective. His rival was older and had more years on the force, but he hadn't gone to college. Would experience outweigh education? They both wanted to prove themselves and stayed close to Crane's heels as they headed to the interrogation room. Roger was pacing the small space when they entered. He wore cowboy boots, faded jeans, and a plaid shirt buttoned to the neck. His hair was long in the back and short on the sides. Wrinkles in his forehead and around his mouth dug deep in his sallow skin. His beard stubble showed gray, but his hair was a solid sandy brown.

Roger sat opposite the three men and removed a cigarette from a pack tucked into his shirt pocket.

"Thank you for coming in, Mr. Markem. I'm Detective Crane, and this is Officer O'Toole and Sergeant Pratt."

"Call me Roger. I'm just a regular hardworking slob." He tapped the unlit cigarette on the table similar to Doreen's nervous habit.

"No smoking in here." Crane placed the folder on the table. Travis sat to his right and stole a glance. The contents had grown thicker since yesterday with additional reports and photos. "What sort of work do you do, Roger?"

"I install carpet." His hands showed no cuts, but they were scarred and calloused. He cracked his knuckles. "I have a working man's hands." He chuckled as he stretched his fingers straight. His pinkie and ring finger on his right hand were bent from being broken, but the injury appeared old.

Crane opened his folder. "Do you know why you're here?"

"Sunday brunch?" Roger's tone was flippant.

Crane stood so fast his chair fell and skidded on the cement floor. He smacked his hands against the table surface and leaned forward, nose to nose with Roger. "You're not here for breakfast, lunch, or dinner. I want to talk to you about your relationship with Christina Porter." His words echoed off the concrete block walls.

Roger went pale and leaned back, balancing on the back legs of his chair. "She was a friend. I was shocked to hear about her death."

Crane retreated. He picked up his chair, righted it, and took his seat. "How did you hear about her murder?"

Roger scratched the stubble on his face. "A couple of friends called to tell me her body had been found in the national park."

"Who were these friends?"

He didn't hesitate to share names. "Lucy Vance and Sue Marino."

The same two women Ken had named.

Crane turned to Adam. "Did you interview them?"

"Saturday," he said. "They work at the Hair-em Salon."

"Tina worked there, too," Roger said.

Ken Porter had told them Christina didn't work.

Who was telling the truth? "What did she do there?" Travis asked.

Adam leaned back and looked at Travis. "Are we allowed to ask questions?"

"If they're good ones."

"Officers," Crane growled a warning. He waited for them to focus on Roger. "What did Christina do at the salon?"

"Nails and hair." He ran his fingers through his layered locks. "She cut mine."

Travis jotted down the information. "Did she color it, too?"

Roger looked annoyed. "She touched up a little gray."

Travis leaned forward. "It wouldn't do to be mistaken for her father."

"No one made that mistake twice," he hissed.

Roger was sensitive about his age. He was in his forties but looked older. "You must have been flattered to have someone young and pretty like Christina pay attention to you."

"She had a crush on me, but we were just friends."

Doreen had another story. "Then why are you and your wife filing for divorce?"

"That had nothing to do with Tina."

Crane took over. "When was the last time you saw Christina?"

"That would have been at the Boot N Scoot Friday night. Lucy and Sue were there, too. We met for drinks."

The Boot N Scoot Entertainment Venue had been built when country line dancing was popular. Now it was the place for greasy meals, cheap beer, and easy hookups for one-night stands. The parking lot was littered with cigarette butts, crushed beer cans, and used condoms. Travis had made his share of arrests at the place. Drunken fistfights were common.

Doreen had followed her husband to the Porter home. "How did Christina arrive at the Boot N Scoot? Her car was left at home." The babysitter and Ken had confirmed that detail.

Roger put the unlit cigarette to his lips, looked at Crane, and removed it. "I picked her up."

Crane leaned forward. "Did you take her home?"

"No." He took a deep breath. "I planned to fish the next day and had to get some sleep. I left the group early. She told me Lucy or Sue could take her home."

Crane drew a line on his notepad. "What time was this?"

"Around eleven."

He wrote the time on the line. "Where did you go?"

"My mother's home. I'm staying with her."

"Can she verify you were at home?" Crane continued the quick-fire questions.

"She was asleep. She's seventy-three and not well."

Travis made a note. *No alibi.*

"You and your wife, Doreen, were married for eighteen years." Crane studied his folder notes. "Is that correct?"

"Yes, sir."

Sir? Roger had gone from being snarky to polite. Was he worried about something? Travis pushed him to answer his previous question. "Why are you getting a divorce?"

He patted his chest. "Eighteen years of hell was enough penance for this man."

Travis didn't need to read the folder to know the

background of their relationship. He'd written it up. "Doreen said you confessed to an affair with Christina Porter, and she filed for divorce citing adultery."

"I had to give her a good reason to part ways. Old Doreen is making me pay. She's the one who got the house and kids."

"A house with a mortgage and two teenagers," Crane said. "I think you received the better deal."

"She demands alimony and child support because the lazy woman won't work full time. She reads reports on the computer at home and calls that employment while I wear my fingers to the bone."

"Isn't your wife also working Saturday and Sunday nights at the local hospital?" Travis asked.

"That's not work. She spends all night drinking coffee and gabbing with her friends."

Crane handed Travis the next report in the folder. It was the call about Doreen disturbing the peace. "Do you know why your wife followed you to Christina's home Friday night?"

"Doreen has trust issues. She was always stalking me and jealous for no good reason. Can I help it if I aged better than her?"

Travis studied his worn-out face. "What do you mean?"

"Doreen aged overnight. No amount of makeup is going to hide her wrinkles." Roger patted his stomach. "Me, I don't weigh an ounce more than I did in my twenties. I have the energy of a young man, too. I'm not ready for the grave like her. I want to have fun before I die."

"Were you planning to marry Christina?" Adam asked.

"I wasn't a fool." Roger's grin exposed crooked yellow teeth. "What man jumps out of a frying pan into the fire? She had two little brats. I've got two of my own. Thankfully, they'll be grown soon. Child support ends at eighteen."

Travis wanted to confirm their affair. "But were you romantically involved with Christina?"

"She had an itch. I scratched it. But she kept our relationship a secret," Roger said. "She said if Ken found out, she would lose custody of her kids. That's why she only went out when Ken was working. I'm no fool. If a woman cheats on her husband, she'll cheat on the next man in her life."

"Was Christina cheating on you?" Adam asked.

The corners of Roger's mouth rose, and he lowered his voice. "I don't think I was the only man in her life."

Crane interrupted. "Do you know who any of these men were?"

"Nope." He leaned back, a smug look on his face. "Maybe one of them picked her up at the Boot N Scoot."

"Didn't you say Lucy or Sue were going to take her home?" Crane asked.

"That's what Tina told me, but what a woman says and what a woman does are two different things. Ain't you ever had a woman lie to you?"

"One more thing," Crane said. "Do you remember what jewelry Christina was wearing Friday night?"

"I don't pay much attention to that junk. It had red stones. It matched her top."

Crane withdrew a photograph of a ruby necklace and matching earrings. "Was this it?"

He studied the photograph. "Yeah, that looks like it."

"Did anyone show interest in her necklace?"

"Why? It's costume crap. That's what she told everyone."

Crane lifted the photograph, but Roger grabbed it.

"Are you saying it was real?"

"I'm not saying anything, but perhaps someone thought it was real. Her jewelry was missing from the body."

"Someone killed her for this worthless junk?" He studied the photograph before dropping it on the table.

Crane gathered his notes. "That's all for now, Mr. Markem. We'll be in contact if we have any more questions."

Roger rose. "You want to know who killed her? Look no further than that greedy husband of hers."

"Thank you for your input, Mr. Markem."

An officer waiting outside escorted Roger from the room.

Chapter Nine

Crane leaned back in his chair and clasped his hands behind his head. "What did you think of Roger?"

Travis chose his words carefully. "Doreen said Roger confessed to the affair on Valentine's Day. That's why she filed for divorce. He claimed he was just friends with Christina and then admits they were more. He can't keep his story straight."

"Why lie about the affair?"

"He's hiding something," Adam said. "He claims he's a ladies' man, but who would give up a rich husband for a jerk like him?"

"Maybe another man was involved," Crane said. "Maybe Roger is full of shit. I still like the husband for this, but I need a motive. Why do you think she was killed, Officers?"

"Ken found out about the affair," Adam said.

"Would she have met him in the parking lot of the Boot N Scoot to discuss their marriage?" Travis asked. "It's not the safest location for a rendezvous. She had to trust the person."

"What if the person didn't show?" Adam asked. "She was alone in a dark parking lot. Maybe it was a rape that escalated into murder."

"I don't think it was a random act of violence," Travis said. "Choking and beating someone to death is personal. This was someone who hated her enough to punish her." He looked at the crime folder on the table. "Did the coroner have more information?"

Crane flipped through the pages. "She wasn't shot or stabbed with a knife, but there were bruises on her torso, arms, and face. She was punched, kicked, and choked."

"That means Doreen could have done it," Travis said. "She had enough anger to inflict serious injury on a smaller woman."

"Anger is key," Crane said. "Roger showed he has a short fuse. That was good work, poking at him for a reaction, O'Toole. But we need motive. Doreen wanted her husband back. Ken claims he didn't know about the affair, but that's probably a lie. Then there's Roger. If he did it, what set him off?"

"He said he wasn't the only man in her life, but that seemed forced," Travis said. "He asked for a divorce. What man does that if the affair is casual?"

"He's on the list of suspects. Do we want to add any others?"

"What about the jewelry?" Adam asked. "Lucy and Sue said she was wearing it the night she was murdered, but none of it was on the body. Robbery could still be a motive."

Crane removed the photograph of the ruby necklace, earrings, and a bracelet. "Ken sent these photos and confirmed the missing baubles were worth nearly six thousand dollars. I'll wager he's already sent a claim to the insurance company."

"Six thousand? And she wore it to the Boot N Scoot?" Adam shook his head and examined the photos. "That proves my theory."

"She told her friends it was costume jewelry," Crane

said. "It's in your report."

"Maybe the thief didn't believe her," Adam said.

"Roger wanted to know if it was real. But why kill her? Just grab it and run." Travis studied the photos. "Doreen said Christina was wearing a bunch of tacky jewelry Friday night, but these pieces look expensive."

"Tacky usually means she can't afford it," Crane said. "I've sent descriptions of the missing pieces to pawn shops and jewelry stores in case it was a robbery and someone tries to sell any of it."

"Then we're done?" Adam rose.

"You can leave if you want, but I have Ken's girlfriend in room two."

Adam paused. "The husband had a girlfriend?"

"He referred to her as his client, but he claims to have spent the night with her." Crane opened his report. "Her name is Talia Shaver."

"The news woman with the big...headlines?" A grin broke across Adam's face as he turned the knob on the door. "I've always been a fan."

Adam was already seated when Travis followed Crane into the other interrogation room. Talia was the stereotype women had to become to star on television. She wore a tight-fitting dress that displayed ample breasts, the size that left no doubt they were artificially enhanced. They were at odds with her bone-thin arms and legs. Her hair was bleached nearly white and was artfully curled over one shoulder and hung to her waist.

Adam wiped the drool off his lip while Crane studied his notes. Travis studied Talia. Makeup was artfully applied on a face that had seen more than one surgeon's blade. The nose was too narrow, and her eyes had a surprised look. She wore an elaborate necklace with matching bracelets on each wrist. They moved up and down on her thin arms every time she raised her hands.

Crane introduced them. Adam leaned across the table and offered his hand. She gave it a slight brush before withdrawing her perfectly manicured nails. Travis nodded instead.

"Do you know any of these people?" Crane placed an array of photographs on the table.

She tapped on Ken's picture. "This is my financial advisor, Ken Porter." Her voice was light and airy as if she were doing a Marilyn Monroe impersonation.

"What about these?" Crane pointed to photographs of Roger, Doreen, and Christina.

She moved her hand in a dismissive wave. "I never met any of them."

He shoved a photograph of a young, well-dressed Christina closer. "This woman was murdered early Saturday morning. You don't know who she is?"

She tapped her nails on the table. "I never met her, but that's Ken's wife. I've seen her picture in the society pages. He called me on Saturday and was extremely distraught."

"Do you know the whereabouts of Ken Porter on Friday night and Saturday morning?"

She leaned forward, pressing her already enlarged breasts higher above the low-cut neckline. "He stayed with me at my place."

"Did you share the same bed?"

She fluttered fake eyelashes so long they touched her thinly plucked eyebrows. "All night long." She said the words slowly and purred to convey a not-so-subtle meaning.

Crane snorted. "He never left?"

"No man leaves my bed before I kick him out." The slow delivery was meant to convey seduction, but her words grated like nails on a chalkboard.

Travis wrote *liar* in his notes.

Crane continued, "So you admit you and Ken Porter are lovers?"

"I prefer to call it friends with benefits. No strings attached, although he does give me the friends discount when he does my finances and taxes."

"How long has he been doing your bookkeeping?" Adam asked.

"Three years."

"Did his wife know about you?"

"If she did, she kept quiet about it, and Ken never complained about her. He knew not to talk about his personal life with me. I'm not a family therapist."

Travis waited for Adam to ask another question. When he didn't, he spoke. "Do you have ambitions to be the next Mrs. Porter?"

"No." She pressed her fingertips against one breast, drawing attention to her ample cleavage. "I was married once, but I didn't like it. I don't know if it was jealousy or insecurity, but my husband couldn't handle how much attention I received when we were out in public. I like my independence. Besides, I have more social followers as a single woman."

"That's a lovely necklace." Travis pointed to the elaborate designed chain with pink stones resting on her breasts. "A gift from Ken?"

"No. This is one I bought from a jeweler in downtown Cleveland."

Crane lifted his phone. "Do you mind if I take a

photograph?"

"Of the necklace or my breasts?" She twittered as if flirting.

The phone shook for a brief moment. "Both unless you want to remove it."

"Don't forget the matching bracelets." She raised her hands.

Crane recorded the jewelry. "That's all for now."

Adam volunteered to escort her to her car.

Travis wasn't done. If Ken was her lover, why wasn't she wearing a gift of his? "Did Ken give you any jewelry?"

She stiffened in the doorway and glanced over her shoulder. "Yes."

"What did he give you?"

"A sapphire necklace and earrings but the clasp broke. He's having it fixed."

"Thank you."

Crane motioned for Travis to wait until Adam and Talia had left. "Good call, O'Toole. I'll wager there's no broken clasp, so why didn't she wear Ken's gift?"

"I hope I'm not overstepping by asking questions."

"That's how we find out who's guilty. Keep it up."

Chapter Ten

When her shift ended Sunday night, Emily yanked her backpack from her locker. The old denim fabric ripped as it caught on the metal frame, and a pen, a miniature flashlight, and a tampon fell out of the new hole. She bent to retrieve her property.

"You need a new bag."

She didn't need to turn around to know it was Doreen. The smell of hairspray filled the air. Even though her hair was short, Doreen sprayed a heavy layer on it to keep every strand in place. Emily had convinced herself Doreen was innocent in Christina's death. She couldn't murder someone and keep quiet about it.

Emily shoved everything inside her bag after covering the hole with a book she had been reading during her break. She examined the damage. "I guess it's time to give up the old bag, but I like carrying it better than a purse."

"You're not going camping. You should carry a cute little purse that moves when you do." Doreen strutted across the room. "If I had your figure, I'd flaunt it. Why is it that the ones with the best equipment have no idea how to operate it?"

"What do you mean?"

"You never know when a cute cop might drop in." Doreen was acting strange. She had shown little interest in Emily's love life before, but she was giving her funny looks and giggling.

"What's wrong with you?"

"Roger wants to get back together." The singsong voice and huge smile on her face declared she was a woman in love. Goofy with romantic fantasies.

A groan escaped Emily's mouth before she could censure her reaction.

Doreen's smile disappeared. "What?"

Logically, whether Doreen got back together with Roger was her business, but she'd been on an emotional roller coaster since February. Didn't she recognize Roger as the cause?

She handed the pager to Doreen who continued her praises of Roger.

"He came by to take the children to dinner and asked me to go along. He was so sweet and asked me all sorts of questions about my day. He said he missed me." A sigh escaped.

Emily couldn't with a clear conscience congratulate her for getting a cheating scumbag back. She stared, trying to figure out something appropriate to say. Nothing came to mind.

Doreen put her hands on her hips. "You think I'm making a mistake, don't you!"

"I didn't say anything." Emily turned her back. "It's none of my business if you want to take Roger back."

"I need him."

Emily turned, and her voice rose to a scream. "Like a hole in the head."

Doreen put her belongings in her locker. "My children need their father. They're miserable without him."

"You said he was a lousy father. He never wanted

children. He's the reason your children have low self-esteem."

"Who said they have low self-esteem?"

She jabbed a finger toward Doreen. "You did. Every time one of them received a bad grade or did something wrong, you blamed Roger."

Doreen's voice softened. "Roger said he loves me."

"Even when he was *doing* Christina?" Emily expected Doreen to get upset, but for once, she kept her emotions in control.

"Roger said it didn't mean anything."

Any respect she had for Doreen disappeared. "You can't possibly believe that lie. You filed for divorce because he confessed to an affair. On Valentine's Day."

"He said it was all a mistake and he never made love to that adulteress."

She shook her head. "You can't call her that if he didn't sleep with her."

"Maybe he did have sex with her, but men are different than women. They need to affirm their masculinity. Especially when they're married to a strong woman." Doreen hauled a box up the ramp. "He needed to assert his dominance elsewhere."

Outrage filled Emily's voice. "The affair is your fault? When did marriage become a competition with the loser seeking a consolation prize?"

"Roger is back on bended knee. I know he has his faults, but he's a hard worker and the only man I've ever loved." Doreen sounded heartbroken as she continued her routine.

"You haven't been separated long enough to meet someone, let alone fall in love with anyone else," Emily argued. "You cannot tell me you're serious about taking him back."

"Give me one good reason why I shouldn't."

"One"—Emily held up a finger—"even if he claims otherwise, he slept with another woman. He may have been in love with her. Two, he wanted a divorce after eighteen years of marriage. Three, he may have killed Christina. Four—"

"I don't believe that. Roger said he was planning to break the whole thing off with her. He saw her with another man a week before her death, and he suspected something was going on."

"You realize you just gave Roger a motive for murder."

Color faded from Doreen's face. "What motive?"

"Jealousy." The same reason the police suspected Doreen might have killed Christina.

"Roger had a temper, but he's mellowed with age. He wouldn't kill her." She sounded unsure.

"Even if he is innocent, what about cheating on you?"

"Don't you think I should forgive him?"

"If you thought he was sincere, you might consider it, but you only have Roger's word for it." Emily shrugged. "For what that's worth."

"He's a good poker player," Doreen said. "Sometimes he plays dumb on purpose, especially if he's hiding something. That's why it took me so long to find out about Tina in the first place."

"He confessed to loving her and asked for a divorce. Why would he do that if it wasn't serious?"

Doreen paced back and forth. "How am I going to know for sure he was through with that temptress and is telling me the truth that he loves me?"

"Christina would be the only other person to tell you if their relationship was over, and she's not speaking unless you believe in séances."

"She worked at a salon." Doreen sat in front of the computer monitors. "There is no topic sacred at a beauty parlor." She unloaded her colored pens and placed them next to her run sheets. "I'm sure she gabbed to her co-workers about her personal life. Sue and Lucy knew Roger. They spent time together at the Boot N Scoot." She stared at Emily, and a scary smile appeared on her face. "I think you need your hair done."

Emily gagged. "Me? I just drag a comb through it once in a while."

Doreen spun Emily's chair around to look at the back of her head. "It definitely needs cut."

Emily grabbed her precious locks. "Why don't you go?"

"They know me," Doreen confessed. "I was a customer and recently stopped in, looking for Roger. I might have broken a few things on my last visit."

Emily sank down in the chair. "Great."

"None of them know you. And you have the perfect excuse for being there. You're not a student anymore. Don't you want to look like a sophisticated woman?" She put her hand on Emily's arm and looked into her eyes. "Help me find out the truth."

Emily threw up her hands. "I don't think you should take Roger back."

Doreen crossed her arms and scowled. "No wonder you don't have a boyfriend."

"What does that mean?"

"All men have faults, Emily. You can't expect them to be perfect. But every man you've dated has failed to meet your standards." She opened the printer door. "Maybe they're too high."

Emily had dated enough men not to be labeled a prude, but no one had made her want to spend the rest of her life with him. And who was Doreen to criticize her choices? "That's better than too low."

"You have to learn to forgive a man his faults."

She did not need a mother hen to give her romantic advice. "Not when it comes to his unfaithfulness. I've broken up with guys for less."

"I'm more tolerant than you." Doreen looked smug.

"I guess you are." Emily swiveled in her chair. Standing by her cheating man was not a trait she cared to endorse. "But what if he's lying?"

Doreen looked worried. "Then help me find out what the other beauticians knew about Tina and Roger."

Emily wanted no part of Doreen's idiotic scheme, but she owed it to her friend to stop her from making the biggest mistake of her life. Besides, a forensic investigator gathered evidence. If she was going to make that her career, she could start on something basic like Roger's involvement with Christina Porter. How hard could it be to prove they were madly in love?

Doreen must have seen that she was weakening. "All you have to do is listen when they talk about Tina and Roger. They would know if the romance was over. That would prove Roger is telling the truth."

"What if their affair was serious and he had every intention of leaving you for her?"

"Then I'd be a fool to take him back."

"And you're not a fool, right?"

Doreen nodded. "Not in this lifetime."

****

Emily tossed and turned all night, wondering how she would carry out Doreen's absurd scheme. She couldn't back out or say no. She owed her co-worker, and it was time to reciprocate a past debt.

If her actions kept her co-worker from taking back Roger, maybe a couple of hours sitting in a salon was worth it. She already knew what they would say. Roger was bonking Christina and was only going back to his wife on the rebound. But Doreen was stubborn. Would she believe her? She had a recording app on her phone she'd used for school. She took the small backpack she had worn jogging to hide her phone and record the conversation. She would play it for Doreen, who was going to meet her after the Monday afternoon appointment.

The salon was in a plaza with other stores, restaurants, and office buildings. She parked in the second row and walked to the entrance.

"Hello!" Emily called out as she entered the empty foyer of the Hair-em Salon. The walls were painted a solid pink and reminded her of the doll aisle in stores. A plethora of scents from shampoo, dye mixtures, and hairspray assaulted her nostrils, and she sneezed.

"I'll be right with you," a woman called out from the large main room.

Emily hung up her coat and sat down in one of the hard pink plastic chairs. She thumbed through a hairstyle magazine, and her fingertips fluttered in a nervous beat. She would never wear her hair in the severe styles of the models. None of them were flattering to less-than-perfect features or easy maintenance. She looked up when footsteps echoed on the gray ceramic floor.

A woman with red hair, in a shade no one was born

with and styled in a short bob, came through the saloon-style doors that swung several times after she passed. She tapped her long talon-like nails on the registration table. Alien life forms had taken over the beauty parlor business. Her pink coat had *Lucy* embroidered with purple thread on the pocket. "What can I do for you?"

"Shampoo, haircut, and style, but I'm not sure what I want. Could we start with a trim?"

Lucy smiled, but it didn't reach her eyes. "We're not busy. Let's see what I can do." She led the way into a large open room with hair dryers on one wall, sinks and reclining chairs on another, and styling chairs in front of a row of mirrors. A beautician, whose coat was embroidered with the name *Sue*, wore her black hair in tight braids along her scalp. Her nails were even longer than Lucy's, if that was possible. These were Christina's friends. Emily hoped they were in a talkative mood.

Chapter Eleven

Emily watched as Sue circled a woman in her styling chair. The beautician wasn't being gentle as she separated clumps of hair and wrapped foil around each section. It looked like mini-antennas were sprouting all over her head. The woman appeared to be in pain.

"Are you coming?" Lucy led her to a pink chair with a sink behind it along the far wall and draped a pink plastic cape around her. "Lean back." She kicked the control on the chair to recline Emily over the hard edge of the pink sink.

Emily gripped the armrest and kept her eyes tightly closed. After spraying her head with hot water, Lucy slapped cold shampoo on her hair and massaged it in. She rinsed and added conditioner before a final rinse. She kicked the chair into an upright position and wrapped a towel around her head.

"Over here." Lucy motioned for Emily to sit in a styling chair where she combed out her tangles in hard, short strokes. "When was the last time you had your hair done?"

"I've been busy with school." Her scalp tingled from the abuse. "I usually wear it in a ponytail."

"Your hair has plenty of natural curl."

Curls that went in every direction, especially with a bad cut.

"What about a few layers to shape it around your

face?" Lucy asked.

That didn't sound so bad. She nodded. A good haircut might help her land a job if she ever received a call for an interview. "I'm looking for a new job, but I may need to wear my hair out of my face."

"I'll leave it long enough to pull back. Will that work?"

Emily took a deep breath and forced herself to relax. "That sounds great."

Lucy pinned several sections of hair to the top of her head and picked up a pair of scissors. "What sort of job are you looking for?" She snipped away at the back.

"I majored in criminology."

"Like a cop?" Lucy lifted the sharp scissors in the air.

She should have lied. "Oh no. I want to investigate crime scenes."

"Like those people on the TV shows with letters instead of a name?"

"Something like that. I like solving puzzles." And saving friends from stepping in dog doo by taking their cheating husbands back.

Lucy released a clip and began working on another section of her hair. "Too bad you're not investigating the murder of our friend. The cops couldn't care less. She wasn't important enough for their time."

Doreen was right. All she had to do was listen. She took a deep breath to calm her voice. "What friend?"

"Tina Porter." Lucy pointed at the beautician license with Christina's photograph tucked into the bottom corner of the large mirror in front of the empty stylist chair next to hers. A black-and-pink bow was stuck to the license like a miniature memorial. "She was one of our employees."

"She used to do my hair all the time, but it's been months since I saw her," said the woman in Sue's chair. "What's your name, sugar?"

"Emily." She didn't think to give an alias.

"Emily is a pretty name." She extended her hand from beneath her pink cape. "I'm Barb. Pleasure to meet you."

"Nice to meet you, Barb."

Sue was shaking a solution in a plastic bottle. Barb tilted her head back like a pro. She had a head full of foil and was now getting squirted with a mixture of hair color that looked like mud.

"Are you sure that's the right color?" Barb asked. "Tina always used a special mix for me."

"I followed her instructions exactly," Sue said.

"The last time Tina did my hair was at Christmas. My friends and family loved what she did with it." Barb stared at the memorial on the mirror and sighed.

Emily nodded toward the license. "What was she like?"

"She was the sweetest woman on the face of the earth. I can't believe someone murdered her. Who would do such a thing?" Barb shook her head back and forth.

"Stop!" Sue was splattered with the mud-colored dye.

"Sorry," Barb said.

Sue grabbed a couple of towels and wiped herself clean.

Emily wanted to ask about Roger but posed a safer question. "Did she have family?"

Barb dabbed at her face with a towel Sue gave her. "Two children she adored and a husband who gave her everything a woman could want."

Lucy gave Sue a knowing look in the mirror.

Barb saw it, too. "I thought he was rich. Wasn't Tina happy?"

"He was very alpha male," Lucy said.

Barb looked puzzled. "Isn't that a good thing?"

"In romance novels when they never go past the wedding vows. Besides, Ken was insecure and had to control every aspect of Tina's life," Lucy said. "She could barely breathe. She worked here part time so it wouldn't interfere with serving her master's wishes. Like that made any difference. He was preparing to kick her to the curb, but until then, she had to abide by his rules."

Barb asked the next question on Emily's mind. "He wanted a divorce?"

"Tina saw the papers in his safe," Lucy said. "Ken wasn't going to let her walk with anything but what she came in with. He had an ironclad prenup that required a ten-year marriage before she received anything. They were on year nine, and he was seeking sole custody of the children."

"The girl is only six, and the boy is around eight." Sue tossed the soiled towels in a hamper. "They were better off with their mother, but Ken didn't care."

"That's awful," Barb said. "Did she have a good lawyer?"

"He didn't give her much of a chance with a prenup." Lucy waved the scissors in the air. "He warned her to avoid anything Ken could use against her in a custody battle."

"That's why she wanted to keep her license current," Sue said. "She knew it was only a matter of time before he stopped paying the bills. Who would have thought he would do something permanent?"

Barb gasped. "Then you think he killed her?"

"You'll have to keep your eyes closed," Sue told Barb as she finished squirting the foul-smelling liquid onto her hair.

Barb shut her eyes. "Is Ken guilty?"

"I don't know. The police haven't made an arrest." Sue squeezed the last of the mixture onto Barb's head. "They've been busy asking stupid questions."

"That sergeant wasted our time questioning us." Lucy ran a comb through Emily's hair, measured the length, and snipped at the ends. "He wanted to know why we didn't leave with her from the Boot N Scoot at one. We were in the ladies' room with beer-filled bladders. She said she had a ride. You don't give up your spot when the line is out the door and they want to lock up the joint. She was gone by the time we went outside."

"We were her best friends." Sue looked at Lucy. "Ken had the motive."

"Will Ken have a funeral for Tina?" Barb looked at the memorial. "I'd like to pay my respects."

"It would make him look guilty if he didn't," Sue said.

"Do you know when?"

"Thursday." Sue threw the plastic bottle away and set a timer. "It was posted online. Tranquility Funeral Home."

Tranquility? They were the largest funeral home in town and Emily's father's biggest competitor.

"Are you going to close the salon?" Barb asked.

"We have to so we both can attend." Lucy combed Emily's hair out to the side and clipped the ends in a jagged pattern. "Everyone was understanding when I rescheduled them."

Barb held the towel to her forehead to catch any drips. "I hate to ask, but will you be replacing Tina?"

"We put an ad in Sunday's paper," Lucy said.

"Already?" Barb asked.

"Tina could only work when her kids were in school, and summer break was coming up, so we were planning to hire someone anyway." Lucy put the scissors down and ran her fingers through the layers she had created.

"It'll be tough to replace Tina," Barb said. "She was so friendly."

Sue cleaned her work area. "Well, Roger didn't waste any time getting a replacement."

Roger as in Roger Markem? "Who's Roger?" Emily tried to control the excitement in her voice.

"One of her secrets," Lucy whispered from behind her.

"I won't tell." Spying was fun. She might have a knack for gaining others' trust and having them open up.

Lucy shrugged as she retrieved a blow dryer. "It doesn't matter now. He was Tina's secret boyfriend."

"Because of the prenup?" Emily asked.

"We hung out in public as friends, but Ken must have become suspicious." Lucy turned on the blow dryer, and everyone paused the conversation until she was done.

"It was Roger's fault," Sue said. "He hung all over her even when she warned him not to be so affectionate."

"Roger," Lucy sneered as she plugged in a curling iron. "He's already back with his wife."

"He's married, too?" Emily knew it was forced, but

no one seemed to notice the high squeak in her shaky voice. "Isn't anyone faithful anymore?"

"Not when he was married to an old hag who wanted to bleed him dry," Lucy said. "I hope the police don't overlook her as a suspect. She was harassing Tina the night she died. She came to her house and demanded to speak to Roger. They had to call the police to get her to leave."

"Did you tell the police about that?" Barb asked.

Lucy picked up the curling iron. "I told the police sergeant what Tina said at the Boot N Scoot. She was upset. The last thing Tina needed was more trouble."

Lucy was nearly finished, and Emily was running out of time. She needed something to convince Doreen beyond a doubt that she was better off without Roger. "What kind of trouble?"

"Roger's wife. What did it matter that her soon-to-be ex-husband was helping Tina out? He loved her," Sue said.

"How do you know?" Emily hoped her voice didn't sound too eager.

"He was like a lovesick school boy when she was with him." Sue waved at another customer, who had entered. "He had his hands all over her no matter how many times she warned him to behave. Who knew if Ken had a private investigator following her?"

"It was a convenient love if you ask me." Lucy released the curling iron, and a steamy tendril fell against Emily's neck. "After we told Roger they had found Tina's body, he came in here crying his eyes out over losing the love of his life. Now he's talking about making up with his wife—the woman he used to call bitchzilla."

"Bitchzilla." Sue laughed. "At least Roger was fun.

He would join us at the Boot N Scoot when Tina could get away from her husband for an evening."

"Only the best from Roger." Lucy put the curling iron down.

"It's not that bad, and it's a great place to dance," Sue defended. "Did you hear back from Butch about a memorial service?"

"He confirmed we could hold a wake for Tina at the Boot N Scoot." Lucy brushed her hair with a big round brush to style it into a long straight bob.

Sue nodded as she checked the timer for Barb's color treatment. "Tina would have liked that."

"When is it?" Barb asked.

"Wednesday night," Lucy said. "We didn't want to do it after the funeral. It would be too depressing."

Silence ensued. Emily couldn't wait to share what she had learned with Doreen.

"How is that?" Lucy handed her a mirror and turned the chair around so she could view her new hairstyle front and back. It was sleek and professional looking.

Emily knew she'd be tempted to take scissors to it once the curl sprang back into it and ruined the smooth elegance Lucy had painstakingly created. She should have told Lucy she liked the curl in her hair. She could scrunch it and go. "It's just what I imagined," she lied.

Emily clicked off her phone app before Lucy removed the pink cape. She searched through her backpack to pay her.

"I'll take it at the front desk."

Emily paid and stashed her receipt. She hoped Lucy and Sue had provided her with enough information to extinguish the flame Doreen was carrying for Roger.

Chapter Twelve

Travis was given the solo assignment of interviewing the owners of the Boot N Scoot Entertainment Venue. The concrete block building had no windows, and a mural was painted on the otherwise dull gray wall facing the parking lot. A stagecoach with six horses, a driver, and an armed lookout graced the surface and sanctioned the western theme of the business establishment. Even though Ohio had never been considered the Wild West, a stagecoach line had traveled through the area and justified the decor.

The double-door entrance opened to a foyer where restrooms were located on one side and a coatrack was located opposite. A sign read *leave belongings at your own risk*. A cardboard box labeled *lost and found* sat on a chair. A single glove, a winter scarf, and a tube of lipstick remained inside, unclaimed.

The main room had a raised stage at one end. Booths lined the walls with a few tables and chairs arranged around the edge of an open wooden floor for dancing. The bar was opposite the stage with an old-fashioned cash register near the door. The low-wattage lighting from hanging lanterns illuminated the mahogany wood of the antique bar that had been polished to a shine. A mirror reflected carefully arranged liquor bottles on shelves behind the counter. The business was in the hands of someone who cared. A man with a scraggly gray ponytail stacked clean glasses on the shelves beneath the bar. It was still early for the dinner crowd, and no one was around except a few men shooting pool in the game room separated from the main area by support columns.

"Is one of the owners in?" Travis flashed his badge for the man with the ponytail.

"I'm co-owner with Jade Carter. She's off today." He wiped off his hand and extended it. "Butch Faris. What can I do for you?"

Travis placed a photograph of Roger on the bar top. "Do you know Roger Markem?"

"He's a regular. Came in with his wife for years, then he came in alone, and since last year he's been joining Tina Porter and her friends."

"Christina Porter?" Travis placed her photo on the bar.

"That's her. Is she really dead?"

"Yes. Why do you doubt it?"

"She was full of life." Butch stared at the photo. "She was a lady but no snob. Friendly and always generous with the tips and compliments. Everyone liked her."

Someone didn't. "Do you remember what she was wearing Friday night?"

"She wore a shiny red blouse that glittered under the lights and a mini skirt. Tina had great legs. I think she was a cheerleader in high school."

"Any jewelry?"

"She always wore glitter, but I couldn't describe it. You should ask Jade. She talked jewelry with Tina all the time. They were close."

Travis placed Ken's photo on the bar. "Did he ever

come in?"

"Never saw him." Butch identified Lucy and Sue. "They came in Friday nights to dance and drink a couple of beers."

Travis gathered the photographs. "Anyone besides Roger pay more than the usual attention to her?"

"She danced with any man who asked as long as he wasn't stumbling-down drunk."

"Were Roger and her a couple or not?"

"They were both married, and Tina was careful not to flaunt any romance. But Roger made it clear she was his girl. He got real possessive when someone acted too friendly."

"Did Roger ever fight anyone over her?"

"Usually I'd bust up anything before it mushroomed into a brawl," Butch said. "We don't like replacing furniture and glass. And if there is a fight, the cops show up and send everyone home. I always tell them to take any arguments outside."

"Did Roger confront anyone in the parking lot?"

"I don't follow the customers out the door unless they leave without paying their bill," Butch said.

"What happened Friday night?"

"It was quiet. Roger and Tina came in together and joined Lucy and Sue. They always sat together to make it look friendly but not romantic."

Travis flipped back through his notes. "Do you remember when Roger left?"

"It was before midnight. I thought it odd he didn't take her outside for a quickie in his truck." Butch smirked. "That's what he usually did."

"How do you know?"

"They had a routine. About a half hour before

closing, Tina would pay the bill, and Roger would take her out to his truck to do the deed. She would return with her hair and clothes messed. Lucy and Sue would join her in the ladies' room, and she would emerge with no evidence Roger had ever touched her. Lucy would take her home in case her husband returned early."

Butch had said Tina paid the bill. "Roger didn't pay?"

Butch laughed. "Roger had a huge loan on a truck and child support to pay, which he complained about to anyone who would listen. He paid for his own drinks but never bought a round and was a lousy tipper."

Travis had hoped for more information. "Did anything out of the ordinary happen Friday night?"

"Roger was in a foul mood. He complained about his old lady following him around. She confronted Tina at her home. By the end of the night, everyone knew about it." Butch opened a crate filled with liquor bottles. "I remember his wife being loud but not violent. Have you talked to her?"

"I can't comment on an ongoing investigation. How mad was Roger?"

"He didn't get into any fights, but most people knew to stay clear of him. Everyone was glad when he finally left."

"Do you know if he came back?"

"If he did, he didn't come in."

"Do you have cameras on your parking lot?"

"No. As far as I'm concerned, what happens outside stays outside. We keep a camera above the cash register and in the storeroom where we keep the liquor. That's my priority."

"Thank you for your help. I'll be back to talk to

Jade."

"We're hosting a wake for Tina Wednesday night. Jade will be serving drinks."

"A wake? She was that popular?"

"It's an excuse to drink and gather with friends. Who am I to judge how the dead are sent off to the afterlife?"

Chapter Thirteen

Emily stepped outside the salon and played back a few minutes of the recorded conversation on her phone. The truth might hurt Doreen's feelings, but Roger was lying to her. He'd been in love with Christina and had cried when he heard the news of her death. She dialed Doreen's number. "I just had a lovely talk with Sue and Lucy. You were right. They couldn't wait to share what they knew—"

"Forget about that." Doreen's tone was harsh.

"I know you don't want to hear the truth, but Roger loved Christina. I have it taped on my phone. He's lying to you, Doreen."

"I know. I need you to drive to the back of the hair salon."

"You know?" Emily looked around. The Hair-em was located on the end of the plaza. Walking would take less time than going to her car and driving around. "What's in the back?"

"I am. Get back here now." Doreen sounded upset.

Was she hurt? Emily jogged around the plaza to the back where deliveries were made. Doreen's SUV was parked in the alley that ran parallel to the back of the buildings. She stood next to an old van parked behind the Hair-em near the employee entrance door. The vehicle had seen better days with rust along the bottom, a dent in the side, and scrape marks along the entire sliding door.

Doreen examined the dent.

"How did you hit a parked van?"

She turned, a scowl on her face. "I didn't hit it."

"Then why are you standing back here staring at it?"

She waved her hand across the battered vehicle. "It's mine."

Emily pointed at the SUV across the street. "I thought that was your car."

"This is my old car." Doreen ran her hands along the metal side as if it were an old friend. "This is the one I totaled in January. Roger said he sold it for scrap. He had me sign the title over, and he gave me two hundred dollars."

Emily studied the van. Unlike auto experts, she couldn't care less what model or year a vehicle was as long as it transported her from here to there. "It probably just looks like your car."

"How many blue vans do you know that are sideswiped? I told you how that driver suddenly came into my lane. I could have been killed."

Doreen had told that harrowing encounter more than once. The driver's side was dented and scraped from the sliding door to the rear where a taillight was broken.

"You think it's your van?"

Doreen pulled her to the back. "Look at the plates. I left the old ones on and got new ones when I bought my SUV." She dragged her back to the front and inserted a key into the door lock.

Emily looked around. "What are you doing?"

"Haven't you been listening? This is *my* car." Doreen unlocked the door. "I have the spare key."

"Why would you keep it?"

"They didn't need both keys to scrap the car." She

opened the door.

"But why do you have the key in your purse?"

She shook it. "Lucky for me I'm not good at cleaning out old items."

Emily had waited until the end of a semester to clean out her bag. "I understand that, but what do you want me for?"

"I need you to drive it out of here."

"Me?" The rational side of her brain was shouting *don't do it.*

Doreen's argument was equally logical. "I can't drive both, can I?"

"What about my car in front?"

"I'll drive you back for it."

This was a bad idea. Emily searched for a reason to say no. "Why do you need to move it?"

"Roger must have parked it here. He's going to come back and claim it now that his lover is dead."

She'd referred to Christina as Roger's lover. At least she was no longer in denial about his relationship with her. "Are you sure it's your van?"

"Yes, and I'm claiming it," Doreen said. "Check the glove compartment if you don't believe me. I always kept the title and registration in there."

Emily went to the passenger door, which Doreen unlocked. She searched the glove box and found outdated proof of insurance, the registration due for renewal in another month, and a title. "If you move it, Roger will find out."

Doreen climbed into the driver's seat. "That's why you need to drive it to your house."

"You mean my parents' house? That's a bad idea. They're going to ask questions."

"You have a parking lot in the backyard."

"That's for my father's business. People don't park overnight. They're going to notice a battered van sitting all by itself."

Doreen shrugged as she opened the caddy between the bucket seats. "Make up a story."

"I can't lie to my parents."

Doreen made a tsking noise and scrunched her face. "How old are you? Three?"

Her parents had raised her to be an honest person. "Do your children lie to you?"

"All the time. That's why I search their rooms and keep tabs on where they go."

That explained the tracking app. "What happened to trust?"

Doreen stopped her search. "Do your parents trust you?"

"Yes." It was the truth and a profound insight. She needed to thank them and certainly not embarrass them by involving them in one of Doreen's crazy schemes. Emily looked around. "There has to be a better place to hide your van."

Doreen snapped her fingers. "The hospital. Cars are parked there twenty-four hours a day. It'll just be another vehicle in the parking lot."

Emily didn't argue. Parking Doreen's van at the hospital was far better than at her parents' house even if it was a funeral home. "Are you sure Roger didn't sell your car to someone?"

Doreen grabbed the papers from Emily and pointed at the information. The title had Doreen's name, the mileage, the make and year of the van, and her signature to transfer ownership but no date. "He told me he sold it for scrap, but here's the title, and here's the van." She shoved the paperwork into her purse.

"But you said Roger gave you money from scrapping it."

"Two hundred dollars." Doreen's jaw dropped, and her voice rose to a screech. "If he didn't sell it, where did he get the money? And if he had that much, how much more does he have?"

Emily searched the alley. A straight-bed truck was backed up to a loading dock behind one of the stores in the plaza, but no one else was around. "Why is it parked here? Maybe we should tell the police about this."

"Tell them I found my van?" Doreen shouted. "Roger was hiding it."

"But why? He has a truck."

Doreen looked at the other vehicles parked in the alley. "I bet Roger let that woman use it."

"Christina? She didn't have a car?"

"She had an expensive one. Brand new," Doreen said. "I saw it parked in the plaza parking lot all the time."

This was a huge step down for transportation. "Then why would she want to drive this wreck?"

Doreen didn't argue the description of her beloved van. She tapped her fingers on the steering wheel. "I bet her husband was tracking her car."

Like Doreen tracked Roger's truck? But the outlandish statement made sense. If Christina didn't want her husband to know where she was going, why not switch vehicles? "Is there anything in here to prove Christina used it?"

Doreen felt under the front seat. "Check the back."

The back seats had stains Emily couldn't identify.

103

"Why can't you check the back?"

"The door on my side doesn't open." The sideswiped door.

Emily slid open the door on her side. A pungent odor overwhelmed her nostrils. She pinched her nose with her fingertips and took a step back. "What's that smell?"

"Kids. They're not careful about food, drinks, or bodily functions."

She looked through the seat opening where Doreen was searching the small compartments in the dash. "What do you mean bodily functions?"

"My daughter used to get carsick."

She backed up a step. "Maybe you should check."

"You're the one who wants to work with dead people," Doreen said. "Don't go all hysterical on me now, Morticia."

She stomped her foot on the pavement. "One of the boys in fifth grade made the mistake of calling me that because I helped place the flowers in my dad's funeral home. Don't make me kick your butt, Doreen."

"Then stop making excuses and take a look."

Emily's pride kicked in. If she could handle the smell of lilies, roses, and formaldehyde, she could handle dirty, smelly, and sticky. She leaned down and peered under the passenger seats. She ignored the paper wrappers, food scraps, and gum stuck to the metal framework. She tossed aside a bag filled with empty aluminum cans. "I found something." She pulled out a backpack tucked under the bench seat in the third row. It was pink with a kitten sewn on the pouch on the front. She climbed into the front passenger seat and placed the bag on her lap. "Does this belong to your daughter?"

"She wouldn't be caught dead with a kitty

backpack."

"Sue, the friendly beautician, said Christina had two kids. Her daughter is six. It probably belongs to her." Emily slowly moved the zipper around the top of the bag.

"It's not a Christmas present or a bomb," Doreen complained. "Unzip it."

Emily opened the bag and pulled the sides apart to reveal what was inside. Boxes of condoms were stacked tightly inside. "Wow! That's a lot of protection."

"Especially for a first grader."

Emily stared at Doreen. "It must belong to Christina and the man in her life." It was another mark against Roger. Hurray!

Doreen examined a box. "Why would Roger need condoms? He had a vasectomy after our daughter was born."

The reason was obvious to Emily. "Protection from STDs. When was the last time you had sex with Roger?" She raised her hand. "Wait, don't answer that." An involuntary shudder shook her body, and she closed her eyes against any image. "You might want to visit your doctor."

"You don't think Roger had sex with her in my van?" Doreen took a sniff. "Do you smell cigarette smoke?"

Smoke haloed Doreen. "Only on you."

She looked to the back. "Did you see a blanket? He kept one in his truck. He liked parking and making out under it."

"No, no, no!" Emily held up her hands. "I do not want to hear about Roger's sex habits. If you want to search for a blanket, be my guest."

Doreen looked at the backpack. "Anything else in

there?"

She unzipped the small front compartment. "There's business cards inside." She handed Doreen a card embossed with the name of the Tally-Ho Hotel and owner B. J. Debrowsky with a phone number below.

"The Tally-Ho?" Doreen handed the card back. "That place rents by the hour."

"Maybe he didn't defile your van." She was taking a shower when she returned home just in case. She tapped on the card. "This address puts the hotel near the hospital."

"Haven't you heard the nurses talk about a place called Penicillin Penthouse? That's one of the kinder names for that dump."

She was thankfully ignorant of the seedier lifestyles of some people. "Good to know Roger only took Christina to the finest places."

"Which proves he didn't love her. It was all about the sex."

"I can prove otherwise if you'll listen to what the women at the Hair-em said about Roger."

Doreen's stubborn look softened. "I know Roger was lying about the van, but maybe he was telling the truth about ending his affair with Tina."

Emily pointed at the kitty backpack. "I have a bag full of condoms. They weren't making balloon animals."

Doreen crossed her arms and leaned back in the bucket seat. "I'll listen to your dumb recording one time, and then I don't want to hear it again."

Chapter Fourteen

Emily played the recording. Doreen grunted a few times, made a few comments, but listened until the end.

Emily put away her phone. "Roger was crying when Christina was killed. I think that's pretty hard evidence he loved her."

"He barely knew her," Doreen argued.

She dropped the kitty backpack to the floor of the van and zipped it closed. "They were having an affair with lots of sex."

"I was married to him for eighteen years. No contest!"

She softened her tone to reason with her. "You know he lied about your van. Why are you defending him?"

Doreen swiped a stray tear away. "Roger had a midlife crisis. He wanted to feel young again, and she was right there, willing to spread her legs." A venomous tone underscored her words. "I never cheated on Roger. I sometimes gave him a hard time, but that was for his own good."

"I'm sorry." Emily patted her hand. "I don't want him to hurt you again. You were a train wreck in February when he told you about her. I know you were happy at one time, but relationships change. You can't go back."

Doreen hesitated, her body rigid. "You just don't get it."

"Get what?"

"I was pretty when I was your age, but I'm forty-six years old now. What man is going to want me?"

"There are lots of men who—"

"I know the stats!" Doreen screamed. "A woman depends on one thing. The man she marries when she's young is supposed to grow old with her."

Doreen was on the verge of tears, but Emily pressed her point. "Do you want to grow old with someone who makes you miserable?"

"Every couple has their problems." Doreen removed a tissue from her purse and dried her eyes. After staring at her reflection in the vanity mirror, she removed a compact to repair the damage. "Maybe Roger isn't so bright, and he has a temper, but I know what I have with him." She sniffled as she dabbed powder on her cheeks and added a layer of lipstick to her mouth. "He said he made a mistake."

How was she going to get through to Doreen? She had to be tough to convince her of Roger's true feelings. "If Christina hadn't died, he wouldn't be begging to come back to you."

"I can't help it. I still love him."

"How?" Emily demanded. "After everything he's put you through, after what others said about him, how can you still love him?"

"Those women don't know Roger," Doreen defended. "You should have heard him on the phone today. He wanted to make sure I was all right and asked if the police were harassing me. Isn't that sweet?"

"Sweet? It's his fault the police are questioning you. Did you ask him if he murdered Christina?"

"Emily!"

It was a fair question. "He drove her to the Boot N Scoot. Why didn't he take her home?"

"He said he left all three of them—Tina, Lucy, and Sue—at the Boot N Scoot because he had to get up early to go fishing." Doreen dropped her lipstick tube into her bag. "He went straight home."

Emily leaned back in the seat and stared at her. "Well, you would know."

"What?" Doreen had a confused look on her face.

Emily pointed at the phone outlined in Doreen's pocket. "You tracked him."

"I only used it to follow him to *that* woman's house." Doreen removed her phone. "He doesn't know I have him on my app, and I don't want him to."

Could it convict Roger? Emily pointed at the screen. "How does it work? Can you tell where he went Friday night after he left the Boot N Scoot?"

Doreen pressed several buttons on the screen. "He left the Boot N Scoot at eleven just like he said."

So much for catching him committing a crime. She wasn't ready to quit. "Where did he go?"

Doreen frowned and refused to answer.

"What?" She tried to take the phone, but Doreen held fast and moved it out of her reach.

"He went to the convenience store across the street from the Boot. He probably needed beer and cigarettes."

Emily peered over her shoulder. "Then what?"

"He stayed there. Maybe he bought something to eat. The food at the Boot N Scoot is eighty-percent grease."

Emily groaned. "Good to know."

"Wait, he returned to the Boot N Scoot around one." Doreen faced her, her eyes round with fear. "That's

109

closing time."

"He went back to pick up Christina. Why else would he wait around?" She leaned in close to view the screen. "Where did he go next?"

"I don't want to know." Doreen turned off her phone.

"No, you don't." Emily grabbed for it.

Doreen stared her down as she clutched her phone.

"Do you want to know the truth or not? He might be a killer."

Doreen turned it back on and brought up the screen. "No!"

Emily leaned in close to see. "What?"

"He took her to the Tally-Ho."

"The one on the card?"

Doreen waved the phone around as if it were contaminated. "They were there until two. Then he took her home."

"Home? He didn't take her to Ida Road and the park?" Emily pointed at the phone. "Check it again."

Doreen took her time reviewing the information. "He stopped at her house for a few minutes and drove to his mother's." She looked up. "The truck stayed there all night."

Emily groaned as she fell back against the passenger seat. "Great, he didn't kill Christina."

Doreen smacked her shoulder.

"Ouch!" The woman was strong.

Doreen jerked her chin up. "You sound disappointed, but I'm not."

A guilty verdict would have kept Roger out of Doreen's life. "He still lied about your van and having sex with Christina Porter unless they played cards at the

Tally-Ho." Sarcasm dripped with every word.

"Come with me tomorrow morning," Doreen begged. "I'm meeting him for breakfast. You can help me find out the truth."

Breakfast wasn't a bad idea. Emily wanted to see Roger's reaction and hear his explanation when confronted with the facts. "Where should I meet you?"

"Friends Café and Coffee House," Doreen said. "It's near the Boot N Scoot." Her expression softened. "Roger and I used to line dance for hours when the place opened."

She was traveling down memory lane, a dangerous trip. She needed to keep her focus on reality and the future. Confronting Roger might convince Doreen he couldn't be trusted. Emily wanted to show her what a sleaze the man was and how lucky she was to be rid of him.

"We'll meet at eight." Emily climbed out of the vehicle, leaving the kitty backpack on the floor. "Don't forget to call the police about the van and bag."

"Why?"

"Christina used it. It's part of the police investigation into her death."

"How?" Doreen looked to the back. "You don't think she was killed in it?"

Who could tell with all the stains? "Do you want to get into trouble with the police?"

Doreen lifted her phone. "I'm calling them now."

Emily paused. "And tell them I was in the van if they check for fingerprints."

"Don't worry. I'll take care of it," she promised.

Emily jogged to the front and drove home.

Chapter Fifteen

Emily chose a skort and lightweight sweater to wear to breakfast with Doreen and Roger. She had her recording and the name of a hotel to prove he'd had an affair with Christina Porter, but he could claim he had seen the light and wanted a second chance. She needed him to say something that would make Doreen realize he hadn't changed. The van could be the factor that tipped the scales.

Friends Café and Coffee House showed its age with duct-tape patches on the vinyl seats of the booths that lined the walls. Small wooden tables filled the remaining floor space. Emily wondered how long it would remain open. Most of the businesses on Main Street were run down and barely hanging on. Too many sported *for lease* signs in empty windows. Most residents of Darrow Falls commuted to work north to Cleveland or south to Akron and shopped at mega-malls near the interstate. The town was losing its identity and its population. Most of her friends had moved away, but she loved her hometown and its rich history. If enough young people stayed, the town could see new life.

The coffee house was named Friends after a popular television show in syndication about three men and three women who sorted out their relationships. The diner served breakfast and lunch and closed at two.

Doreen was at a booth near a window overlooking

the parking lot with her back to the entrance. She was wearing a long cotton dress. The weather woman had said it was going to be sunny with a high in the seventies, and for once, she was right.

Emily took the seat across from Doreen and looked around. "Where's Roger?"

Doreen stopped playing a game on her phone and nodded toward a black truck pulling in to the parking lot. She grabbed Emily's hand. "Don't mention finding the van. I called a place that buys cars for scrap, and they'll give me four hundred dollars for it."

"The police are going to let you sell it?"

Doreen didn't answer.

"Doreen! You promised to call the police. You can't withhold evidence in a criminal investigation."

"The van has nothing to do with Tina's murder."

"You have to let the police decide that."

"I'll tell them, but don't mention the van or anything we found in it to Roger."

Without the van, condoms, and business cards, she had nothing but the recording on her phone. How was she going to convince Doreen he was no good? "Are you going to confront him about Christina?"

"Not now. He wants to reconcile. Try to be nice."

Was she crazy? So much for talking sense into her. "Maybe I should leave."

"Don't," Doreen begged. "I won't find out the truth if I confront him directly. Don't you know anything about using feminine wiles?"

Doreen was the most direct person she knew when it came to dealing with others. "You have feminine wiles?"

Doreen's eyebrows came together in a frown but

rose with a wide smile as she waved to Roger when he passed their window and entered.

He wore blue jeans, cowboy boots, and a wrinkled button-down shirt. He hadn't shaved. On some men, stubble looked rugged, even handsome, but on Roger, it looked like he'd spent a restless night.

"I thought we were meeting alone." He stared at Emily sitting across from Doreen. "Not that I'm complainin'." His good-boy charm was emphasized by a display of imperfect teeth that were badly stained, likely from coffee and tobacco. "Any friend of Doreen darlin' is a friend of mine."

On a young man a look conveying interest could be flattering. On an older, married man like Roger, it made Emily shudder.

Doreen either didn't see the lust in his eyes or chose to ignore it. She smoothed out the collar of his shirt as he sat next to her. "You look like hell. You need someone to take care of you."

Why was Doreen being so loving? Had she forgotten all the evidence they'd accumulated against him? Even if she wanted to find out the truth with wiles, she didn't have to slobber all over him.

"How do you know Doreen?" He had suspicion in his voice. Had he figured out it wasn't a friendly visit?

"You've met Emily. She works second shift at the hospital in my department," Doreen said. "We chat between shifts."

"Do you work part time, too?" A hint of anger was in his voice.

"Yes, but I'm looking for a full-time job," Emily said.

"I've told Doreen she needs to work more hours."

Emily took advantage of the opening. "She may have to if you don't pay child support."

Roger put his arm around Doreen's shoulders. "I hardly think I'll need to pay anything since we're getting back together."

Emily took her jab. "So you're only reconciling to save money?"

Roger squinted, replacing a frown with a broad smile, too forced to be natural. "I'm returning for love. After eighteen years the flame hasn't gone out."

She poked, hoping he'd react. "It must have been flickering when you were seeing Christina Porter."

Doreen looked like she was going to kill Emily but kept her anger contained to a condemning glare. She would thank her when the truth came out.

"I told you we were just friends." Roger hugged Doreen around her shoulders. "You understand, don't you, darlin'? A man needs to have a beer and relax after a long day of working with his hands. If a woman smiles at him, he just naturally smiles back."

Doreen ran her hand up his arm and rested it upon his shoulder as she met his gaze. "I knew you were going through a midlife crisis. You wandered a little, but now you're back."

"I couldn't stay away from my wonderful wife."

Doreen gave Emily a smug smile at his answer. "I told you he wanted to reconcile."

Roger's eyes narrowed a bit as he studied Emily. "You don't believe me?"

"I hardly know you. I'm here to support Doreen. I wouldn't want her to make a mistake. If you've put your relationship with Christina in the past, you won't be attending her funeral," Emily said in what could only be a challenge.

He didn't answer.

Doreen slapped him on the back of his head with her palm. "Don't even think about it! You're not going to that harlot's funeral!"

Emily gasped as spoons clanged, and a few customers turned in their direction. "Calm down." She'd been hoping for a reaction from Roger, not Doreen. But at least Doreen was acting like her normal self.

"What's wrong with you, woman? It's just a funeral!"

"You said it was over between you," Doreen shouted.

"I'm just showing my respect." He unwrapped the paper napkin around the silverware. "She was a friend."

"With benefits. You were banging her in your truck!"

More dishes clanged. One of the waitresses headed to the back, likely to notify the manager.

Roger's features hardened at her words. "You don't understand," he said slowly and deliberately. "I feel it's my duty to attend."

"You don't need to go!" Doreen ordered. "She's dead."

"This is not something we can discuss." He signaled the waitress to bring coffee.

"You're right." Doreen turned her cup over for the waitress who had appeared at Roger's side. "There is no discussion because you are not going."

"No woman tells me what to do." His voice was low and threatening.

The waitress poured Roger and Doreen coffee.

Emily left her cup overturned. "Hot chocolate,

please."

"Anything else?"

Roger ordered eggs and hash browns with sausage and toast. Doreen ordered the same. Emily ordered a cinnamon roll.

"Welcome, Officer," another waitress called out near the front door as a uniformed police officer entered. It was Travis, and Emily sank in her seat, glad Roger and Doreen had their backs to the door. The manager approached him and nodded toward their booth. Had he called for help? Another officer arrived, and they talked to the manager, who nodded and returned to the back. At least they weren't going to throw them out.

She gave Travis a nod to thank him for intervening. He walked toward her and stopped by their booth.

"Look who's here!" Doreen pointed at the empty spot next to Emily. "Take a seat."

Travis sat beside Emily who moved her backpack to the wall.

"Good morning." He nodded toward Doreen and Roger. "I didn't know you were all friends."

"I know you! You're the cop who was with the detective when he questioned me about Tina." Roger looked around. "What's going on?"

"Nothing is going on," Doreen explained. "He's Emily's boyfriend."

"What?"

Doreen kicked Emily under the table before she could correct anyone.

"We just want to have a friendly chat, don't we, Emily?" Doreen nodded. "Two happy couples having breakfast together."

Emily reached beneath the table and rubbed her

throbbing shin. "Sure. What do you want to talk about?"

"I want to know about the investigation into Tina's murder," Roger said.

"I can't discuss an ongoing case." Travis draped his arm across the top of the booth, and his fingertips touched her shoulder lightly as he whispered in her ear. "Is this for your friends or mine?"

The other officer was looking their way. No, he was staring. Travis gave him a casual wave.

"I'm not sure what Doreen is up to, but your co-worker acts like he's never seen you with a woman," Emily said, hoping to deflate his fun.

"Not one who looks as good as you."

It was a compliment, a good one. "Thank you."

"Let's talk about the funeral of Tina Porter," Doreen announced. "Do you expect a crowd?"

"We expect a large group of mourners, including gawkers and those curious about her death. The police force will be present to keep order."

"Roger thinks he should attend, but Emily and I both agree that would be a mistake," Doreen cooed. Did she hope Travis would join their side?

Roger must have understood the team stacking. "There's no law saying I can't attend, is there, Officer?"

"No, but do you think it's a good idea to attend the funeral of your mistress?"

"Even the police believe she was your lover." A few dishes rattled after Doreen's loud comment.

"She was my friend. It would be disrespectful not to attend." Roger crossed his arms and scowled at the others at the table.

Doreen crossed her arms and sulked.

Emily offered an alternative. "Why not pay your

respects at her wake instead?"

Doreen straightened. "What wake?"

"Wednesday night at the Boot N Scoot," Emily said. "Her friends are paying their respects."

"How'd you know about the wake?" Roger asked.

"I had my hair done," Emily said. "Sue and Lucy told me about it."

Travis tugged on a strand. "You went to the Hair-em?"

"I needed a new look. I have job interviews." She hoped.

"Then we should all go," Doreen said. "I'd like to pay my respects to the homewrecker. Besides, it's been a long time since I've been at the Boot N Scoot. Ought to be fun."

"It's a wake, not a gala," Emily said. "You need to behave."

Travis looked around. "Where's our waitress?"

"She already came and went." Emily pointed. "There she is."

He waved her over.

She smiled and took out her pad. "What can I get you, Officer?"

"You can get me more coffee, sugar," Roger said with a leer.

Travis gave his order, and she headed toward the kitchen. Roger nearly twisted his head off, watching her depart. She had on soft-soled white shoes but walked like she was on a fashion runway, her wide hips bouncing from side to side.

Roger was hardly behaving like a man who wanted to reconcile with his wife. Doreen was busy stirring sugar into her coffee. Was she blind?

Chapter Sixteen

Travis watched Emily studying the waitress. "Do you know her?"

She reddened. "No. I'm glad I never had to work for tips. I don't think I could move like that."

She underestimated her attraction. "You'd make plenty of tips, Em."

She blushed and stammered a reply. "You have to say that because you're my *boyfriend*."

He touched her fingertips. Static flew between them. "Since we're dating, are you free Friday night? We can have dinner and go to a show."

She looked shocked. "A show? Like in a strip club?"

He laughed and placed his hand over his heart. "You cut me to the quick to think I would take any woman to a strip club. I have sisters. One of them is in a local theater production of Shakespeare's *Much Ado About Nothing*. I promised I'd attend, but if you want to do something else, we can skip the show."

Emily's mouth dropped open. "You do know who Shakespeare is, right?"

"No relation, but I've heard of him."

Her mouth formed a smile. She didn't mind being teased. Verbal foreplay was his second favorite pastime.

"Sounds entertaining."

"I'll pick you up at five thirty."

"Do you know where I live?"

"I have it programmed into my GPS."

She glanced at Doreen. "Wonderful thing about GPS. It can give you directions to a destination, the mileage, and track how long it took for the trip."

Doreen gave Emily a little shake of her head. Was she giving her a silent warning against saying anything more?

"Tracking sounds like an invasion of privacy." Doreen shoved her phone into her purse. "I would never do anything illegal."

Emily winced and jerked her leg against his. Had Doreen kicked her?

"You can track a car you own, but there's some discussion about the legality of tracking someone else's automobile," Travis said. "That's why the police have to obtain a warrant to look at GPS history or track the vehicle of a suspect."

"Why would you want to know where someone drove?" Roger fumbled with his coffee cup.

Although Travis had initially responded to the reported disturbance at the café, he wasn't going to pass up an opportunity to interrogate Roger. Crane was seeking a warrant to examine Roger's truck, Doreen's SUV, and Ken's car to track their whereabouts on Friday night. "Sometimes suspects lie."

"And if they lie, they're usually guilty." Emily looked at Travis.

"Right." He looked at his watch. "Aren't you normally at work, Roger?"

"No jobs until ten. I'm taking some personal time to spend with my wife." He leaned over and smacked Doreen on the lips with a loud, slobbering kiss.

She giggled. "Oh, Roger."

The awkward silence was broken by the waitress delivering breakfast. Travis had ordered blueberry pancakes and a side of bacon. He added butter and syrup. Emily picked at her cinnamon roll.

"That doesn't look like much. Do you want one of my pancakes?"

"No, but I'd love half a slice of bacon."

"Take a whole one."

She broke off half and nibbled away on it. Her action made him want to nibble on her lower lip. She smelled like a fresh breeze. She looked like sunshine. And she had agreed to go out on a date. He should have thought of something better than his sister's play, but maybe they would leave at intermission. His thoughts were interrupted by the sound of animals feeding at a trough.

The Markems were digging in to their meals. Roger had poured a thick layer of ketchup on his eggs and hash browns and was shoveling his food into his mouth, which he had trouble closing while he chewed. A glob of ketchup escaped to his chin and hung on the hint of his beard. He didn't seem to feel it. Did manners dictate Travis point it out?

"Roger!" Doreen laughed and dabbed at his face with her napkin. "You must be starving."

Roger pulled away like an angry child having his face wiped with his mother's spit. He gobbled the remaining food on his plate and asked for a refill of coffee.

Doreen finished her meal, and a loud belch escaped. "Excuse me."

"You said the police would be at Tina's funeral, but I hope the police aren't attending Tina's wake," Roger said as if their previous conversation hadn't been interrupted by the meal. "Everyone there liked Tina. The only person who didn't was Ken Porter. I told you her husband killed her."

A few heads turned, but the café was thinning out. Travis kept his voice calm. "And we appreciate your input, but we can't arrest someone without evidence. Besides, we have several people of interest." He hoped Roger told him something he hadn't said in his earlier interview.

"Cut the crap," Roger remarked in a manner identical to Doreen. "Ken threatened her all the time."

Travis leaned forward. "How?"

"He said she'd lose her kids and walk with just the clothes on her back if he divorced her," Roger said. "Tina was scared of him. I guess he didn't stop at threats."

Travis kept his voice smooth and direct. "Did you ever hurt her?"

"I loved—" Roger caught himself as he glanced at Doreen. "I'm a lover not a killer."

"I checked with the owner. You've been in a couple of fights at the Boot N Scoot."

"With men. I'm usually defending a lady's honor." He squeezed Doreen's shoulder as if she were the lady.

"I'd imagine putting down carpet builds upper-body strength."

"I like to stay in shape," Roger defended. "I don't want anyone mistaking me for a donut-loving cop."

Maybe a cop with a potbelly would have been offended, but Travis ignored the insult. Roger was a chain smoker like Doreen and had a gray pallor to his skin. He also had sunken eyes with dark circles under them, so he looked like he didn't sleep well. But his arms and hands were strong enough to beat a woman. Ken

Porter's work involved a pencil or computer, but he outweighed Christina by a hundred pounds. He could inflict damage as well. Which one had the stronger motive and the opportunity?

"I hope you've ruled me out as a suspect," Roger said. "I went home at eleven from the Boot N Scoot."

"That's not true. Ouch!" Emily bent down to rub her leg. Why was Doreen kicking her under the table?

Doreen grabbed her purse. "I think I need to go to the ladies' room. Why don't you join me, Emily?"

They stared each other down before Emily grabbed her backpack. The men stepped out to let them exit the booth.

"That was interesting," Travis said. "Why would Emily think you were lying?"

"Because females lie all the time. They expect men to do the same, but I left the Boot N Scoot at eleven like I told you and the detective."

"Doreen seems to think you're getting back together. Are you lying to her?"

"If it saves me child support, I can tolerate her until something better comes along."

Tolerate. Doreen was looking for love in the wrong place. "You don't think much of women."

"I try not to."

He'd misunderstood his meaning. "It must be difficult for you to lose someone like Christina Porter. She was young, beautiful, and sophisticated. A little bit out of your league."

"Women are all the same. Some have more polish on the outside, but they serve the same purpose."

"Did she serve your purpose the last few months?"

"I served hers. Tina wanted to have fun," Roger

said. "Ken Porter's idea of entertainment was balancing his checkbook."

"But you were both married."

Roger stared at a waitress and chuckled. "Nothing wrong with tasting a side dish, especially when the entrée is old and dried out."

Travis looked beyond Roger. "Your entrée is returning."

"If you ever get tired of your entrée, I'll be happy to make her a side dish."

Emily was too smart to believe Roger's lies. He rose and let her slide in. Roger moved to the inside, and his wife sat on the edge.

Doreen reached for her coffee cup, sipped, and made a face. "That's cold. What have you boys been talking about in our absence?"

"Fine dining," Travis said.

Roger stabbed a finger at Travis like they were conspirators about the value of women. "You've got that right."

The waitress placed their checks on the table, removed their dishes, and offered to refill their cups. Doreen and Roger took her up on the offer. They were staying. Emily declined, and Travis stood to let her out.

"It's been a pleasure talking to both of you again," Travis said. "I'll see you both at the wake."

"I wouldn't miss it," Doreen said.

"You don't even know her," Roger argued.

"We had a lovely chat Friday night," Doreen said. "Before you took her to the Boot N Scoot."

His face reddened. "What were you thinking, following me to her house?"

Her voice rose above his in volume. "I wanted my

child-support check."

"It was in the mail!"

The manager had returned and was heading their way, but Travis nodded toward the police officer who stopped him. Anyone would have thought Doreen and Roger would control themselves with two armed police officers in the same room, but they were in their own little world of war.

"Did you call the cops on me?" Doreen demanded.

Roger didn't answer, but he leaned back with a smile on his face.

"You scumbag!" She moved to the other side of the booth.

Travis would find out nothing in a shouting match and escorted Emily to the checkout.

The other officer joined them and pointed toward Roger and Doreen. "Who are they?"

"Suspects in a murder case," Travis answered without turning. "What do you think about the Markems?"

"They're married?"

"To each other," Travis added.

"They're getting a divorce," Emily said.

"Are you sure?"

"Do you think I should stay?" the officer asked.

"You could watch from your patrol car. They should leave soon. Separately."

He took his coffee mug and left.

Travis handed their bills to the cashier.

Emily gave Travis money to pay for her meal.

"You're my girlfriend," he said. "I expect to pay."

"I don't like to be indebted to a man."

He leaned close and whispered in her ear. "Afraid

I'll try to kiss you?"

She blushed. How would she react when he did kiss her? He had Doreen to thank for the boyfriend status. He was going to make the most of it.

"I'll pick you up for the wake."

She looked back at the booth. "It ought to be interesting with Doreen and Roger attending."

"Luckily, they have a bouncer at the Boot N Scoot."

"Will you provide one for the funeral?"

"I thought we talked Roger out of going."

"You don't know them very well." Emily looked toward the booth where Roger was staring at the other women in the diner while Doreen sulked. "They both like to win. When one says white, the other says black. She told him not to go, so it's a good bet he'll show up."

"What about Doreen?"

"She'll go. It would be the perfect opportunity to obtain revenge on the woman who stole her husband."

"But she's dead."

"It's her image she wants to tarnish. Doreen knows Christina stole her husband, but she won't be happy until everyone else knows what she did."

"It takes two people to commit adultery. Why doesn't she blame Roger for his cheating?"

"Doreen is afraid of what life might become without Roger in it," Emily said. "She tends to view him through rose-colored glasses. I'm hoping to tarnish his image."

"How?"

"My task is to gather evidence."

"This isn't your case."

"I'm not doing it for any criminal case," she explained. "I'm doing it to save Doreen from making the biggest mistake of her life. She wants to take Roger back because she can't see the possibilities without him. But he's lying."

"What do you know?"

"I can't tell you." Emily reddened under his stare. "It might not be legal."

"Geesh, sweetheart. What are you up to?"

"Roger may not be a killer, but he's a manipulating scumbag, and Doreen is my friend."

"How do you know Roger isn't the killer? Did it have something with Doreen turning your legs black and blue?"

Emily glanced at her legs. "What's wrong with them?"

"Nothing, but I like them better without bruises. Doreen landed several hard blows to silence you. What's going on, Em?"

She chewed her bottom lip and shrugged. "I can't tell you, but if you want to be a detective, you'll find the answers."

He watched her drive off and followed.

Chapter Seventeen

During their bathroom break Emily had promised Doreen not to say anything to Roger about the van or tracking him on GPS, and she kept her word except for calling him a liar. She knew Roger was telling a partial truth when he said he left the Boot N Scoot at eleven. He hadn't gone home. He had gone back to pick up Christina and then had taken her to the Tally-Ho Hotel. After an hour GPS showed him going to her home before heading to his mother's house.

How much time had elapsed between Roger dropping Christina at her doorstep and someone killing her? The tracking meant Roger couldn't have dumped her body in the canal, but maybe he knew something that would help the police.

She couldn't tell Travis without breaking her promise to Doreen, but the police had to have thought about tracking their suspects' vehicles. Travis had mentioned a warrant. They'd find out legally whether Roger was innocent of murder or not. Her job was to prove Roger was guilty of cheating with Christina and they were more serious than he claimed. If he could lie to the police, he'd lie to his wife. Maybe he or his friends would reveal something eye-opening during the wake, but she had a new idea on how to convince Doreen not to take him back.

She had a location for their trysts and headed for the

Tally-Ho Hotel. She needed to talk to B. J. Debrowsky and see if Christina and Roger were regulars at his establishment.

She could record the conversation and confirm Roger had taken Christina to the hotel and was her lover in every sense of the word. If necessary, she'd drag Doreen to the Tally-Ho to confront the staff about the truth of their affair.

Even though the Tally-Ho Hotel was two blocks from the hospital, she had barely noticed the building except for its neglected appearance. Rooms were located on two floors with numbers hand painted on the doors. The concrete walls had cracks zig-zagging down the seams, and chunks of cement were missing from the second-floor balcony. Graffiti messages decorated the outside cement stairway. The iron railing was rusty and broken. Wind swept trash into piles in dark, vermin-friendly corners.

She hesitated to enter, but the idea of Doreen falling for Roger's lies and taking him back gave her courage. He had a power over her that made no logical sense. Doreen viewed the arguments and fighting as part of a normal relationship, but Emily couldn't let Doreen ruin her life by settling for an abusive partner. She owed her that much. She started the recording app on her phone and cautiously entered the main entrance beneath a rusty awning.

The hotel lobby was small and cluttered. A sign offered to rent rooms by the month, week, or day. She saw no hourly rate posted, but that didn't mean it didn't exist. Dust covered two unmatched end tables next to a red leather couch that sagged in the middle. A magazine from last summer was on the table. The pages were well-worn, and the cover featuring a happily married Hollywood couple was torn. The couple had recently divorced.

Emily tapped on a bell that rang with a high-pitched ding. Stains were visible on the carpet, the curtains, and the furniture. Even the desk was stained with coffee rings that formed a chain across the worn wooden surface. Someone had carved their initials with a knife. She kept her hands away from any surface. How long should she wait? "Hello?"

A door behind the counter opened, and a middle-aged, balding man emerged from the room where computer screens provided the only light. His clothes were wrinkled and stained, and he rubbed his face before focusing on his guest. His eyes widened, and he licked his lips. "How can I help you, pretty lady?"

Did he think a compliment made him more appealing? She recalled the name on the card in the backpack. "I'm looking for B. J. Debrowsky. Is he in?"

He grinned to reveal a gap in his teeth. A drool of slobber escaped. "That's me."

Why would Christina Porter have a stack of this man's cards in a kitty backpack? How was she going to encourage him to talk without arousing suspicion? Different lines of dialogue ran through her brain.

"You want a room?"

"No." She raised her hands and stepped back. "I was a friend of Christina Porter."

He stared as if undressing her with his eyes. "Her friends called her Tina."

"Like Roger?"

"Who?"

"Her boyfriend," she clarified.

His bushy eyebrows touched as he chuckled. "Where do you know Tina from?"

She said the first thing that popped into her head. "The Boot N Scoot. We hang out with Lucy and Sue."

"You're a beautician?"

"No, I like to dance."

He peered over the counter and examined her in a way that made her feel dirty. "I bet you do."

She needed to change the topic. "I'm going to the wake. Are you going to be there?" Why had she asked that? He might think she was interested in him.

"I'm sorry I can't enjoy your company," he said. "I'm working, but tell Jade hello for me."

"Who's Jade?"

He narrowed his eyes and stared hard, suspicion in his voice. "You don't know Jade?" He grabbed her wrist and pulled her against the counter, his foul breath making her cringe as she fought to escape.

"Let her go." Travis made his way to the counter with a taser drawn. "I'll drop you where you stand, and this thing creates a nasty mess to those it encounters."

Debrowsky released her and raised his hands. "We were just talking."

"You can talk to me."

He lowered his hands and backed up. "I have nothing to say."

"Do you see the uniform I'm wearing?"

Debrowsky's eyes narrowed before a grin revealed his missing teeth. "I thought you might be a stripper auditioning your performance."

Emily bit down to stop from laughing. "How did you know? Have you caught his act?"

Debrowsky leered at her. "I'd catch yours."

Emily backed up into a solid wall of Travis O'Toole standing behind her. She looked up at him. "How did you find me?"

"I followed you from the café. You were over the speed limit."

She stepped away. "You're going to write me a ticket?"

"It depends. What are you doing here?"

She waved her hand at Debrowsky. "This is personal business."

"Personal? Do you know what this hotel specializes in?"

"I run a respectable joint," Debrowsky said.

"For prostitution and narcotics." Travis turned to Emily. "What business could you possibly have with this guy?"

"I'm helping a friend. This may have been where Roger and Christina met."

His eyes widened in surprise. "What makes you think they met here?"

"Doreen found a card with this hotel's name on it. She's thinking of taking Roger back, and I don't want her to make a huge mistake. I thought Mr. Debrowsky could prove Roger and Christina were regulars here."

His blue eyes twinkled with mischief. "You girls had a long talk in the ladies' room."

"It's what we *girls* do." She sighed and turned to Debrowsky. "Did Roger Markem and Christina Porter meet here?"

"Who?"

Travis narrowed his eyes in a *don't mess with me look* and placed photos of Christina, Ken, Roger, Doreen, Lucy, and Sue on the counter. "Let me help refresh your memory. Have any of these people graced your fine establishment?"

Debrowsky scratched his cheek as he studied the photos. He pointed at Roger Markem. "This guy came in Friday afternoon. He wanted a room on the first floor in the back."

The back of the hotel faced the hospital. "What's so special about that room?"

"It's the cheapest room I rent."

That sounded like Roger. "Did he have someone with him?"

"Not when he paid for the room. He came in after our lunch crowd, took the key, and left."

"You serve lunch?"

Travis choked on his laughter.

Emily wanted in on the joke. "What did I say?"

He waved at Debrowsky to continue as his chest shook.

Debrowsky grinned. "Do we serve lunch? You're cute."

There was no restaurant in this hotel. The lunch crowd consisted of businessmen who wanted a quickie on their breaks. She must have sounded like a stupid ingenue. "I was kidding. What better time to cheat than in the middle of the day? Is that why Roger was here?"

"No. He didn't use his room until after midnight."

Travis pointed at Christina's picture. "Was she with him?"

Debrowsky shrugged. "Only the man registered, and he was alone. I don't know about later. He parked in the back, and I don't take attendance." He searched his computer. "The key card records when the door is opened. Once at one twenty and again at two. Forty minutes. That's a little better than average."

"Do you have security cameras?" Travis asked.

Debrowsky laughed. "No. People who come here don't want to be recorded coming and going. I use technology where it's needed."

Travis looked around. "Has the room been cleaned?"

"I have two girls who do housekeeping every morning. They strip the sheets and wipe down the toilets. I run a clean joint."

Travis tapped on Roger's photo. "How often did he rent a room?"

"That was his first time."

"But he's been having an affair for months." Emily snatched Roger's picture from the counter and pressed it close to Debrowsky's face. "Are you sure you haven't seen him in here before Friday?"

He shook his head. "He was never in here before then. I swear it."

Travis lifted the photo of Christina. "Are you sure this woman wasn't with Roger?"

"I didn't see her with him."

"Do you know who this woman is?"

Debrowsky studied the picture. His voice trembled. "She's the one who was murdered, but she wasn't killed here."

"How do you know? Roger could have killed her in the room, carried her to his truck, and driven off with you none the wiser." Travis gathered the photos. "Do you have a receipt for Roger's stay?"

"He paid cash. I don't print receipts unless they ask for one."

"I bet the IRS loves that. Did you copy his ID?"

"Not when they pay cash."

Travis pressed his hand against Emily's back. "Time to go." He called Crane while Emily waited by his police car.

"Am I under arrest?"

"Not yet, sweetheart." He leaned in close. "I told Crane about the Tally-Ho and Roger's visit. He wants to know how you knew since the GPS tracking report only arrived on his desk ten minutes ago." He pinned her against the side of the police car. His body was warm and hard as his hands massaged her shoulders, his breath hot on her neck. "Where did you get your information?"

"Doreen found a card with the hotel's name on it."

"How did you know he visited?"

Emily's insides turned soft and compliant under his seductive touch. His masculine scent filled her nostrils and created a desire to be touched as his hands worked magic. Her limp body molded against his frame. It had been a long time since a man made her feel grateful to be a woman. Her resolve loosened as did her tongue. "Doreen has an app to track her son's car. She added Roger's truck to it."

He gripped her arms and stared into her eyes. "Is that what you meant by not legal? You shouldn't withhold evidence."

She shrugged. "It won't help."

"Why not?"

"When Roger left the hotel, he took Christina home and headed for his mother's place. He never went near the Ida Road towpath parking lot. He couldn't have dumped Christina's body."

"The babysitter said no one came home during the night. She was on the couch and claims to be a light sleeper."

"If Christina never made it to her front door, someone was waiting for her outside."

Travis searched her face. "Doreen?"

"No." She thought about the possibility. "She went home."

"If she was tracking Roger's truck, she knew he went to the Tally-Ho and could have followed him back to Christina's home."

"She couldn't overpower Roger and Christina."

"She could have waited until Roger left and forced Christina into her car."

"How?"

"Christina's alcohol level in her body would have meant she was legally drunk. It wouldn't have taken much for Doreen to put the smaller woman in her car and drive her to the Ida Road parking lot."

"Doreen's not a killer." She pushed against his chest. "I don't like your theory."

He leaned in close. "Give me a better one."

"This isn't the first time Roger has lied. He wove a fairy tale about Doreen's van."

"What van?"

"Doreen found her old van behind the Hair-em yesterday. She promised me she'd call the police and report it."

His hand slid downward along her waist to her hip. His fingertips brushed the bare flesh of her thigh. "She never called. Tell me about the van."

"I can't think with your hands on me."

"I don't want you to think. I want you to answer my questions."

"Is this how you question all your female suspects?"

"No, but I find it's effective with you. And enjoyable. Besides, you're my girlfriend. We shouldn't have secrets."

She sighed. "Doreen doesn't want Roger to realize she knows about the van."

He kissed her neck. "Knows what?"

Emily took a deep breath to slow her fluttering heart. "Doreen totaled her van in January, and Roger said he sold it for scrap and gave her two hundred dollars. She thought that was the end of it until she found her van parked behind the Hair-em. We think Roger gave it to Christina to drive."

He paused his assault on her senses. "But Christina had a car."

"Doreen tracks her son's car so she knows where he goes. What if Ken did the same thing to Christina? He owned her car, so it would have been legal. Maybe she didn't want him to know where she was going."

"How do you know this?" He tugged on her hair. "Salon talk?"

"Lucy and Sue said he was tracking her every move. She needed a secret car, and Roger gave her Doreen's van."

He stepped back, his brows forming a frown. "Do you know where Christina was going?"

"Doreen didn't track the van." She shrugged. "She thought it was in a junkyard."

"Roger sold the van to Christina without Doreen's knowledge?"

"No. Doreen signed over the title, but it was never transferred."

He took out his phone. "And this van is behind the Hair-em Salon?"

She nodded. "Yes."

He called Crane to update him. "Crane's going to check on it."

"Then you're done with me?"

"Not yet." He leaned in close, his hand brushing her hair back from her face. "Why are you so loyal to Doreen? Isn't she just a co-worker?"

"Did you check my background?"

"Crane did."

She looked up and concentrated on the fluffy clouds floating overhead. "Then you don't know about the assault."

"What happened?" His voice was full of concern.

She'd been lucky but still trembled at the memory. Sharing the experience had been part of her therapy. "I was nineteen. I had only been working at the hospital for a few months. It was late in my shift, and I was delivering reports. A man grabbed me and pulled me into the men's bathroom and began groping me and tearing at my clothes."

He looked distressed. A cop would have investigated the worst of assaults on women.

"He didn't rape me," she reassured him. "Someone made a noise in the hall, and I ran. Doreen found me crying in the break area in the computer room. I was a mess. You never imagine anything violent happening to you, and when it does, your sense of safety is shattered. She called security and the police and took care of me when I was most vulnerable."

He stroked her cheek with his fingertips. "And you're taking care of her."

"It's what we girls do."

He pulled her close, and she absorbed his strength.

His phone rang. "No van?" He looked at Emily. "The van is gone."

Emily called Doreen and put her voice on speaker. "Doreen, is Roger with you?"

"No, he's at work."

"Did you move the van from the Hair-em?"

"I had to," Doreen barked. "Roger could have taken it."

She felt a headache starting. "You promised to tell the police."

"They don't need to know."

She looked at Travis listening to the conversation. "They do know. Where is it?"

"How did they find out?" Doreen demanded.

She rested against Travis whose hand held her waist in a light embrace. "Officer O'Toole tortured the information out of me."

"I thought you said good-bye at the café."

"He followed me to the Tally-Ho."

Doreen shrieked. "What are you doing at that dump?"

She chose her words carefully since Travis was listening. "You found a card with the hotel's name. I was checking to see if Roger was at the place Friday night. Debrowsky rented a room to him."

"I know that from my app. Did you find out anything new?"

"You're tracking your husband's truck," Travis interrupted, "which is illegal if he doesn't know. I think you should cooperate, Ms. Markem."

"What didn't you tell them, Emily?" Doreen demanded.

"I'm sorry, but they think it's linked to Christina's

murder. Do you want to be the reason they don't find her killer?"

"Doesn't the app prove Roger is innocent?"

"Which is why we should come clean. Where's the van?"

"After the Hair-em closed, I drove my van to the hospital and left it in Lot B. Cars are parked there twenty-four seven, so I figured no one would notice," Doreen said.

"You can meet us at the hospital," Travis said. "And bring proof of ownership and the key, or we'll break in."

"I'll be there in ten minutes," Doreen said. "But Roger is the one who lied about selling it."

"We'll talk to Roger." Travis stepped away and made a phone call.

Emily turned off the speaker and lowered her voice. She didn't want to scare Doreen by telling her she was a prime suspect, but she wanted to warn her. "Did you go out after confronting Christina at her home Friday night?"

"No."

"Can you prove it?"

Doreen's voice was defensive. "What do you mean?"

"Did either of your kids wake up? Can they give you an alibi?"

"Do they think I killed that woman?" Her voice was a mixture of anger and fear.

"Doreen, do you have a lawyer?"

"Emily, what did you tell them?"

"They're drawing their own conclusions. I'm warning you to be careful."

"Noted."

Chapter Eighteen

Travis waited for Emily to finish her phone call, noting she whispered her message. How much was she telling Doreen? When she put her phone away, he stepped forward. "Is she meeting me at the hospital?"

She looked worried. "Don't you mean us?"

He escorted Emily to her car. "You should go home."

"But Doreen may need me."

"Crane will be there, and you're up to your pretty little neck in this murder. If Doreen is guilty, you could be charged as an accomplice."

She pulled away and glared at him. "I don't like your accusation. I was helping her."

"Which is the definition of an accomplice."

She bit her bottom lip. "As a friend, I was helping her make a decision about her marriage to Roger."

"That should be a no-brainer."

She sighed. "She's blinded by love."

"Have you ever been blinded by love?" Did he sound worried? No matter how much she was involved, he was still interested in knowing her better.

"I keep my eyes open, but I tend to look at the best side of someone until I can't make any more excuses for bad behavior. My romances tend to be short term."

"Are you in a relationship now?"

"I wouldn't have agreed to go out with you if I was.

I date one man at a time."

He valued fidelity. "Good to know."

She studied him. "What about you?"

"I'm not in a relationship. My job keeps me busy. If we don't solve this murder, we may have to postpone our Friday night date."

"Then solve it." Her voice was low and full of promise. He leaned in, but she put a hand on his chest. "Doreen won't get into trouble tracking Roger's truck, will she?"

He forced himself to relax. "They're still married. I'll convince Crane to let it slide, especially since we have our own report."

She patted his chest. "Thank you."

"I'll pick you up tomorrow night for the wake."

"What are we going to do there?"

"I'd like to sit in my car in the parking lot and neck with you, but if we don't have a suspect in custody, I'll have to interview people."

"Then it's not an official date." She sounded disappointed.

He leaned in. "That's why there won't be any necking."

"Too bad." She studied his mouth. "What sort of kisser are you?"

"I believe in fresh breath, no slobber, and I can hold my breath for a long time."

She swiped her tongue across her lips.

"Hell." He grabbed her, pulling her tight against his chest, and kissed her. He meant it to be quick and a surprise she wouldn't be able to reject, but her mouth melted against his and forged them into a passionate embrace. His hunger grew and the heat with it. He tickled his tongue against her lips, parting them, and dove inside. A moan escaped and vibrated against his flesh. He pressed her body against the side of her car, and his hands outlined the curves of her body. Her hand slid to his butt and squeezed. She wanted him as much as he wanted her. A car honked its horn, and he pulled away. He was in uniform and in a public place. He had it bad to risk an official reprimand for a kiss.

He opened her car door. She fumbled with the keys.

"What are you doing tomorrow before the wake?" He wanted to spend some personal time with her.

"I have a job interview with the county medical examiner's office. I know it's a long shot, but if I don't get the job, I can look at alternatives."

"You'll do great. You deserve your dream job."

His dream job rested on whether or not he helped solve this case. He waited for Emily to leave before heading to the hospital. He drove around the building, located Lot B, and spotted the beat-up van with a license plate registered to Doreen. Crane arrived, followed by the criminal search team's van.

When Doreen arrived, she flew at Travis. "What are you doing to my van?"

Crane stepped forward. "Do you have the key?"

Her jaw dropped, and her eyebrows rose to her hairline. "You haven't already broken in?"

"We were hoping for your cooperation." Crane held out his hand.

Doreen handed the key to him, and the technician opened the door.

Crane returned the key. "What is your van doing parked here?"

Doreen jerked her chin high. "I work here."

Crane surveyed the wreck of a van. "And you're driving this vehicle?"

She only hesitated a moment before answering. "I needed a place to store it for a few days."

"Where was it before you moved it here?"

She looked from Crane to Travis. "I thought it had been sold by my husband, but when I was passing the Hair-em, I recognized it and moved it here."

Travis gave her points for not outing Emily.

"You should have reported your find to the police," Crane said. "Christina Porter worked at the Hair-em."

"You don't think that woman was killed in it." Doreen made a face. "I was planning to sell it for scrap."

"You said you thought your husband sold it," Crane said. "Can you prove this is your van?"

"I have the title right here." She searched her purse and waved the paper in Crane's face.

He examined the document and returned it.

"If Roger asks about the van, could you tell him you took it from behind the Hair-em?" She removed a cigarette from her case. "He doesn't need to know I found out about it, does he?"

"Don't you think that's up to your divorce lawyer?" Crane asked.

"We may not be getting a divorce. Roger wants to reconcile."

Emily had good reason to worry about her friend.

"Do you know why Roger parked the van at the Hair-em?" Crane asked.

Doreen shrugged. "You'll have to ask him. I was shocked when I saw it."

"I might have a theory." Travis shared Emily's explanation and watched Doreen's reaction. "Ken may have been tracking Christina's car. It's easy enough to do, and he was controlling."

"She needed another car so he wouldn't know what she was doing, but what was that?" Crane asked. "What was our victim hiding?"

"Do you think her co-workers at the salon know?" Travis asked.

"Pratt interviewed them Saturday, but we need to do a follow-up. We'll talk to them next."

Travis turned to Doreen. "Do you know where Christina was going in the van?"

She shrugged. "I thought it was scrap metal."

"But you were tracking Roger's truck," Travis said.

She stared daggers at him. "I should have warned Emily about confiding in cute cops."

Doreen was still a suspect. "She doesn't want you to get into trouble."

"What do you know, Ms. Markem?" Crane asked.

Doreen removed her phone from her coat pocket. "I was only tracking Roger's truck to make sure he went to work and could pay child support."

"What about Friday afternoon?" Travis asked.

"I didn't check his location until later that night," Doreen defended in a calm voice. "I admit to confronting Tina at her home, but that's all I did. I was home the rest of the night."

"I can't use your spying on your husband in court, but I can use the report I requested through a court order," Crane said. "It confirms Roger left the Boot N Scoot at eleven but stayed in the area. He then returned to the Boot N Scoot and likely picked up Mrs. Porter. They went to the Tally-Ho Hotel, and then he stopped at her home before driving to his mother's house south of town. The report doesn't explain how her body ended up in the canal."

"I didn't take her," Doreen screeched.

Crane leaned into Doreen. "You didn't track your husband's truck from the Tally-Ho to Christina's home?"

"I was asleep." Her voice rose in volume. "But I was right to confront him about owing me child care. He was spending it on a cheap hotel room."

Crane raised his voice to match hers. "You never tracked your husband to the Tally-Ho or other hotels?"

"No," Doreen answered in a smug tone. "His truck was his love nest."

"How long have you been tracking him?" Crane asked.

"Since February when he told me about Tina."

Crane didn't hide his surprise. "He told you?"

"He had a lapse in judgment. He's regained his senses," Doreen said. "How much longer will you be with my van?"

"We're almost done," Crane said. "We'll lock up if you want to leave."

Doreen headed for her car.

Travis followed. "Will you be going to the Boot N Scoot tomorrow night for the wake?"

"I wouldn't let Roger go alone."

He opened her car door. "I'll see you there, and thank you for not mentioning Emily to Crane."

"Emily is my friend. I don't want her in any trouble."

A friend like Doreen caused trouble. Travis joined Crane who was talking to a search technician.

"The van has trash, food stains, and plenty of

fingerprints," the technician said. "We bagged the gas receipts and these business cards."

Travis grabbed the evidence bag. "These are all for the Tally-Ho. Why would she need more than one card?"

"Maybe she received a discount for promoting the place," Crane said. "I'll need you to talk to Debrowsky."

"I already did." Travis flipped through his notebook. "He identified Roger. He paid for a room with cash Friday afternoon but didn't arrive until after one in the morning. Debrowsky said he didn't see Christina with him, so we have to prove she was in his room. But why else would he stop at her home afterward?"

"See if you can get Roger to admit Christina was with him at the Tally-Ho. Lie if you have to. I want to put the two of them together. He was the last person to see her alive."

"What about Ken Porter?"

"GPS shows Ken's car was parked at Talia's place all night." Crane snorted through his long nose. "I don't like eliminating him or Roger as suspects. Even Doreen's SUV remained at her home. We must be missing something."

"We've talked to everyone involved." Travis closed his notebook. "Now what do we do?"

"We talk to them again. Roger lied about leaving the Boot N Scoot. He's hiding something. And Ken must have suspected his wife of something if he was tracking her car."

Figuring out who murdered Christina was proving harder than Travis thought. "What do you want me to do?"

"We'll visit the Hair-em and find out why the van was parked there."

Chapter Nineteen

Travis followed Crane to the Hair-em Salon and parked his patrol car next to the detective's unmarked vehicle. He was shocked by all the pink when they entered. "Wow, this is a girl's place."

"That's why I go to a barber." Crane waved to a beautician who had just finished with a customer. "That's either Lucy or Sue."

Her smock had *Lucy* embroidered on it. After she rang out the customer, she turned to them.

Crane introduced himself and Travis.

"I thought we answered all the sergeant's questions."

"We've uncovered new information," Crane said. "Did you notice a damaged blue van parked behind the building?"

She looked toward the back wall. "That van belonged to Roger Markem. He loaned it to Tina."

"Did you see who took it?"

Lucy looked worried. "I assumed Roger took it after her death. Are you saying it was stolen?"

"It wasn't stolen." Travis looked at Crane for permission to speak. He nodded. "Christina had a car. A good car. Why would she need a battered van?"

Lucy set her lips in a thin line.

"You can tell us here or down at the precinct," Crane threatened.

She grunted and motioned them to a corner near the sinks. "Tina said Ken was tracking her car. I mean Ken's car. Everything was in his name. That was one of the reasons he didn't want her to work. She told him she was shopping or having her hair or nails done. The only cash she had was what she made here."

"Was she on the payroll?" Crane asked.

Lucy's shoulders slumped. "He would have taken her paycheck. I paid her cash on top of tips for any work she did."

"How many hours did she work?" Travis asked.

Lucy straightened bottles of shampoo and conditioner on a shelf. "She had a few customers but was gone most of the time."

Emily had been right. "In the van Roger gave her?"

"She'd park her car in the mall, and Ken wouldn't know she was gone."

"Do you know where she went? What she was doing?"

Crane put a hand on his shoulder. He needed to calm down. He took a deep breath. He didn't want to scare Lucy into silence.

She turned to face him. "I know what it's like to be in an abusive relationship. Shame, secrecy, and desperation. She was my friend. I was helping her escape."

"Abusive? Did Ken hit her?" Crane asked.

"A man doesn't have to hit a woman to torment her. Ken was an expert at emotional abuse. He knew Tina's weak spot."

"Which was what?" Crane turned to Travis. "You're good at asking questions, but I have a few of my own."

Lucy twisted a towel from a clean stack on the table

next to the sink. "Her children. She would have done anything for them. That's why she stayed with Ken even though she didn't love him anymore. She described his touch like dry ice. A part of her shattered every time he demanded his marital rights."

"Why didn't she divorce him?" Crane asked. "He had a mistress."

"Ken had an ironclad prenup that prevented Tina from receiving more than a pittance if they divorced before their tenth anniversary. Nothing if he caught her with another man. I think that's why he was waiting to serve divorce papers. He wanted evidence she was cheating."

"Then why was she having an affair with Roger?" Travis didn't hide the shock in his voice. The last thing Christina should have been doing was flaunting another man in her husband's face.

"It wasn't like that. Roger was flattered a younger woman was interested in him. Tina needed his help. She asked for a car so Ken couldn't track her, and he provided a van. She was grateful."

"Her relationship with Roger wasn't sexual?"

"Men expect sex. Roger was no different, but he admired and respected Tina. She had class. He wanted to help her escape from Ken. They had a common goal."

One that had failed. "When did she meet with Roger?"

"Mostly Friday nights when Ken worked late or all night." Lucy pointed toward Sue. "We'd hang out at the Boot N Scoot. They'd make love in his truck, and I'd drive her home."

What about the Tally-Ho? "They never went to a hotel?"

"Roger was cheap, and Tina didn't know if Ken had hired a private investigator."

Travis looked at Crane. "If she wasn't meeting Roger, where was she going during the day?"

"I know she met with a lawyer, but I don't know what else she did."

"How long was she gone?" Crane asked.

"She would drop the kids off at school, park her car next door, and go to her locker. She would always be back in time to switch cars and pick up her kids from school."

"We're going to need to see her locker," Crane said. "We need to bag everything in it."

Sue joined them as they headed for the back room. "What's going on?"

"Do you know where Christina went in the van Roger gave her?" Travis asked.

"I think she went to the gym," Sue said.

"Why do you say that?"

"She carried a gym bag, and sometimes her hair was damp when she returned."

Crane looked at both women. "Why didn't you ever ask her where she went?"

"Tina said it was better we didn't know, especially if Ken asked questions," Lucy said.

A lock secured the locker. "I'll get the bolt cutters." When Travis returned, Sue was waiting on a new customer, but Lucy had remained with Crane, who had his hands covered. Travis also put on latex gloves and cut the lock.

Crane dropped it into an evidence bag. "You can do the honors." He opened the door to the narrow metal locker.

A change of clothing was neatly folded on the top shelf. He lifted each garment and handed it to Crane. He unzipped a gym bag on the floor. Inside was lacy underwear and an assortment of sex toys. He accidently hit a button, and a vibrator began to hum. He hit another button, and the beaded dildo moved in a rhythmic wave. "How do you turn this thing off?"

Crane backed away. "You're asking the wrong man."

Lucy pointed at a button. "I think it's that one."

Travis stopped the vibration and dropped the sex toy back inside. "What was she doing with these?"

Lucy shrugged. "She was a fun girl."

"She was a safe girl." Travis removed a box of condoms from the gym bag. "Was Roger the only man Christina was dating?"

"As far as I know."

Travis zipped the bag. "Seems like a lot of toys and condoms for one man."

"I know it wasn't for Ken," Lucy said. "They had separate bedrooms."

Travis was curious. "Then why did she marry him?"

"She fell in love and wanted a home and children. He swept her off her feet, and everyone told her she was marrying up," Lucy said. "She was a middle-class working woman, and he was a rich businessman. Have you seen *My Fair Lady* or *Pretty Woman*? He transformed her. She was his creation. Only it was more like *The Bride of Frankenstein*. She didn't mind having no life of her own, but she wanted her children to have the freedom to make their own decisions. Ken had everything mapped out for them with private schools and college funds."

"She could guide their decisions as much as Ken," Crane said.

"He was pushing her out of the picture," Lucy said. "She found documents from a divorce lawyer. She knew she wasn't going to get any money from him, but he was trying to take the children from her. The lawyer was helping him gain full custody. That's why she kept her relationship with Roger a secret."

"What were her plans?" Crane asked.

Lucy didn't answer.

"Was she going to kidnap the kids and skip town?" Crane demanded.

"It wasn't kidnapping. They were her kids," Lucy said. "She told me she was going to leave with the children on Monday in the van. She wouldn't be back."

"Two days after she was killed." Crane strutted around Lucy as his head bobbed. "Could Ken have found out about her plans?"

Ken wasn't the type to allow his wife to best him. His motive was looking stronger. Travis made notes while Crane waited for an answer.

"He must have." Lucy's shoulders sagged, and she sniffled. "She was so close to starting a new life. I feel sorry for the kids. Ken barely spent any time with them. They were props for his image as the perfect husband and father."

"If Christina left Ken secretly, how was she going to take care of her kids without alimony or child support?" Travis asked.

"She didn't share," Lucy said.

Travis didn't accept that. "But you were her boss and friend. She didn't say anything to you?"

Crane lowered his voice. "What was Christina

hiding?"

"She didn't want to involve us any more than she had to. Ken could be persuasive."

"I thought you said he wasn't violent."

"Normally, threats were enough, but she had a little too much to drink at one of those lavish parties he insisted they attend. She already knew about his divorce plans and didn't feel like sucking up to his friends. He found fault with her behavior and claimed she embarrassed him in front of his business friends and colleagues. When they reached home, he smacked her around. She wore extra makeup to hide the bruises."

"She didn't file charges?" Crane asked.

"No. Ken apologized and gave her some jewelry. He said it was a gift, but he kept it locked in his safe. She could only wear it when he wanted to show off his wealth. She wore costume pieces when she went out with us."

"How do you know it was costume?" Travis asked.

"She showed me where the gold paint had come off one of the pieces she bought at a yard sale. Tina was no fool. She'd never wear the real stuff. Ken would have a fit if anything happened to his precious heirlooms."

"Heirlooms?" Travis looked at Lucy for an explanation.

"Some of the pieces were handed down through his family. He was planning to leave them to the children in a trust. Tina wasn't going to get any of it."

"What was she wearing Friday night?" Crane asked.

"A fancy necklace with red stones," Lucy said. "She wore matching earrings and a bracelet. Tina knew how to accessorize."

Crane removed photos of the jewelry from his folder

and placed them on a table.

Lucy tapped her nail against one. "That's what she was wearing."

"Thank you." Crane gathered the evidence bags and stepped outside.

"The picture you showed Lucy was of the real thing," Travis said.

"Yeah. The insurance company authenticated all the jewelry five years ago, but Christina told her best friends and boyfriend her jewelry was worthless. Why?"

Travis didn't have a good answer. "She didn't want to be robbed?"

"Then why tempt someone by wearing the real stuff?"

"Lucy said Christina scraped the paint off. Do you think the jewelry could have been fake and Ken was ripping off the insurance company? Five years gave him plenty of time to switch costume knockoffs for real. Maybe she threatened to tell the company the truth."

"That's one theory. I'll check into his financials. We'll let Ken bury his wife Thursday, and then we'll bring him in for questioning. I don't think Lucy and Sue were telling us everything they know. They'll be at the Boot N Scoot Wednesday along with Roger and Doreen. I want you and Pratt to record your interviews and relay them to me. Someone knew where Christina was going in Doreen's van." He lifted the bag. "Find out who the toys were for."

"You don't think they were for Roger?"

"They had sex once a week in his truck."

"I wonder why he took her to the Tally-Ho on Friday."

"That's another question you can ask."

Chapter Twenty

Emily had changed into three outfits before settling on a denim skirt, a peasant blouse, and a pair of soft leather boots. She was debating a fourth choice when she saw Travis arrive.

Instead of honking and expecting her to emerge, he headed up the outside staircase. She grabbed her discarded choices, stuffed them into the closet, and secured the door. She glanced around and decided nothing too personal was exposed.

Travis knocked, and she welcomed him inside.

"I thought I was at the wrong address. The funeral home is Quinn and Sons. Isn't your name Stevenson?"

"My father didn't want to change the name. The business was nearly a hundred years old, passed down from one generation to the next."

"Why did they sell?"

"They ran out of children who wanted to carry on the business. My dad worked part time for them when he was in college. After working in sales for a pharmaceutical business, he bought the place when it went on the market. I know it sounds like a weird career choice, but he loves helping people through one of the most difficult times of their lives. He knows how to comfort others."

"And you live here?" He looked around the large room. "How about the nickel tour?"

She walked around the open space and showed him the kitchen with a long counter and stools for guests to gather and eat. A couch, recliner, and large screen television created an entertainment area. She waved toward the bed at the other end of the room. "No need to tour the bathroom, closets, or elevator."

"Elevator?"

"This was storage for caskets, which are heavy. My dad remodeled the space for my brother when he decided to go to college. With two schools within an hour's drive, it was cheaper for him to live here than pay dorm fees. When he moved out, I moved in."

"My dorm room was no bigger than a closet, and anyone over the age of twelve should not have to sleep in a bunkbed. The glamour of college life is grossly exaggerated."

"I'm glad I'm done with that phase of my life." She held out her arms and slowly turned. "Do you think this outfit will pass for country western?"

"It's more appropriate than mine." He wore a button-down denim shirt, loose leather jacket, and blue jeans. He wore biker boots instead of cowboy boots. "Does the jacket hide my gun?"

"And I just thought you were happy to see me," she teased.

"My gun is under my armpit, sweetie, but thanks for noticing the other package."

Some men were threatened by a woman's boldness. "I've always admired jeans that fit just right. I'm sure you notice a woman's figure."

"For the record, I noticed your legs first. By the time I reached your face, I was a goner."

He was equally bold. "Cops. You flirt with every

female you meet."

"Not me. I'm a professional on the job."

She might argue, especially after he pinned her against his police car and frisked her, but she didn't want to ruin the playful mood. "What are you going to do tonight?"

"Crane wants us to blend in and find out more information. He thinks someone is hiding something. He hopes the drinks will loosen tongues."

"Blend in?" Even if he wasn't a cop, he wouldn't go unnoticed. His jeans molded to the muscles of his thighs and calves, and his jacket accentuated his wide shoulders. Then there was his face. Thick dark hair framed sky-blue eyes and a mouth carved by angels. She already knew the magic of those lips. She was getting warm and moist and needed to change the subject. "Do you think you'll make detective?"

"If I don't do anything stupid."

"You haven't so far. How many cops will be there?"

"Adam and me. Crane is wading through Ken's financials and inventory but expects updates." He removed his phone. "I'll let you know when I'm recording."

"Will Doreen be there, or did you arrest her?"

"She was very cooperative. All she asked was to tell Roger that the police found the van at the Hair-em so he wouldn't know she had taken it. She wants to sell it for scrap."

"The police don't need it?"

"No, and she kept your name out of the details when she talked to Crane."

"See, you misjudged Doreen."

"She surprised me. She considers you a true and

loyal friend."

"I know Doreen has faults, but she's someone you can count on." She dumped her backpack on the counter. "She said I should start carrying a purse." A box of condoms fell out with her other belongings.

"It's good to know you're prepared." He removed a sticky note from the box. "In case you get lucky."

How embarrassing. It was one of the boxes from the kitty backpack. Had Doreen put it in her backpack in the bathroom at the Friends Café? It was her loopy handwriting on the note. "It was a gag gift for graduation," she lied. "I tended to pass up parties to study. Now I can party all I want." She raised her hands into the air and gave a little shout of joy.

She reached for the box, but he lifted it out of her reach.

"Those are mine."

"Christina had this same brand."

"Must be a popular choice." Her excuse sounded weak.

His eyebrow shot up. "You and Christina just happened to buy the same condoms. Did you go shopping together?"

Doreen hadn't tattled on her. She felt the same obligation. Besides, it was one box. What difference would that make to the investigation? "I never met Christina before you fished her body out of the canal." She shoved the box back into her backpack along with the other items she wouldn't need. She lifted her tampon box. "Did she buy the same brand for these?"

He backed up. "That is too much information before the first date."

First date. If he kept thinking she was guilty of some

crime, there wouldn't be a first date. Ever. Her hands shook as she sorted through the contents, gathering her wallet, a lip gloss, comb, and other necessary items, and placed them in a small sequined purse. "I'm ready to go."

"It's getting cold out. You might want a coat."

She grabbed a denim jacket she had selected earlier and made sure her keys were in the clutch before she led the way outside. He opened the car door, and she slid onto the bucket seat.

"I know you can't share information about an ongoing investigation, but can you tell me what the medical examiner's report said? How did Christina die?"

"It's public information now. The newspaper will have it in a story tomorrow morning that Christina Porter died of injuries as a result of a beating," Travis said. "You saw the bruises on her throat, face, and arms, but those injuries didn't kill her. The marks on her abdomen were from a smooth, heavy object that tore her insides apart. She bled internally but didn't die right away. The ME puts her death between one and four Saturday morning."

Emily swiped at a stray tear. "Why would anyone viciously beat her? She was petite. Hardly a threat."

"Anger. Hate. Revenge. Someone was making a statement with that level of violence."

"The man who grabbed me attacked two other women before he was arrested. He went to jail for a long time." She met his gaze. "Make sure this man pays."

Travis nodded.

They talked about anything but the case until he pulled into the large parking lot of the Boot N Scoot. The entrance was lit, but the cars and trucks were shrouded in darkness. Her heels echoed on the asphalt, and the shadows made her shiver. This was no place for a woman alone. Why had Roger made Christina wait for him to return Friday night? Why didn't he want anyone to know he was taking her to the Tally-Ho? Was it her suggestion to keep her husband from finding out about the affair?

Travis opened the heavy metal door to the Boot N Scoot, and the smell of beer, barbecue, and loud country music assaulted her. This wake was a far cry from organ music and whispering voices.

She looked for Doreen but saw no sign of her, Roger, Lucy, or Sue. "We must be early."

He nodded toward the dance floor. "How about dancing?"

She looked at her clutch. "What do I do with this?"

"I can put it in my jacket pocket."

She handed it over. He led her to the dance floor, his hand on her back. The light touch was more erotic than a heavy hand taking control. He stood facing her, his right hand under her armpit and his fingers resting gently on her back. She placed her right hand in his left.

"Ready?" He nudged her, and they began a country two-step.

She had taken dance in college as an elective, and it came back under his guidance. He added turns as they moved around the room.

He turned her into a cuddle. "You're good."

"My sisters taught me. They needed a partner to practice, and I didn't think I had a choice."

He danced her around the floor until the music ended. They clapped and looked around. Travis nodded. "Looks like Roger is here."

She followed his gaze toward the door. Roger looked around before turning back toward the entrance.

Doreen emerged from the ladies' room and took his arm. They appeared to be a happily married couple.

"Now the real fun begins."

"Let's dance again and let them settle in." Travis led her back onto the floor as they circled with the other dancers.

Doreen gave her a big shout and a thumbs-up as she passed. Emily returned a wave before Travis turned her in the opposite direction.

Lucy and Sue arrived and took a booth close to Roger's table. They stared and frowned.

"They look like they recognize you," Emily said. "Did you interview them?"

"Yes. Crane and I asked why Christina needed the van. They claimed she drove it to her gym or to see a lawyer. Maybe you can find out more."

"Me?"

"I'm discovering that women don't like to confide in cops or men. Maybe you'll have better luck."

"Anything else I should know?"

"Besides condoms in her work locker, there was lacy underwear and lots of sex toys."

"Sex toys? What were they for?"

He grinned.

"What kind is what I meant," she said, hoping to hide her embarrassment.

"I'm an old-fashioned guy when it comes to making love, but some of them looked interesting. I don't understand why she needed so many. Is Roger into kinky sex?"

She closed her eyes. "I don't know, and I don't want to know."

"There were oils, restraints, and a feather."

He was tormenting her. "Don't look at me to explain," Emily said. "All I have is a vibrator to satisfy an itch when I get one."

"Isn't that what a boyfriend is for?"

Her voice rose in disbelief. "You think you can convince me to throw away my vibrator?"

He grinned wider as he turned her. "I'm thinking of new ways to use it."

They finished dancing, but Roger was leading Doreen onto the dance floor, and a conversation would have to wait.

"Now would be a good time for you to talk to the Hair-em crew." Travis nodded at their booth. "We can join the Markems when you're done."

She left Travis surveying the crowd and headed for Lucy and Sue. The booth had a clear view of the room. "Hello. Remember me? Emily."

Lucy narrowed her eyes. "You came to my salon."

"And I love what you did with my hair." Her voice was a high-pitched singsong that made her cringe at the unnatural sound. She cleared her throat. "May I join you?"

Lucy moved over. "Do you know you were dancing with a cop?"

She borrowed attitude from Doreen. "He asked me. I said yes." She held out her hand. "We're not engaged."

"He's investigating Tina Porter's murder with Detective Crane," Lucy said. "You were awfully interested in her death at the salon. What gives?"

"I was curious." She lowered her voice and looked around. "You see, I was jogging on the towpath Saturday morning and discovered Christina's body in the canal."

"You found her?" Sue screeched.

Lucy hushed her.

"Scary, huh? I called 911. Officer O'Toole responded." She sighed and shook her head. "He's been hitting on me ever since." That would explain the dance. "The detective thinks I might be involved. I never met Christina Porter before Saturday morning. I'm sorry about your friend."

Lucy narrowed her eyes. "So why did you come to the salon?"

"I wanted to know Christina better. I felt connected to her." She took a deep breath. She needed to gain their confidence with the truth. "I should also confess I work with Doreen Markem."

"You what?" Both women had screamed the question, but the music muffled their outcries.

"She'd been talking about Roger and Christina for months. I didn't know the woman I found in the canal was Christina at first. Officer O'Toole came to the hospital where we work to interview Doreen. He said she may be involved. You don't know how nervous I feel working with a possible killer."

Sue gripped her hand. "You poor child. That woman hated Tina. What did Doreen say about her?"

Emily shook her head. "Doreen was horribly upset her husband was having an affair with her."

"It wasn't an affair," Lucy said. "Roger was in love with her. He was doing everything he could to convince Tina to divorce her husband and be with him."

"You can't tell by the way Roger is treating his wife now," Sue said. "Bitchzilla."

Chapter Twenty-One

Emily followed their vehement stares to the happy couple two-stepping around the dance floor. She needed to find out about Roger. "I was outside, and it's scary at night. Why didn't one of you give Christina a ride home on Friday night?"

"Tina said she had a ride," Lucy said. "We were in line for the bathroom. If I'd known she was in danger, I would have insisted she wait for us. Then we would know who picked her up."

She saw no reason to be subtle. "It was Roger."

Sue stared daggers at Roger. "He lied to us!"

"He said he was going fishing early in the morning and needed to sleep," Lucy said. "Are you saying he came back for her?"

"Yes. He lied to the police, too, but Officer O'Toole said the police checked the GPS on his truck. They discovered he went back to the Boot N Scoot around one."

Sue frowned. "Why wouldn't Tina tell us Roger was taking her home?"

"He didn't take her home. Not right away. He took her to the Tally-Ho Hotel and rented a room." Emily watched their expressions.

Sue cringed. "That slum. Did Roger think he was impressing her with a rat hole?"

"It was risky," Lucy said. "What if Ken's spies saw

them there? Or his truck?"

"Then why be seen with Roger at all?"

"She was careful not to give Ken any evidence of the affair," Lucy said. "She danced with any guy who asked. Roger wasn't allowed to kiss her in here. Outside, it was too dark for photos, and they weren't the only couple steaming up windows."

Emily attempted to block that image. "When were they going to court?"

"I don't know." Sue looked at Lucy.

"In June." Lucy examined her nails. "Ken wanted the children to finish school before he kicked Tina out."

"Did Christina have a lawyer?"

"I remember someone named Amanda Wright," Sue said. "Tina said she had to visit her."

"That wasn't a lawyer," Lucy said. "She owns the Wright Stuff. It's a new jewelry store in the same plaza as the Hair-em. Tina loved bling and would stop in there to dream."

Sue pouted. "Then who was her lawyer?"

"I don't know, but she talked to someone," Lucy said. "She was depressed because he didn't give her much of a chance after she showed him the prenuptial agreement she signed. But she was more upset about losing custody of her kids. She said she would do anything to keep them from Ken's cold hands."

Sue brushed a tear away. "Why don't they let Tina rest in peace?"

Emily leaned in closer. "Don't you want them to find her killer?"

Lucy jabbed her finger in her face. "Ken Porter killed her."

"Why? What did Christina do that Ken would kill

her?"

"I don't know, but Ken loved money." Lucy rubbed her thumb against her fingers. "With her dead, he saved a fortune in divorce lawyers, and he doesn't have to worry about custody of the kids. Tina said most judges award custody to the mother, and Ken might do something to guarantee he got it."

Sue pointed at Doreen dancing around the crowded floor with her husband. "I wouldn't rule out Roger's wife. Tina was upset when that woman came to her home demanding to talk to him. Roger was furious all night. Even Tina couldn't cheer him up. He nearly bit her head off when she tried."

The music ended. "I appreciate you ladies talking to me." Emily left the booth and joined Roger and Doreen at their table where they fought to catch a breath after the exertion of the dance.

"Emily!" Doreen grabbed her hand. "Come with me to the ladies' room."

Emily pulled her hand from Doreen's sweaty palm. "You don't need to drag me."

As soon as they were in the bathroom, Doreen searched the stalls and, finding them empty, burst into tears.

Only one person could upset her this much. "Roger?"

She nodded.

Emily patted her on the back. "He isn't worth crying over."

"I thought he loved me, but one minute he's treating me like his favorite honey bear, and the next he's screaming at me like a banshee from hell. I don't know what to think."

"You're trying to pick up where you left off, but you can't go back."

"Why not? We had some good years together."

"And a few more bad years," Emily said. "Don't forget he had an affair with Christina."

"Don't mention that woman's name! Besides, she's dead now."

"Which is the only reason the affair is over. What makes you think he won't have another affair? And another?"

"He had his fling, and he's over it. Roger needs someone to take care of him. He wants to move back in." Doreen searched her bag and removed a tube of mascara to repair the damage to her makeup.

Emily couldn't keep her mouth shut. "You have to decide whether you want him back."

"Of course I do."

Emily let out a frustrated huff. Doreen wouldn't listen to common sense.

"It would make things easier financially," Doreen said.

"This isn't a decision about money. It's about your happiness."

Doreen opened the door. "What makes you think Roger won't make me happy?"

Emily stayed behind to count to ten. She had said her piece. It was up to Doreen to make a decision. She was the one who would have to live with it.

Roger was draining a bottle of beer when she joined the couple. He grinned at Emily. "How would you like to dance?"

"That'll have to wait. I'm investigating Christina Porter's death." Travis pulled out a chair for Emily and sat next to her.

She hoped her smile conveyed how grateful she was for his rescue.

Roger looked around the crowded room. "Everyone here loved Tina."

"Someone didn't," Travis said. "She was beaten to death. It was a slow and painful way to die."

"I thought it was a robbery," Roger said. "Wasn't her jewelry missing?"

"That tacky stuff?" Doreen asked. "Who would want it?"

"The detective wouldn't have photos of costume crap," Roger said. "How much was it worth?"

"Who cares?" Doreen said. "It's gone."

Emily turned to Travis. "Was it robbery?"

He tapped on his phone. He was recording the conversation. "I can't comment on an ongoing investigation."

"If it wasn't a robbery, why kill her?" Doreen asked.

"It comes back to motive," Emily said. "Who wanted Christina dead?"

"I had no reason to kill her," Roger said. "We were friends."

"Just friends?" Travis looked from Roger to Doreen. "She was making plans to leave her husband. You were seeking a divorce. Were you leaving with Christina and her children?"

"Leaving?" Doreen straightened in her chair. "What does he mean?"

"I had no plans to go anywhere." Roger put his arm around Doreen's shoulders. "I plan on staying right here with the woman I love."

"Then why did you give Christina your wife's van?"

Travis asked. "It was found parked behind the Hair-em."

"My van!" Doreen screeched. Her outrage sounded authentic. "Why did you give that rich bitch my van?"

"Doreen," Emily pleaded as she looked around. Her outburst had attracted attention. "Remember this is a wake for Christina. These people were her friends."

Doreen leaned back in her chair and crossed her arms. Her gaze bored a hole in her husband. "Do you want to explain yourself?"

Roger looked at Travis. "Tina said her husband was tracking her to dig up dirt on her. She didn't want him to know she was meeting with a lawyer." He glared at his wife. "I loaned her a vehicle I was planning to scrap."

Doreen made a grunting noise.

"Do you know who her lawyer was?"

"A man named Dobson."

Doreen leaned forward. "That's your divorce lawyer."

"He's the only lawyer I know. She wanted to keep her meetings with him a secret."

"And what secrets are you keeping from me, your wife?"

"We know you took Christina to the Tally-Ho Hotel the night she died," Travis said. "Debrowsky confirmed it."

Emily searched her memory. Debrowsky had said he never saw Christina. Travis was lying.

"We went there to talk," Roger stammered. "She was worried about Ken. She wanted my advice."

Roger had just admitted they were together, and Travis was recording it. Emily was impressed. Maybe Crane would be as well.

"Advice?" Travis asked. "You took her to a hotel.

171

Are you sure all you did was talk?"

Doreen bellowed her objection, but Travis studied Roger's reaction.

Emily did the same.

Roger clenched his fists in anger. He looked at Doreen. "They want to make me their scapegoat."

"He didn't care enough about that woman to kill her," Doreen said in a shaky voice.

"Exactly." Roger leaned across the table. "Ken had motive. He was having an affair with some hottie newswoman. He wanted to get rid of Tina."

"Ken has an alibi." Travis pointed at Roger. "You, on the other hand, were the last person to see Christina alive. We know you left the Boot N Scoot at eleven, but you didn't go home. You waited across the street and returned at one. You took her to the Tally-Ho where you claim to have had a heartfelt talk. What time did you and Christina leave?"

"I dropped her off at home after two in the morning." Roger's voice rose in anger. "I don't know what happened after that."

"What was her condition when you left her?"

Roger hesitated, flexing his hands before hiding them beneath the table. "What do you mean?"

"You *talked* for almost an hour. Was she elated, disappointed, happy, sad?"

"She was alive."

Travis continued his questions. "Did you go inside?"

"It was late. I needed to get home."

"But you went inside earlier," Travis said. "Why didn't you show up on the front porch camera when you picked Christina up?"

Roger looked smug. "Tina turned it off so Ken couldn't spy on us."

"Everyone is spying on everyone else, but nobody knows what happened," Travis said.

"I want to know something," Roger demanded. "When are the police going to return my van?"

"It's my van," Doreen corrected.

Roger patted her hand. "I'm looking out for your interests."

"Like you did when you told me you sold it for scrap? Why did you lie to me?"

His voice rose to match hers. "I gave you money."

"Two hundred dollars. Well, now I'm going to sell it and keep all the money."

"You owe me, Doreen. Between child support and lawyer fees, I'm broke."

"And whose fault is that? You're the one who wanted a divorce."

"Calm down," Travis said. "This isn't the place to air your grievances."

"This is a private conversation," Roger said. "I don't remember inviting you to join us."

"They're my guests," Doreen said.

Travis stood and extended his hand to Emily. "There are some empty stools at the bar. Maybe we should let the Markems work things out alone."

Emily clasped his hand as they crossed the room. "Why can't she see that he's all wrong for her?"

"Love is blind?"

"It should never leave you in the dark." She took a seat on a stool. "Please find Roger guilty so he can't ruin Doreen's life."

"I'm afraid both Roger and Ken have alibis."

"And that leaves Doreen as your prime suspect." She crossed her arms. "Maybe Christina never got out of Roger's truck. Roger could have left her body farther south in the canal."

"Too far away. There was just enough water in the canal for her body to float a few yards from the Ida Road entrance where we think the body was dumped," Travis said. "Roger drove in the opposite direction from the park."

"Then he left her at home."

"She never went inside," he said. "The alarm system was set and the pass code never entered. Besides, the babysitter said no one was in the house until Ken arrived in the morning."

"What if Ken was waiting for Christina when Roger dropped her off?"

"We checked his GPS. His car never left his girlfriend's garage."

"What about his girlfriend's car? Did you check it?"

Travis stared, his eyes growing big. He kissed her. It started as a peck, a symbol of gratitude, but his lips lingered on hers, and she responded, sharing his passion as the kiss deepened, spreading to areas that tingled and throbbed. He finally allowed enough space for her to breathe.

"The car," she reminded him.

He stared as if trying to understand the importance. "The car. Her car." He removed his phone. "I need to call Crane." He leaned in close. "Stay here. Let me mark my spot." He kissed her again. "I'll be back."

He moved toward a quieter area.

Chapter Twenty-Two

Emily perched on the tall bar stool, her legs crossed and her hands in her lap to hide the turmoil of emotions tumbling inside. Her body reacted every time she was near Travis, but that was a physical reaction caused by hormones. She had learned that in biology class. But she liked him. She enjoyed his company. Was she rushing into a relationship, or was this the man she had been waiting for after discarding the other men in her life?

She cleared her tangle of thoughts and concentrated on the people reflected in the large mirror. Roger and Doreen were a couple, if only temporarily. Sue and Lucy were co-workers and friends. But how many were strangers hoping to find a sympathetic ear, a new friend, or the perfect mate? What had Christina been looking for?

"Is this seat taken?" a burly man with a full beard asked. He smelled of whiskey and pungent cigar smoke.

Some women found the masculine smells attractive. Emily's eyes teared up. "My boyfriend is coming back." She pointed at Travis in the distance.

"Lucky man." He turned to the bartender. "Hey, Jade. Can I get a refill?"

Jade. Debrowsky had mentioned the name regarding Christina. Jade filled the man's glass. She was into Goth with heavy lines outlining her brown eyes. Her nails were painted black with a skull painted on her index finger. Her ears were filled with sparkling stones in a series of piercings, and a diamond stud penetrated one nostril. Tattoos decorated her arms with medieval fantasy images.

"I'm going to miss Tina. She was the only woman who looked at me twice."

"I looked at you twice, Cowboy, or don't you remember?"

"Yeah, but you don't offer comfort now that you own this place. I should get a free drink for my contribution."

Jade granted him a wide smile. "I would lose the place if I gave every man a free drink who contributed to my enterprise."

"Jade, let me feed the dragon one more time for old time's sake."

Her warm smile turned into a thin line of black. "I have a new reputation to maintain. This is your last drink, Cowboy."

"But the night is young, and I'm all alone."

His whining was not attractive. Emily gave the woman what she hoped was a sympathetic look.

Jade signaled a man who had to be the bouncer. He was over six feet tall and pushing two hundred and fifty pounds of muscle. He escorted the man toward the door.

Emily watched them go. "Some guys don't take no for an answer."

"He comes in every night, hoping I'll say yes. I don't mind going to bed with an older man if he can perform and has money, but Cowboy is lonely. I don't have time for a puppy following me around whimpering for a treat."

The description seemed cold but practical. Charles

had been insecure and clingy. Not admirable traits. Emily didn't know any way to steer the conversation to the Tally-Ho owner but directly. She glanced around as if looking for someone. "Do you know a B. J. Debrowsky?"

Jade froze, her gaze cold, her voice full of suspicion. "Who's asking?"

"Emily Stevenson." She extended her hand and smiled. "Debrowsky said you were friends with Tina, and I should talk to you." Would linking their names produce a response? She was fishing with the smallest of bait.

Jade's eyes widened. "*You* want to replace Tina?"

Emily hesitated. What sort of work had Christina done for Debrowsky? "He said you'd give me details."

Jade shook her head. "I never would have pegged you for that line of work. You must need money pretty badly."

Tina had needed money. That must be the common thread for the job. "I just graduated from college. I am in debt up to here." She put the side of her hand in front of her nose. "And no job offers."

"I can sympathize. Plenty of girls pay for college working for Debrowsky."

Some of Emily's friends had called her dense and naïve when it came to life's darker mysteries. She had led a sheltered life, but she'd heard about college girls who worked as escorts, mistresses, and prostitutes. But she had to be wrong. Christina Porter was a mother. Would she be so desperate she sold her body? Her imagination was in overdrive. Someone like Christina wouldn't sink that low. Maybe she was an escort, but the clientele at the Tally-Ho weren't the type to need a beautiful woman on their arm at charity events. Ken had married her for that role.

Emily needed to know more but not tip her hand she was clueless. "Can you explain how it works?"

Jade placed a card on the counter. It was the same one as the stack in the kitty backpack. She scanned the room. "If a guy wants to hook up, you give him a card. He calls Debrowsky and sets up a date and time at the Tally-Ho. Debrowsky collects the money and gives you your share in cash."

She had said *hook up*. That meant sex, and receiving money meant prostitution. Poor Christina. Emily slowly inhaled and exhaled to calm her racing heart. *Don't blow it.* She leaned an elbow on the counter. "How much is my share?"

"Debrowsky takes a third for every job."

"A third? That doesn't sound fair. Doesn't the woman do the important work?" Emily's outrage was genuine.

"It's better than a boyfriend who would take everything. Besides, he provides the bed and schedules the customers. All you have to do is show up with a smile on your face."

Others had warned Emily about how her expressions were as transparent as glass. Everyone knew what she was thinking or when she was lying. It was one of the reasons Charles quizzed her on his performance in bed or lack of. She needed to focus on not reacting and lowered her voice to a whisper. "Isn't it illegal?"

"The cops are only interested in drugs. If you stay clean, they'll leave you alone." Jade sighed. "It's a good-paying job."

"You do it?" Her voice couldn't hide the shock.

Jade looked around. "I worked as a waitress here. A year ago the owner wanted to sell the place, but I didn't have the money. I worked for Debrowsky until I earned enough to buy in. Now I'm co-owner. I had a goal. So did Christina. She was only going to work until she could leave her husband and start a new life. Someone changed her plans."

"Who wanted the divorce? Ken or Christina?"

Jade looked startled. "You know Ken?"

"His name was in the obit under grieving husband," she said with a heavy layer of sarcasm.

Jade nodded. "Tina told me Ken was planning to divorce her and take her kids from her. She was going to leave before the axe fell but needed money. You're young. Life is unfair to women, especially when you depend on a wealthy man. He had an image to maintain. I bet he found out about her fundraising efforts."

"You think her husband killed her? Couldn't it have been one of her customers? It sounds like a dangerous job."

"It can be, but Debrowsky has cameras. He likes to watch, but he came to my rescue more than once."

Debrowsky had emerged from a dark room with monitors. What had he been watching? Emily shuddered. She tried not to judge. Christina needed money and quickly. "Did she make enough to leave her husband?"

"She could only work during school hours. That's five hours and about ten customers but only if Debrowsky fills the schedule."

"Ten men?" Emily's voice was near a screech.

"Some book an hour, but these aren't businessmen and doctors." Jade looked around at the crowd. "Debrowsky had to keep the fee reasonable for his clientele."

Was it enough to start a new life with two children? "You and Tina were friends?"

"We helped each other," Jade said. "She wanted to leave her husband. I wanted to become a partner in this place. She gave me the name of a good business lawyer, and I hooked her up with Debrowsky to raise funds for her cause."

She thought of her attack and unwanted hands on her body. She shuddered. "Wasn't there an easier way?"

"You'll never make it in this business if you think too much. When a man forces a woman to be used by other men, it degrades her, but when a woman chooses the man, it gives her power. Sex can be a means to an end. That's why you need a goal. Once met, you get out."

"But can you forget?"

"You don't." Jade wiped down the countertop. "I was raped when I was fifteen. He told me nobody would want me, but I still valued myself for other things than my virginity. Every experience, good and bad, becomes part of who you are."

Her assailant was in jail, but she would never forget the attack. "But what about past clients like Cowboy?"

"Men like him are looking for a connection they can't find anywhere else, but don't get emotionally involved. Cowboy thinks of me as his girlfriend, but it was all business. Men who fall in love with you are dangerous. They don't like sharing."

"Was anyone in love with Christina?"

"Men liked her. A few may have been in love with her."

She looked toward the table where Doreen and Roger were arguing. "Was Roger Markem one of them?"

"Roger was besotted." Jade laughed. "Tina encouraged it because he was useful, but he had no money."

Travis was returning. Emily rushed to intercept him before he could reach the bar. "Pretend we're hooking up."

"What?"

She grabbed his sleeve. "Follow my lead."

He put his arm around her waist. "Great suggestion about the car. Crane is having it checked out."

"I bet he was impressed by your idea."

"Mine?" He had a puzzled look on his handsome face. "I told him you thought of it."

She stared. "What?"

"Why would I take credit for your idea?"

"Because it makes you look smart and will help you get the job of detective." Charles had always taken credit for her ideas.

Travis looked confused by her answer. Her heart seemed to grow three times its size. She had the urge to bear his children.

"Why are you looking at me so strangely? Did something happen?"

She glanced toward the bar where Jade was studying them. She placed her fingertips on his lips. "Don't let her know you're a cop."

"Who?"

She nodded toward the bar. "Jade."

"Jade, the co-owner? I was planning to talk to her."

"She has an interesting entrepreneur story you'll want to hear." She took his hand and led him to the stools.

"I might have a client," Emily whispered to Jade.

"What would you two like to drink?"

"Two beers," Emily said.

When Jade turned to fill the glasses, Emily saw a tattoo of a forked tail on her back that disappeared into the belt of her short skirt. "What is that?"

"A devil?" Travis guessed.

Jade placed a napkin on the counter and a glass on top for each of them. "It's a dragon tattoo." She turned to model the artwork.

Travis frowned. "Just the tail?"

Jade winked. "It costs extra to see the rest."

Feed the dragon. "That's what Cowboy was talking about!"

"Who's Cowboy?" Travis asked.

Emily ignored him and lowered her voice as she spoke to Jade. "I thought you quit that line of work."

"A girl still needs to feed the dragon, and old habits die hard, especially when I'm strapped for cash. Besides, I can afford to be particular." She looked at Travis and slid a few cards to Emily. "Why don't you give this handsome man one of these?"

He examined the card. "This is for the…"

Emily squeezed his thigh to silence him. He groaned instead.

"You're here for Tina's wake," Emily coached. "You must have been friends."

"Yeah," Travis answered. "I knew her."

Jade filled several beer glasses and loaded them on a tray. "Then you'll be happy to know that Emily's thinking of taking Tina's place."

Travis looked at Emily for an explanation.

"At the Tally-Ho."

"Doing what?" he whispered.

"She needed cash." Emily patted his chest. "I have college loans to pay off. Jade says it's a great way to get out of debt and make men's dreams come true at the same time. Tell me your fantasy. Does it have anything to do with handcuffs?"

His mouth dropped to his chest.

"Just because you're interested in replacing Tina, I'll show you my dragon no charge." Jade turned and lifted the short-pleated skirt to expose bare buns. Tattooed across each one was a dragon wing in full flight.

Travis looked puzzled. "Where's the head?"

"Feeding the dragon costs extra, and I choose the meat." Jade smiled at Travis. "You interested, handsome?"

He gulped. "Just the drink."

"Let me know if you need a refill." Jade sauntered off with the tray of beers.

"What happened?" He shook his head. "Did she proposition me for money?"

"She's semi-retired." Emily lifted the stack of cards from the counter. "Jade explained that Tina passed out cards to men who were interested in a little paid recreation. They called Debrowsky who set up a time and day in her schedule. Then he paid her in cash."

He frowned. "So where's the cash?"

"You didn't find any?"

"No." He texted something on his phone. "Crane will meet us there."

"Where?"

"We need to talk to Debrowsky."

She looked around. "Tonight?"

"It's a hotel. He'll be there."

How had she become part of the police investigation? "I don't have to go inside, do I?"

"Debrowsky liked you. He doesn't like cops. Besides, you can tell him how you want to replace Tina."

"What?"

He grabbed her hand and led her to the door. "I'll tell you my plan on the way."

Chapter Twenty-Three

Emily had barely contained the contents of her stomach on the first visit to the Tally-Ho. Now her belly did somersaults as Travis pulled into the nearly full parking lot. "This is a popular place for a dump."

"I don't think couples come here for the ambiance. It's a quick in and out."

"Yuck."

He acted innocent about the double entendre.

She could hold her own. "What sort of man pays for sex?"

"Men in unhappy marriages, single men who don't like to date, ugly men who—"

Emily held up her hands. "I get the picture."

He leaned toward her. "You don't approve of sex between strangers?"

"It's OK as long as I'm not the stranger."

Travis grinned as his hand slid toward her and rested on her bare knee. "How long do you need to know a guy before he's not a stranger?"

Her private parts were humming. She was in heat. She needed to slow things down before her neglected sex drive made her do something she regretted. She lifted his hand. "I'll let you know."

Crane pulled into the spot next to them. They gathered around his vehicle.

"Why am I here?" Crane asked.

Travis nodded in her direction. "Emily talked to Jade. They're BFFs now."

"Who's Jade?"

"The co-owner of the Boot N Scoot. I didn't talk to her until tonight," Travis said. "She was friends with Christina Porter."

Emily looked at the hotel. "Jade used to work for Debrowsky, the owner of this lovely establishment, and recommended Christina do the same when she needed quick cash."

Crane let out a long whistle. "I take it not as a maid."

Travis nodded toward the building. "Have you seen the inside of the Tally-Ho?"

"I've arrested enough drug dealers in Debrowsky's place to send him a thank-you note for my last commendation."

"He knows I'm a cop, too, but he likes Emily. Jade recommended she replace Christina. I have a feeling Debrowsky will like the suggestion."

Crane's head bobbed, and his mouth dropped open.

She put her hands on her hips. "I'm not planning to take the job. No matter how much it pays."

"He's already admitted Roger was here Friday night," Travis said.

"And Roger admitted he brought Christina here," Emily interrupted.

Travis grinned at her and turned to Crane. "Debrowsky claims he didn't know Christina, but if she worked for him, he was lying."

"Men like Debrowsky want to impress a pretty face. We could send her in and listen," Crane said. "If he admits to running a prostitution ring, we can pressure him to tell us what he knows about Christina's death."

Did Crane just volunteer her to be bait? "Are you sure it's safe for me to go in alone?"

"Get Debrowsky to admit Christina worked here, and I'll join you." Travis removed her purse from his pocket. "Call me on your phone."

Emily tapped in his number.

Travis picked up. "Say something."

"I want to make it clear I'm doing this under duress and only because it will make Roger look bad to Doreen."

"Loud and clear," Travis said. "We'll be listening in."

Emily walked toward the lobby. Darkness didn't disguise the decaying appearance of the building. She saw something scurry across the floor and stifled a scream. She wasn't afraid of the dead, but something alive and able to crawl up her leg terrorized her. No one was at the counter, but the door behind it was open. Emily could hear two people groaning in increasing volume. Was Debrowsky watching customers doing the dirty deed? She was never going to rent a hotel room again. She turned to leave.

"Can I help you?"

It was Debrowsky. He stood in the doorway scratching himself. At least that's what she told herself. How could anyone work for someone who was utterly disgusting?

"Hi. I don't know if you remember me, but I talked to you yesterday before we were interrupted."

"By a cop. Did he pressure you?" He made a motion with his finger going in and out of his other hand.

She raised her hands to block the view of his obscene gesture. "None of that. He's a parasite, but I got

187

rid of him." *Are you listening, Travis?* "I just came from the Boot N Scoot, and Jade said I might be able to make some quick cash. I have college debts to pay." She huffed in disgust and shrugged. "Do the banks think grads can land a job in a month?"

"This job will pay your debts and then some." He drooled. "It's a sweet deal."

She backed up a step and watched the spit drip from his chin. "I have a few questions about the work."

"What's to know?" He coughed, hacking up part of his lung by the sounds. "You give a customer one of my cards, he calls, I set up the appointment, and we split the money fifty-fifty."

Had she heard correctly? "Nice try. Jade said you took twenty-five percent."

"Twenty-five? I take a third, and that was for Tina. She used the rooms during the day when I don't have as many customers."

She leaned her elbows against the counter and felt something sticky. She jerked upright. "I can do the same."

"You want to work days?"

"I can take Tina's clients. Same arrangement."

"Her clients keep calling, so I guess you can service them." He moved his hand from his crotch to his nostril and began digging.

Please don't find anything.

"You're hot like her, and she had a bunch of loyal customers. They'll like you." He wiped something on his shirt.

Emily looked away. A dead body didn't leer and smack its lips as if she were its next meal. She took a deep breath and gathered her courage. She had to keep talking until Travis and Crane arrived. Where were they? "I'm worried about whether one of her customers killed her. What type of protection do you provide?"

"She used a room in the front, and the men had to pay me first. I'd call her and let her know her date was coming. I made sure he left when his time was up."

Date? She glanced toward the room behind him. "Do you have a camera in the room?"

He chuckled. "For security and her protection. I wouldn't let any of the men rough her up."

There was nothing funny about her murder. "Then how did she end up beaten to death?"

"Beaten?" He looked shaken.

"The cop told me she died of internal bleeding."

"She walked out of here Friday afternoon with a pocketful of cash. If she was working for someone else, I didn't know about it."

Travis and Crane came through the door. Emily let out a sigh of relief.

Debrowsky turned to her. "Are you setting me up?"

"We're investigating a murder, Debrowsky," Crane said. "We want answers."

"I only rent rooms. As far as I know, no one murdered anyone in my hotel."

"Christina Porter went to the Boot N Scoot Friday night with her friends," Travis said. "One of them was Roger Markem. The man you identified earlier. You said he rented a room here and then lied when I asked if Christina was with him when he returned."

"I didn't lie. I only saw him earlier in the day, so I didn't see if he brought anyone to the room later. He didn't register a guest."

"Did Roger ask any questions when he rented the

room?" Crane asked.

Debrowsky wiped a sweaty hand on his shirt. "He asked about a little afternoon delight. I gave him a card and said he could set up an appointment. He wanted to know what the girls looked like."

"Why?"

"He didn't want a dog," Debrowsky said. "I showed him Tina's picture. She was the prettiest of my girls."

"Let's see it."

He retrieved a picture from beneath the counter. It was Christina in a lacy red teddy in a pinup pose on a bed.

Crane studied it. "How did you get this?"

"I took it."

"Off a video," Emily said. "It's too grainy to be a snapshot."

Debrowsky backed up. "What video?"

Emily pointed behind him. "The ones you're watching now."

Crane headed toward the room.

Debrowsky moved to block him. "You're not allowed in there."

Crane ignored him. "He has three screens videotaping three rooms." He turned to Debrowsky. "Did Roger rent one of these rooms?"

"No. Like I said, he rented a room in the back. No cameras there."

"You lied when you told me Christina Porter never came to your hotel," Travis said.

"I told you she never came in with Roger, which was the truth," Debrowsky said. "Friday was the first time for the man. I didn't know he knew Tina. He never said anything when I showed him the picture."

Emily was interested in Roger and his relationship with Christina. "How did he react?"

"He got all excited and red in the face like he was already enjoying her." Debrowsky grimaced.

"In lust or anger?" Travis asked. "If Roger found out his girlfriend was turning tricks, that's a good motive for murder."

"For some men," Crane said. "Others might find it to be a turn-on."

Had Roger cared enough about Tina to be upset about her extracurricular activities, or had he demanded to share in the experience? Or both?

Crane turned to Debrowsky. "I want to see both rooms."

"Anything you want, Officers, but the rooms were cleaned. I run a respectable establishment here."

"That's debatable," Crane said. "Show us the room she entertained her customers in first. I'll need a list of all of the men who were her johns."

"Most of them are under aliases. I don't ask for IDs if they pay cash."

Crane made a call. "The tech department will copy your video files."

"You're going to need a warrant for that."

Crane grabbed his dirty shirt. "Right now, I'm ignoring the fact you're operating a bordello. But is that the smell of an illegal substance in the air? Are you going to cooperate, or do we shut this place down?"

"I provide an important service to the public." Debrowsky looked at Emily. "Are you still considering the job?"

How dare he ask. "I'd rather work with dead people than you."

He had a strange look on his face.

"She didn't mean sex with dead people," Travis said. "Get the key cards to the rooms."

Debrowsky led them outside and unlocked the door to the room in front near the office. The first thing that assaulted them was the pungent smell of body odors and flowery perfumes. Emily backed up into Travis.

He put a hand on her shoulder. "Steady, Em."

His touch did anything but calm her.

Debrowsky flipped on the light switch. The walls were painted an army green with a faded blue-and-green spread on a queen-size bed. The carpet was a dirty brown. A small television sat on top of the dresser opposite the end of the bed, and in the corner was a table and two chairs that didn't match. A faded print of sunflowers hung on the wall.

Emily remained near the exit. "Maybe I should just hold the door open and let in some fresh air."

"And you want to be a forensic investigator." Travis put on a pair of gloves and offered a pair for her. "You can't do the job standing outside."

He was right. Emily wished for a nose plug and plunged inside. "It's not so bad," she lied. Standing in the middle of the room, she was unsure of what to do. "What are you looking for?"

"Clues, Detective Stevenson," Travis taunted. "If this was Christina's room like the innkeeper said, there might be something she left behind."

Crane paused and looked at her. "When did you become O'Toole's partner?"

Emily shrugged. "Our paths keep crossing in different investigations."

Crane had a mystified expression on his face. "What

are you investigating?"

Emily cautiously opened a dresser drawer. "I'm gathering proof Roger doesn't love his wife so she doesn't take him back."

Crane looked at Travis. "I saw your video of them together at the Boot N Scoot. They were awfully cozy for a couple heading for divorce."

"Initially, yes. Their relationship runs hot or cold." She opened another empty drawer. "Which is why I'm trying to find out why he wants to reunite with his wife after kicking her to the curb."

"His reason for being single is dead," Crane said.

Emily agreed, but that didn't make the decision to forgive and forget the right one. "I think she's better off without him."

Travis pulled back the drapes. "I don't see any blood stains."

"Christina's injuries wouldn't have left blood splatter." Crane examined the walls near the bathroom. "I don't want to know what some of these other stains are from."

Travis pulled down the covers on the bed. "I can smell the bleach." He rubbed his eyes. "That destroyed any fluid evidence."

Crane pointed at the floor. "Is there anything under the bed?"

Travis got down on his knees and lifted the bottom of the torn bedspread. "I think I see something."

"What is it?"

He brought out a torn condom package. "I'm glad it's just the wrapper."

Crane offered an evidence bag. "This is the same brand as the one in Christina's locker at the Hair-em."

Travis bagged the wrapper and looked at her. "Popular brand."

It was the same type he had seen in her backpack. But why were they talking about condoms in Christina's locker? The condoms she knew about had been in the kitty backpack. She needed to talk to Doreen.

"We're going to have a long list of suspects if one of her johns didn't like her quitting and killed her," Crane said.

"They liked Tina," Debrowsky said. "I know she wasn't killed in here. Her last customer left at two thirty, and she took a shower, dressed, collected her money, and drove off."

Emily pointed toward the bathroom. "Do you have a camera in the shower?"

"No, but she dressed in here." Debrowsky pointed at a camera in the corner near the ceiling. "She didn't have any bruises when she left."

Crane stared at the camera. "We still need to talk to her clients."

"I can give you a list, but like I said, they use aliases," Debrowsky said.

"It's a start." Crane turned to Travis. "You and Pratt can take the IDs of every man who attends her funeral tomorrow and check their aliases and alibis."

"What about Ken?" Travis asked. "Is he still a suspect?"

"We'll know after tomorrow if he used Talia's car." Crane looked at her. "O'Toole said you thought of that. Are you sure you don't want to apply to the police force?"

Would she have to work for Crane? "I'll let you know."

Crane turned to Debrowsky. "Show us the room Roger Markem rented."

He led them around the building to the back where the parking lot was dark. The room was the last one near the dumpster.

"When was trash pickup?"

"Monday."

"Great. If he threw anything away, it's long gone." Crane waited for Debrowsky to open the door. "Why are there no cameras in here?"

"I usually rent these rooms in the back to men who want to sleep."

They searched the room but found nothing, not even a condom wrapper.

"If he came here to do the nasty, he didn't leave anything behind," Crane said.

"But why even come here?" Emily turned to Debrowsky. "Are you telling the truth when you said Roger never came here before?"

He raised his hand in an oath position. "As God is my witness."

"But how did he know Christina was working here?"

"Debrowsky showed him her photo," Crane said.

"But why stop in and ask?" Emily said. "Christina kept that part of her life as secret as possible. That's why she used Doreen's van."

"The van!" Travis smiled at her. "That's how Roger knew."

Crane looked confused. "Knew what?"

"No, that can't be." She turned to Debrowsky. "You said Roger rented the room in the afternoon on Friday. He should have been working."

"The job was canceled," Crane said. "His boss sent him home early. Our GPS report had him picking up lunch next door."

"That's when he saw the van parked by the room in front and recognized it," Travis said. "Roger went in, and Debrowsky showed him Christina's photo. He rented a room and planned to bring her back later that night. Secretly."

"That's why he didn't tell Lucy or Sue," Emily added.

"You two are scary." Crane stared at them. "Roger stays on the list of suspects until we find out what happened in here."

Travis lowered his voice. "Doreen knew about him going to the hotel."

"She didn't kill him." But what if she was wrong?

"We have another problem," Travis said. "What happened to all the cash she was earning?"

Chapter Twenty-Four

Travis tugged on his coat as he stepped out of his car. The black jacket was snug, especially with a gun and bulletproof vest underneath. He entered the Tranquility Funeral Home and walked along a long hallway leading to different showing rooms. A sign-in book was placed outside each door with the name of the deceased spelled out in plastic letters that fit into a grooved holder. Christina Porter was the only body on display this afternoon. A paper booklet offered basic information—name, date of birth, date of death, and a Bible verse. Ken had opted for Psalm 23.

Sergeant Pratt greeted him. They interviewed every man before he entered the funeral parlor and asked their whereabouts early Saturday morning. Most of the men were genuinely sorry about her death and wanted to cooperate.

Debrowsky had been right. Her customers had nothing to complain about and no motive to kill her. But they had to cover all possible suspects.

They had spent hours in the morning viewing Debrowsky's videos. He had been honest about using the cameras to protect his girls. Christina had worked Friday from nine thirty to an hour before school let out. She had been an enthusiastic partner in bed, but between men, alone in the room, she had stared off into space, an empty expression on her face. She ended the day with a shower that took fifteen minutes, the steam so thick it caused the lens of the camera in the outer room to cloud over.

The number of guests slowed, and Travis entered the parlor's showing room. The walls were a tranquil blue with polished oak floors. Ken stood near the casket. His young children were absent. Relatives and friends sat in chairs arranged in rows facing the casket or mingled in small groups. A short line stretched from Ken around the corner of the chairs. Flower arrangements were placed on each side of the casket with a large spray of white roses on the bottom half of the oak box holding Christina's body.

In the back of the room were a few local reporters and Crane, who studied the crowd. Everything seemed under control. It would remain that way unless Roger and Doreen showed up. Hopefully, they wouldn't turn the solemn occasion into a three-ring circus.

Travis returned to the hall and saw Emily walking toward him. She wore a black lace dress that was more sexy than somber. He watched her approach. The high heels gave her body a graceful bounce only women possessed when they walked.

She stopped up close and straightened his tie. "You look nice."

"We make a handsome couple. Too bad it's being wasted on a dead woman."

She looked around. "Have Roger and Doreen arrived?"

"Not yet. I hope you're wrong and they don't show."

"I saw you interviewing the male guests."

"I've been getting to know Christina's customers and matching them to faces from Debrowsky's tapes."

"Did you learn anything from the videos?"

He could take the question as an innocent inquiry, but he liked teasing her. "I'll demonstrate some of the more interesting lessons at a future date."

She made a cute guttural sound as a blush rose in her cheeks but recovered to reply. "You sound like you had fun."

"It was educational and answered a few questions about the sex toys in her locker."

She patted his chest. "I'm glad you cleared that up. How's the case coming?"

"Slow." He ran his fingers up her bare arms. "We have an abundance of liars."

"I'm sorry I keep butting in to your case."

"I'm not complaining," he said. "We make a pretty good team when we're on the same side."

Her eyes darkened. "When haven't I been on your side?"

"Breakfast with Roger, not reporting the van, visiting Debrowsky…"

"I was helping Doreen."

He pulled her close. "I know, and I may have resisted initially, but I appreciate your insights."

"There's something I didn't tell you." She grimaced as she pulled away. "I honestly didn't know about it until I saw the box of condoms in my backpack."

"The one that matched Christina's?"

"We found a pink kitty backpack full of them," she said in a quick burst. "I thought Doreen left it in the van and you found it when you searched it."

He shook his head. "No kitty backpack."

She shrugged. "Sometimes she ignores my advice."

"That would explain why she's with Roger. I'll tell Crane, but we have a box of condoms in evidence. I don't see how any could be linked to Christina's murder."

"Then I can keep the box Doreen gave me?"

He put his hand on her waist. "We might find a use for them."

She blushed a pretty pink.

Now was not the time to find a dark closet and make out. He was on duty and looked toward the viewing room. "I should pay my respects while things are slow."

She slid her hand into his. "I'll join you."

The poor woman had been beaten and left floating in the canal. Why had Ken opted for an open casket? They stared at the corpse.

"She looks a little better than the last time I saw her," Travis said. "But I bet they had to apply her makeup with a putty knife."

"I'm sure they tried, but no amount of cosmetics is going to make her look like that." Emily pointed to a photograph positioned in front of a bouquet of red and white roses nearby. "Sometimes it's better to remember someone as they were in the past. But some people need closure. They have to face death to accept it."

Although Christina's features could scare small children and a few adults, she was dressed in an elegant gown.

Travis pointed at the corpse. "Is she wearing jewelry?"

"The family usually removes personal items before the casket is closed and sealed. Did you ever find the jewelry she was wearing the night of her death?"

"No, but Crane sent photos to every jewelry store and pawn shop." Nothing had been reported.

"You had photos?"

He nodded toward Ken. "He has every piece of

jewelry inventoried, photographed, and insured."

Emily's jaw dropped. "Was it that valuable?"

He put his hand around her waist and pulled her close to share the information. "According to Ken's meticulous records, the collection is worth half a million dollars."

Emily gasped but kept her voice low. "Then why was she working at the Tally-Ho?"

"The jewelry belonged to Ken. He kept it locked in a safe."

"But she was wearing jewelry Friday night according to Doreen. Tacky by her description, but could it have been real?"

"Ken says yes. Lucy and Sue say no. She told everyone it was costume jewelry, but what she wore looks exactly like Ken's inventory photos."

"Then someone robbed her."

"What happened to her wasn't about robbery," Travis said. "A thief would have grabbed the jewelry and run. The person who beat her was angry. Her customers have alibis or swear they loved Christina and were sorry she won't make their afternoons a little brighter."

"Did Ken know his wife was a working girl?"

Travis looked around to make sure no one was within hearing distance before answering. "Crane wanted to give him today to bury his wife before he dropped that bombshell. He's waiting on a few more results to confront him with when he comes in tomorrow for an interview."

"Like the whereabouts of Talia's car?" Emily chewed on her bottom lip. "You're not afraid he'll run?"

He studied her mouth. "Crane has an officer sitting on him. He won't go anywhere."

She tapped her fingers on the casket lid. "It doesn't make sense that Ken would take the jewelry. It belonged to him. If she lost a piece or it was stolen, he had it insured."

He tapped the side of her head. "Insight. But maybe he found out his wife was a working girl and didn't like it."

"Debrowsky never saw Ken at the Tally-Ho."

"That man is an unreliable witness. Ken isn't good at hiding a lie. When Crane confronts him about his wife's secret occupation, we'll see how he reacts."

"I'd like to see that."

"You are not a cop," he reminded her.

She crossed her arms. "I could apply to the police academy."

It sounded like a threat. "Are you serious?"

"If I don't get a job as a forensic investigator, a career as a cop could be an alternative."

"You'll get the job."

"And if I don't?"

"If you joined the force, we couldn't date." He stroked his fingers along the top of her hand. "But as a forensic investigator, we could end up working together on future cases. If I make detective."

"I've enjoyed working with you," Emily said. "You don't make competition a priority."

"What do you mean?"

"Men are competitive by nature. They have to win. Even if they don't play a sport, they have a favorite player they brag about and defend. They also compete in the job setting. If they don't make it as CEO, they're in the upper hierarchy and can brag about their paycheck or playing golf with the boss. In courtship they fight for the prettiest girl and then show her off so all the other men can be jealous."

"And women don't compete?"

"They may compete for a man who can give them more than any other man. That's why the hero in romance novels is always handsome, rich, and powerful. He can have any woman he wants, but he chooses the sweet, naïve heroine. Christina Porter expected to live happily ever after. Instead, she found herself married to a narcissistic, controlling, alpha-male brute."

He looked toward Ken. "She was planning to escape."

Emily stared at the corpse. "So how did she end up here?"

"Someone didn't like her plans."

She looked up and past him. "Looks like Lucy and Sue are heading our way."

The overpowering scent of hairspray preceded them as they met halfway. He sneezed. Lucy hugged Emily. He hoped she didn't choose to hug him. The daggers in her eyes put that fear to rest.

"It's so sad," Lucy wailed. "Have you found her killer?"

Emily stammered.

"Not yet," Travis said, "but we have several suspects." Crane was signaling him. "Excuse me, ladies." He hastily made his departure.

Chapter Twenty-Five

Emily couldn't take her gaze from Travis as he moved gracefully across the room. Tall, strong, and easy on the eyes. She was growing fonder of him every day. He was definitely interested in her. Talk of sex toys and explaining videos had made her more curious than she dared to admit. Maybe those condoms would come in handy after all. She jumped at the sound of a secretive voice intruding on her scandalous thoughts.

"I need to talk to you," Lucy whispered from behind her.

Emily pulled her to a secluded spot behind an arrangement of fragrant lilies. "What is it?"

"The police aren't telling us anything, and they're asking us questions we don't know the answers to. They searched Tina's locker and found some odd items."

"The sex toys?"

Lucy's shocked face reddened. "You know?"

Emily lowered her voice to a whisper. "Do you know what Christina was doing when she wasn't at the salon?"

"I know she was earning handfuls of cash. She asked me to keep it in my safe at the salon." She looked toward her fellow beautician. "Sue didn't know."

"You didn't tell the police about the money?"

"They didn't ask."

"Do you know how she was making the cash?"

Lucy stammered. "She gave me a phone number to call if Ken or Roger came in looking for her. I had to call it once."

"Who was it?"

She didn't answer.

Emily watched her face. "The Tally-Ho Hotel?"

Lucy gasped and looked around before whispering, "Yes. That place has a horrible reputation. Why would she go there?"

Emily studied her. "You don't know?"

Lucy looked defeated. "I can guess. The lingerie and sex toys convinced me I was right. How could she prostitute herself?"

"She needed a lot of money to leave Ken."

Lucy began to cry.

Emily offered her a tissue. "You're going to have to turn the cash over to the police."

"I can't because the money is gone." Lucy blew her nose. "Tina made weekly withdraws and took out what was left on Friday."

"What else haven't you shared?"

"That's it. I told the police she was going to leave town with the kids on Monday. Ken works late on Mondays to catch up from the weekend, so she would have a head start before he missed them."

"Was there enough in the safe to start a new life with two kids?"

"I don't think so." Lucy rubbed her temples. "Everything she did has become muddled. I need a chance to remember everything she said and did before she was killed. Come by the salon tomorrow morning, and I'll tell you everything I can recall."

Sue interrupted. "What are you doing back here? I

want to view Tina's body." She pulled Lucy away.

Emily started to follow but saw Roger and Doreen enter the room. They headed for the casket. This was the moment everyone dreaded, but nobody reacted.

Crane was talking with Travis in the far corner of the room. Ken was listening and nodding to a man near the flower arrangements opposite her and had his back to the receiving line. Lucy and Sue were at the head of the casket staring at the body. Emily was the only person aware that the Markems were approaching. She moved close to Lucy, hoping to block the beauticians from the new arrivals.

Doreen bumped into Emily with Roger behind her, his hands clenched at his sides. Doreen rested one hand on the opening of the casket. "This is the tramp you left me for? She looks terrible."

"Doreen!" Emily reprimanded as everyone turned toward them.

Doreen had announced her presence. "I'm just giving my eulogy." She wore a flowery yellow dress that contrasted against the somber clothing of others.

Roger wore a suit, but the tie was a little string western type, and the shiny metal toes of his cowboy boots were visible beneath his cuffed pant legs. He solemnly stared at Christina's body but said nothing.

Lucy and Sue turned toward the Markems with Emily the only thing between them. She could feel the animosity rising around her.

"Have you no respect for the dead?" Sue demanded.

"I have no respect for whores unless they are dead!" Doreen announced in a booming voice.

"Whore?" Lucy gasped.

Doreen knew nothing about Christina's secret

occupation. She was referring to her affair, but Lucy didn't know that. She looked at Emily as if she had betrayed a trust. Emily wished she could explain the misunderstanding.

"Bitchzilla!" Sue called her.

Doreen might have been able to take Lucy, who was older, but Sue was questionable. Emily had never been in the middle of a cat fight, and she was the only one without long nails.

Ken had turned at the sound of the raised voices and headed toward them.

"Now is not the time for this," Emily reminded Doreen as she looked around for help.

Travis looked in her direction and, thankfully, headed toward her.

"You don't understand," Doreen explained. "We needed closure."

"She wasn't a whore," Ken told Doreen in a quiet controlled tone.

"Yes, she was!" Doreen announced. "She broke up my marriage. That makes her one."

"That's adultery," Emily said, her gaze locked on to Lucy's. "Nothing more."

"Christina made a mistake." Ken squared his shoulders and turned his attention to Roger. "How dare you come to my wife's funeral."

"She was our friend." Roger waved at Lucy and Sue.

"Then say your good-byes and leave." Ken mopped his forehead with a handkerchief.

Travis took up a position near Roger while Crane stood next to Ken. Adam was behind the women. Emily was in the middle and defenseless.

Doreen had her talons drawn. There were going to

be casualties if something wasn't done to stop it. "If she was just a friend, why did you take her to the Tally-Ho?"

Emily looked back at Ken. He had a shocked expression on his face. Of all the questions Doreen could ask, she had to ask that one. Lucy looked betrayed, again.

Roger looked surprised for a brief moment before shrugging. "She was tired of doing it in my truck."

"Then you weren't just friends," Doreen said. "Don't think I won't use that in the divorce."

The divorce was back on. Emily smiled. Maybe something good had come out of the funeral.

"Darlin'," Roger cajoled. "You're the only woman I've *really* loved. How could I love a lyin' whore?"

"You were in love with her," Lucy said. "You said it enough times these past few months."

He sneered. "A man will say anything to remove a woman's panties."

Ken took a step closer to Roger. "That's my wife you're talking about."

"You don't know the first thing about your wife," Roger said.

"I want the truth!" Doreen shouted as she lunged for Roger, who easily sidestepped her attack. Her foot slipped off the backless shoe she wore, and she fell toward the casket. As her hand came into contact with Christina's corpse, Doreen screamed in horror. She jerked her hand away, but her nails caught on the delicate diamond necklace and snagged it. As if in slow motion, the decoration was pulled from Christina's body, flew past Doreen's hand, and arced over her head before crashing to the floor. Doreen shook with repulsion. "Roger!"

Emily watched the events unfold as if viewing a

slow-motion video and cringed.

Roger stepped away from the casket and Doreen. Whether intentionally or accidentally, he stepped on the necklace sprawled on the floor. His thick high heel crushed the stones, and when he lifted his foot, broken fragments sparkled across the oak flooring.

Doreen pointed and laughed. "It's glass! I knew her tacky jewelry was worthless."

Ken stared at the debris scattered on the floor. "That necklace was real. I took it out of the safe this morning." He knelt and gathered the remains of the necklace in his handkerchief. "I bought this from a well-known jeweler. I paid eight thousand dollars for it."

"Eight thousand bucks for glass? It looks like you overpaid." Roger turned to the others gathered around him. "What a loser!"

Ken leapt to his feet and grabbed Roger by the coat collar. "You know something. What happened to the real necklace?"

Roger pushed Ken away with enough force that he stumbled. Crane braced him from falling.

"Tina only wore costume junk," Roger said. "I bet there isn't any real jewelry."

"I have receipts and the insurance company's confirmation it's real." Ken went pale and stabbed his finger toward Roger. "You took it, you thief!"

"Me? What would I do with a bunch of trinkets?"

Crane stepped between them. "Maybe you should step back, gentlemen."

"Tell him the jewelry is real," Ken said. "I gave you the paperwork confirming its worth."

Crane confronted Ken. "Is there any way the real jewelry could have been exchanged for fakes?"

Ken shook his head. "I'm the only one who had access to the safe."

"That proves you switched them," Roger said. "You're a liar and con artist. You're accusing me of stealing them so you can claim the insurance money. What a scam!"

"I want you to throw this man out of here." Ken's voice wavered with barely suppressed anger.

"What's wrong?" Roger taunted. "Can't you do it yourself?"

Ken slowly removed his glasses.

Crane leaned down to face Roger. "Get out of here, Mr. Markem, and don't show up at the burial."

Doreen grabbed his arm and pulled him away. "We should go."

Roger shook her off and stared at Ken. "No wonder Tina preferred other men."

Ken was replacing his glasses and jerked his head up. "What other men? I thought you were her only mistake."

His surprise looked genuine. Maybe Ken didn't know about the Tally-Ho.

Roger stepped back with his arms spread wide. "She certainly preferred my company, but we weren't exclusive."

"You said you were only friends," Doreen said. "Did you love her?"

"What does it matter now?" Roger said.

"It matters to me," Doreen said. "How can I trust you if you lied to me?"

"Everyone lies, Doreen. Get over it."

"It's one thing to lie about a stupid necklace. It's another to lie about sleeping with another woman. Just because you can't put a dollar value on being faithful doesn't make cheating excusable."

"I agree," Roger growled. "Faithfulness is important. Just like trust and honesty. And a woman who betrays a man..." He looked at Christina's body. "She lied to you and betrayed you, Ken. No wonder you wanted her dead."

Ken gathered the broken necklace he had left on the floor. "This is a nightmare," he remarked to no one in particular.

"Just breathe." Emily patted him on the back.

He shoved the handkerchief at her. "Take this worthless piece of junk."

Travis put the remains of the necklace in his pocket.

"We'll have a jeweler examine all the jewelry in your home," Crane said. "We want to know what is real and what is fake."

"What if it's all fake?" Roger taunted from a safe distance.

Ken looked at Crane. "Then you need to find the real jewelry. It's worth half a million dollars."

"What?" Roger moved toward Ken.

Crane blocked him and waved to Adam. "Escort them out of here."

"It's time to close the casket," the funeral director announced. He looked pale as he straightened his tie. "Everyone please be seated for the eulogy, which will take place in a few minutes."

Ken took off his glasses and swiped at a few tears. "I'm going to need a moment before we proceed."

The director handed him a box of tissues and closed a sliding partition to allow Ken some privacy. Emily and Travis remained with him. He removed the remaining jewelry from his wife's body and placed it in a velvet-lined box. "I invested a fortune in jewelry. What if it is all fake?"

"You don't look well," Emily said. "Maybe you should sit down."

He ran his fingers through his thin hair. "If someone stole it, you need to recover it. I don't want the insurance money. I want the jewelry." He snarled. "And I know the first person you should investigate."

Travis pulled her away. "We'll leave you alone."

Emily paused in a side hallway. "He's pretty shaken."

"It's not from losing his wife." Travis removed the broken necklace from his pocket. "How did diamonds turn into glass and paste?"

She examined the intricate work. "It's beautiful even if it is fake. I would never guess it was glass."

"I wonder who made it?"

"Wait. I might know." She searched for Lucy and Sue. They were near the door talking to Roger. He looked in their direction and headed for the exit. Emily touched Lucy's arm. Lucy pulled away as if hurt. Her face was pale, and tears glistened on her lashes.

"What did Roger say to you?"

Lucy shook her head and sniffled. "Nothing important."

"We need to find our seats," Sue reminded Lucy. "They're starting the eulogy."

"One question," Emily begged.

Lucy waved her hand at Sue. "Go ahead. Save me a seat."

"You mentioned a jewelry store in the same mall as the salon that Christina liked to visit," Emily recalled.

"The Wright Stuff."

Travis looked it up on his phone. "Owned by Amanda Wright. Finely crafted jewelry."

Emily looked at him. "Let's see what she knows."

"I'll tell Crane where we're heading," Travis said.

Lucy took a step and searched for Sue.

"I'll see you tomorrow morning. Around eight?" Emily reminded her.

"That's when I open." Lucy glanced back. "I'm honoring Tina today, but I'll tell you anything you want to know tomorrow if you don't find out before then."

Emily didn't have time to dissect the cryptic message but told Travis about the meeting when he joined her.

Chapter Twenty-Six

Travis drove to the outdoor strip mall next to the Hair-em. The shops were arranged in an L with the Wright Stuff near the corner. Shoppers strolled along a covered sidewalk to enjoy the window displays. Amanda's business provided fine jewelry made to order.

Travis took Emily's hand. She didn't pull away but gave him a curious look.

"We're a couple looking at engagement rings."

She relaxed and leaned closer. "I wear a size seven."

What did she mean? "It's a jewelry store, not a dress shop."

"You've never bought a ring before." She raised her free hand and wiggled her fingers. "They come in sizes."

Small, medium, and large he understood. What was a size seven? They stopped in front of the Wright Stuff and stared at the glittering opulence in the window. Handcrafted necklaces, bracelets, and rings sparkled on velvet bedding behind the glass.

He whistled. "I'd worry about getting robbed with all this displayed." He opened the door to the shop. The tinkling of a bell signaled their arrival.

"Hello," a middle-age woman with straight chestnut hair and huge jeweled earrings greeted them. She had equally ornate jewelry on her hands and around her neck. She was a walking advertisement for the merchandise. "I'm Amanda Wright. How may I help you?"

Emily broke free and placed her hands on the glass counter as she stared at all the glittering trinkets. She had the same look on her face that children sported in a candy store. "You have so many beautiful things."

"All handcrafted, but I know what you are looking for," Amanda said with a wide smile. "When two people are in love, they can't hide it from anyone."

Travis moved next to Emily and squeezed her waist.

"You can do better than that," Amanda scolded.

Travis didn't need any encouragement. He pulled Emily so she faced him, tilted her chin, and lowered his mouth over hers. He expected a little resistance to a public display of affection. Instead, she kissed back, her lips softly plucking at his, tiny nips that sent chills down his spine. When he pulled away, her arms slid from his shoulders, and she had a pretty blush in her cheeks.

"Better set the date soon," Amanda told them with a lilt in her voice as she removed a tray and set it on the countertop. "What size carat are you looking for?"

Travis looked at Emily who provided the information. "About a third."

"Respectable but not opulent," Amanda remarked. "Round, oval, square, or diamond shape?"

"Round."

"White gold or yellow?"

"Yellow."

"Size?"

"Seven," Travis interjected.

Amanda placed a few rings that matched their requests on the black velvet ring holder. "Slip one on her finger," she told Travis. "It will be good practice."

He looked at the selection and chose one. Emily held out her hand, and he slipped it on.

"No backing out now, darling," Emily cooed as she admired the ring.

"How much?" he asked.

Amanda didn't hesitate. "Three thousand six hundred."

He stopped breathing like he'd been gut punched. Emily gave him a slight pat on the back. He started to breathe again. "A little ring costs that much?"

"Jewelry is an investment," Amanda explained. "It appreciates, unlike so many other things, and the return is much better than anything you would get at the bank these days, especially with the price of gold and natural stones."

"How much would a diamond necklace be worth?" Emily asked.

"It depends on many factors," Amanda said. "The type, quality, and weight of the gold, the size and clarity of the stones…"

Travis pointed to one in the window. It resembled the one Christina had worn before Roger stepped on it. "What about that one?"

"That is worth about thirty dollars."

"Thirty dollars? What's wrong with it?"

"Everything in my window is costume jewelry," she explained. "I made the mistake of putting the real stuff in the window once. Thieves smashed the glass and made off with a small fortune before I could react. Now, if they rob me, they get nothing of real value."

His patted the fake necklace in his pocket. "Do you make duplicates of all the real stuff?"

"I make copies of my work for my displays for security reasons." Her voice was cool and no-nonsense.

Emily twisted the ring on her finger. "Have you ever

made duplicates for customers?"

Amanda hesitated to answer. "Why would a woman want a copy of the real thing?"

"I didn't say a woman, but what if she wants to replace a ring her husband gave her and sell the real one for cash?" Emily asked.

Amanda gave her a warning glance and then laughed lightly. "You would never have a reason to do that."

"But maybe Christina Porter did." Travis removed the broken necklace from his pocket and placed it on the counter with his police badge. "We're investigating her murder. Her husband claims he purchased real jewelry, and he has receipts from reputable jewelers, but this necklace turned out to be costume."

Amanda's hand shook as she examined the broken necklace. "I only did what I was asked."

He met her gaze. "Which was what?"

She hesitated before replying. "I made copies of her real jewelry. Christina said she liked to go out to places that weren't upscale, and she was afraid to wear the real stuff, but that was a lie."

"How do you know?"

"She'd bring a few pieces every morning and pick up the originals before three. She never left them overnight. She'd bring the same pieces until I finished the duplicates and then bring a different grouping. A woman doesn't copy that many pieces if she's worried about theft. Usually, a woman makes copies of a few favorites she likes to wear every day or in public. Some of the pieces Christina had copied were too fancy for that. They were crafted to impress the rich elite and worth a small fortune." Amanda nodded at the broken necklace. "Like the real version of that one."

"When did she start bringing items in?"

"January, but I worked on pieces every day. She paid me in cash."

He looked toward the back room. "Do you have any of the real pieces here?"

"Not anymore. Once I finished copying a piece, she would leave the real item in my safe and take the copy, but last Friday she took all the real jewelry with her in a gym bag. It was a haul. She said she wouldn't be back. She thanked me for all my work and gave me a bonus. Was she killed because of the jewelry?"

"I can't discuss a case, but we may need your help," Travis said. "If we brought in some jewelry, could you tell if it was real or fake?"

"Of course."

"Expect a visit from Detective Crane. He's going to want your expertise."

"Do you know where she went after she left your place Friday?" Emily asked.

Amanda pointed across the line of buildings opposite her window. "She went to the Hair-em. She worked there part time. I saw her go inside. Later I noticed her car was gone. She always leaves around the same time to pick up her son and daughter from school."

"Could you make a list of what you made for her?" Travis asked.

"It'll take a while to go back through my records," she explained. "Could I email it to you?"

"The address is on my card." He handed her a white business card. They headed for the door, but it wouldn't open.

"The ring," Amanda reminded them.

Travis slipped it off Emily's finger and handed it to Amanda. "Thanks for the practice."

She looked at Emily waiting at the door. "You'll be back."

In the past, the thought of marriage had terrified him. But as he looked at Emily, no panic rose in his chest. Instead, a peace settled on him. She was the one he could picture spending the rest of his life with. But marriage? That would be a topic to discuss in the future. They had yet to go on their first real date.

He drove her to the funeral home to retrieve her car.

"I need to update Crane on what we found out." He called and put the conversation on speakerphone for Emily. "We talked to Amanda Wright. Christina had nearly all Ken's inventory copied. He's probably in possession of a few hundred dollars of intricate costume jewelry. She's sending the information to me."

"Maybe he found out," Crane said.

"How? Christina removed the jewelry in the morning, took it to Amanda's store, and returned the real stuff before her husband returned home from work. She only replaced the real pieces with copies when Amanda finished them. And they were good fakes. She left the real stuff in Amanda's safe until Friday."

"And that's when she was killed," Crane said.

"Someone found out what she was up to," Travis said. "She carried the jewelry in a gym bag, but we didn't find any in the one she left in her locker."

"If Ken's calculation is right, someone robbed Christina of nearly half a million dollars in jewelry," Crane said.

"That's a big motive."

"And if Ken did it, he could file an insurance claim

and keep the real valuables for liquidating in the future," Crane said. "That's double the motive."

"What if someone else took the valuable pieces?" Emily asked. "Roger acted suspicious at the funeral, trying to throw blame on Ken. I wouldn't rule him out, especially if he thought the jewelry that she wore was real."

"Thank you for your input, Emily, but I'm aware of your prejudice," Crane said. "I'll have Ken send the paperwork on the entire collection. Then I'll alert pawn shops and jewelry stores about the additional pieces in case someone brings any of it in to sell. That should cover all our bases if Ken isn't our man."

"Lucy admitted to Emily she kept Christina's cash earnings in her safe but handed it over on Friday," Travis said. "Emily is talking to her tomorrow morning. She may have other secrets. I think it's a good idea if I meet her there."

"I agree," Crane said. "I'll bring a search warrant if Lucy doesn't want to cooperate with the police."

Chapter Twenty-Seven

Emily had forgotten about meeting Lucy at the Hair-em and phoned to say she would be late, but her call went to voice mail. She threw on a skirt and sweater with strappy sandals and headed for the salon, hoping she arrived before the first customer. Maybe Lucy would be in a talkative mood. She certainly knew more than she was revealing.

Travis had said he would meet Emily there, and a police vehicle was parked in front with two other cars. She parked in the mall parking lot and hurried through the front door. She froze as she surveyed the damage.

The Hair-em was a disaster. The front counter had been cleared of all contents and the drawers pulled out and dumped on the floor. One of the swinging doors was broken off and thrown on a pink plastic chair, which had been turned on its side. Containers of different sizes were tossed aside with curlers, hairpins, and combs scattered over the gray ceramic tile.

"Don't move!" Crane had his gun drawn.

Two people were on the floor. She recognized Ken Porter. Crane had him spread-eagled face down. He pulled Ken's hands to his back and slapped cuffs on his wrists.

"Why did you do it?" Crane demanded.

"Lucy called me to come to the Hair-em," Ken argued. "It was like this when I got here."

The other person on the floor didn't look human. Her face was bathed in blood, and her red hair looked darker than what Emily had remembered. "Lucy!"

Lucy made a guttural noise.

"We need an EMS unit!" Travis shouted the location into his radio as he knelt beside Lucy. "Grab some towels." He nodded toward a pile on the floor near an overturned cart.

Emily grabbed a stack and knelt next to Travis.

"Put these on." He handed her a pair of protective gloves.

She slipped them on. She had been in the ER enough to know not to panic. While rebooting a computer or delivering a report, she had watched the nurses work on patients and had learned a few things about caring for an injured person.

"Lucy!" she called to her in what she hoped was a calm, clear voice. "It's going to be all right."

Travis had wrapped Lucy's head in a towel, but it was already stained with blood. Both her eyes were puffy, and her bottom lip had a gash. She turned her head.

"Don't move," Travis told her, but Lucy spat out blood and took a deep breath. Her nose was a swollen blob in what used to be the center of her face.

"She can't breathe through her nose." Emily wiped the blood dripping from the side of her mouth. Lucy reminded her of Christina, only worse. If it was the handiwork of the same person, the violence had escalated.

Crane yanked Ken to his feet. "Why did you beat her?"

"I didn't. I told you the place was torn apart when I

entered. Lucy was on the floor. I knelt down to check for a pulse and called 911." Ken had blood on his knees, hands, and loafers. He was visibly shaking.

"You're a lousy liar, Porter," Crane told him. "Where's the jewelry and money?"

"I don't know. She didn't say anything except on the phone. She said she found the jewelry. The real jewelry," Ken emphasized.

Crane pulled Ken's pockets out. A key attached to a soccer ball and some change fell and rolled on the floor. "If Lucy had the jewelry, where is it now?"

"There wasn't any here." Ken sobbed. "Whoever did this took everything."

"You don't need to worry about your job, kids, or any assets anymore," Crane said. "Ken Porter, you're under arrest for the murder of Christina Porter and the assault on Lucy Vance."

Ken's voice was shrill. "I didn't kill my wife, and I found Lucy this way."

"That's your theme song, and I'm tired of the refrain." Crane yanked Ken's cuffed hands and pushed him toward the door where Adam stood, taking in the scene. "Get this piece of garbage out of my sight."

The paramedics arrived as Adam left with Ken. They wheeled in a stretcher and opened a medical bag. Emily and Travis stepped back to allow Mo Wagner and her partner to work with efficient hyperactivity. Travis put his arm around Emily's trembling shoulders, and she drew comfort from his embrace. She swiped at tears streaming down her cheeks.

"It's one thing to nearly kill a woman, but why torture her?" Mo remarked as she inserted an IV catheter into the top of Lucy's hand.

"What do you mean?" Travis moved forward with Emily.

Mo turned over Lucy's hand. "Someone burned her fingers." The ends were blistered.

"With what?" Emily asked.

Mo glanced around and pointed to an object on the floor. "A curling iron."

Emily picked up the instrument of torture. She had once accidentally burned her scalp with one. "It's cold." It took a while for a curling iron to cool down. Was Ken telling the truth about coming upon the scene?

Travis took the iron from her. "I'll have to bag it."

"Let's stabilize her and move her to the ER," Mo told her partner. She forced a smile in Emily's direction. "Looks like your friend just might make it."

Friend? Emily barely knew Lucy, but was friendship measured by time or by experience? Lucy had cut her hair. They had talked about Christina and gone to her funeral. Emily realized she fit the definition of friend and felt a sudden sadness. She should have done more.

"Are you all right?" Travis asked Emily as the paramedics loaded Lucy on the stretcher. He stripped off his gloves.

Tears blurred her vision. "Why would someone do this?"

"You mean why would Ken Porter do this?" Crane corrected. "After the funeral, he handed over everything in the safe to be appraised. Except for the wedding rings, the jewelry was worthless costume garbage. Christina must not have told him where it was hidden, so he tortured Lucy to find the real jewelry. We were waiting on a warrant to search the Hair-em when this call came in."

"But you searched the Hair-em before," Emily said. "Didn't you find any jewelry then?"

"We searched Christina's locker," Travis said. "Lucy could have moved the jewelry or had it in her safe. Maybe that's what she was going to tell us."

Emily looked toward the office. "Did you find anything in the safe?"

"It was open but empty just like the cash register drawer," Crane said.

"But Ken had nothing on him," Emily reminded him. His pockets had contained no cash or jewels.

Crane looked around the room. "He could have hidden it before we arrived."

Her logic fought Crane's narrative. "But isn't the jewelry rightfully Ken's?"

"Don't feel sorry for him." Crane kicked loose curlers across the floor. "The GPS on Talia's car came through this morning and shows he drove it back home, waited for Roger to drop Christina off, and then took her to the Hair-em. They were here for forty minutes the morning of her murder. She doesn't have a key to the building, and security didn't go off, so we believe they didn't get in. He stopped in the park in the Ida Road parking lot before returning to his girlfriend's apartment. That proves he killed his wife and dumped her body in the canal."

Emily removed her gloves. "He killed her? Why?"

"The oldest motive in the world. Money. She was stealing a fortune from him and leaving worthless junk behind. If that wasn't enough, she was planning to run and take the children with her."

"But why did he confront her Friday night?" Emily asked. "How did he find out?"

"Does it matter?" Crane spat out. "We have our killer. And I appreciate your help. Now we need to prepare our reports and submit them to the district attorney so she can bring official charges against Porter."

"You want me to stay here?" Travis asked.

"The technicians will gather any evidence from the salon. I'm going to search the place for the loot and find out when Lucy will be able to talk to me. We want to tie up all the loose ends for an airtight case."

"What about Sue?" Emily asked. "Has anyone notified her?"

"I'll call her." Crane turned to Travis. "I want you to talk to Talia."

"Is she coming in?"

"We want it to be friendly. We haven't told her Ken took her car. If she knew, she may be an accomplice. Take Stevenson with you to Talia's place. Arrest her if she played any role in this."

Travis looked surprised. "You want Emily to go with me?"

"Talia is a charming woman," Crane warned. "Emily won't fall in love with her."

Chapter Twenty-Eight

Travis followed Emily home so she could park her car. He followed the directions to Talia's apartment while she sat quietly next to him. She looked nervous. Crane suggesting Travis take her along with him on the interview had surprised him. "Crane likes you."

Her eyes widened, and she gasped. "Should I be worried?"

Did she think he meant romantically? He muffled a laugh. "I mean he trusts you. He wouldn't have asked me to take you along if he didn't think you could help. He's come a long way from his first impression of you."

She laughed in a way that made him smile. "Like when he was suspicious of me because I didn't burst into tears at seeing a dead body?"

He shook his head. "He's a bit old-fashioned."

"It amazes me that most people think a woman should become hysterical or burst into tears when confronted with a crisis or trauma. I remember when my brother broke his arm, my mother found a board, braced his bent arm against it, and drove us to the emergency room in rush-hour traffic. I was in awe at how efficiently she handled the situation. I wanted to be just like her."

"I think you can handle any problem."

"You saw me cry like a baby afterward."

"And up to that moment, you were a rock."

"I'm not always brave, but I'm braver when I know

227

someone is standing next to me."

"I'm happy to be your wingman."

She placed her hand on his thigh. "The feeling is mutual."

He needed a distraction and paused as they came upon the Ida Road entrance to the park. "This was Ken's route. He dumped her body in the canal before returning to Talia's."

She turned toward the parking lot. "That's cold. Maybe she made some bad decisions, but Christina was his wife and the mother of his children. How can someone treat another person like trash?"

"We'll be judged by how we treat others," Travis said.

She studied his face. "Is that an Irish saying?"

"That's a Mama O'Toole saying. You'll like her. She never fainted at the sight of blood or became hysterical because of a broken bone."

"Yours?"

He shrugged. "I was an adventurous lad."

She settled back into her seat. "I don't want to think about what I saw at the Hair-em. Distract me. Tell me about your wild youth."

"If you'll share yours."

By the time they reached Talia's apartment, the tales had taken on grandiose proportions, each trying to outdo the other.

Emily had tears in her eyes from laughing. "You're quite the fibber. I mean storyteller."

"Fibber? When it comes to telling tall tales, you win hands down," Travis said. "You're quite the competitor."

"I enjoy a friendly contest when I play sports and games. I don't like people who have to win at all costs."

She paused, and a frown replaced her smile. "Someone like Ken. He wanted his money, children, and girlfriends. Christina had to be desperate to do what she did."

"It was dangerous, but he'll blame her for her own death." He parked his car. "Men like Ken don't take responsibility for their bad decisions. It always the fault of others."

Talia's apartment was in an expensive townhouse in the historic downtown of a rich suburb. Parking was available on the street, and a private garage was located on the bottom level for the tenants. The lobby was small with mailboxes and intercoms. Travis had called Talia to schedule the visit to make sure she would be available. He buzzed her apartment, and she released the lock on the inner door. Stairs ascended to the right. An elevator was located to the left. They took the stairs.

"I wonder what Talia will have to say."

"Remember, she's a suspect." He knocked on the door and announced himself.

Talia opened the door wearing a casual wrap dress, but it was obvious she had forgotten underwear. She looked startled by Emily's presence but ushered them inside.

He put his hand on Emily's back and whispered, "Thanks for coming."

"I'd be scared too if I had any testosterone."

Her remark made him relax. He looked around. Talia's apartment was decorated to impress, but his taste ran toward functional and comfortable. The white carpet and delicate pastel furnishings looked intimidating. What if he left a stain? Or snagged something with his equipment belt? He removed his notebook from his pocket and remained standing to conduct his interview.

Emily relaxed in a powder-blue chair opposite Talia, who lounged on her crème-colored sofa. Both women appraised each other. Emily won hands down.

"I already talked to Detective Crane and the officers." Talia stared hard at him. "Weren't you one of them?"

"Yes, but I have some follow-up questions."

She leaned forward to display her impressive assets. "What more can I do to cooperate?"

He took a few seconds to find his tongue. "We arrested Ken Porter for his wife's murder."

"Ken? I can't believe he would harm his wife. Or any woman." She stroked a necklace that was lost in her cleavage. "He loved her."

"That's a funny thing to say coming from his mistress," Emily said. "How long have you and Ken been an item?"

Talia narrowed her eyes. "Who are you?"

"Emily Stevenson. I'm part of the investigative team."

Talia turned her attention to Travis. "Ken and I are not an item. There are no emotional ties between us."

Emily's interruption had restored his brain to functioning. He concentrated on Talia's eyes. "Besides taxes and accounting services, what else has Ken done for you?"

"He escorts me to social functions." She crossed her legs in a seductive move that drew his attention. "A woman doesn't like to go out alone at night."

He turned to Emily. She had nicer legs. Her skirt had ridden up enough to display a healthy portion of firm thigh. She sat demurely with her legs crossed at the ankles. Sexy without trying. Emily raised a dainty eyebrow. What was she signaling?

"Did you want to ask me something more?" Talia wetted her lips with a swipe of her tongue.

He nodded, trying to recall his next question.

Emily turned to Talia. "When you go out on these social functions, do you use Ken's car or yours?"

"Mine is more luxurious," she purred.

Emily leaned closer to her. "So he knows where the keys are."

"They're in a silver bowl by the door. Why?"

Emily turned to Travis and smiled. "Do you want to tell her the bad news or should I?"

He had recovered from whatever had turned his brain to mush. "We checked the GPS on your car, and it proves Ken took it home and waited for his wife to return. Since she didn't go inside, we believe she went with him to the place she worked. He stopped at the park where Christina's body was found before returning here."

"I can't believe it." Talia ran her hands down her bone-thin arms. "Ken isn't a violent man."

"Violent? We just came from a salon where he assaulted the owner. You wouldn't recognize her after the beating he gave her." He wasn't going to spare her any of the gruesome details. "He burned her fingers with a curling iron. He tortured her."

Talia gagged. "I think you should leave." She balanced on four-inch stilettos and pointed toward the door.

"We can talk here, or you can come down to the police station. You could be charged as an accessory to murder. It was your car Ken drove when he killed his wife."

"I didn't know he took my car." She lowered herself to the sofa and resumed her pose. "I was asleep."

Travis pulled a chair from a table in the adjoining room and sat in front of her. "Then it's in your best interest to cooperate and tell us everything you know."

She swiped at tears that had suddenly appeared on the tips of her false lashes. "I knew he had a temper, but I can't believe he's capable of murder."

"How bad a temper?" Emily moved to the edge of her chair and leaned forward. "Verbal or physical?"

"I never saw him hit anyone, but he could make someone feel small and worthless with an insult or cutting remark. He viewed servants and the poor in a paltry way. He bragged about firing incompetent subordinates. During a social event we attended, he demanded a food server be shown the door for dropping a tray when it was obvious he had knocked it from her hands."

Emily retrieved a box of tissues from a small table and handed it to Talia. "What happened Friday night?"

Talia dabbed at her tears. "He told me not to say anything, but we had a huge fight." She glanced at Travis.

He turned to a clean page in his notebook. "What was the fight about?"

She rose and poured herself a drink. "We had an argument about some jewelry he gave me."

He looked up from his notes. "Why? Most women appreciate jewelry."

She offered to pour a glass for them, but Emily declined.

"I'm on duty," Travis said. "Tell us about the argument."

Talia downed a second drink and resumed her seat. "Two weeks ago, he brought me a necklace with matching earrings. After he left, I examined the box it came in. Underneath the velvet display was a receipt. It was five years old. I figured it was a gift to his wife originally and he was regifting it to me. I should have been insulted, but the original price was nearly four thousand dollars. I took it to a jeweler to have it appraised. It had to be worth more now. Only the jeweler said it was gold plated with glass stones. It wasn't worth more than fifty bucks."

"He gave you costume jewelry in a fancy box?" Emily asked.

"I thought he left the old receipt in the bottom to fool me," Talia said. "When he visited last Friday, I let him have it. I threw the box in his face and told him his expensive gift was a cheap imitation."

"How did Ken respond?" he asked.

"He didn't believe me," Talia said. "I showed him the report from my jeweler. I wanted to make sure he knew I wasn't lying. That's when he became furious. He grabbed the necklace from me and examined it. Only he couldn't tell."

The necklace had to be one Christina had replaced with a fake. "How did you prove you were telling the truth?"

"I showed him how my diamond ring left a mark on his piece of glass. I even scraped off the thin gold plating to reveal copper underneath. You should have seen his face. Either he's a great actor or he didn't know."

"Are you sure he thought the necklace was real when he gave it to you?" Travis asked.

"He's never been cheap about gifts before. My

jeweler said it was a great knock off. Whoever did the work was a craftsman. I believe he was genuinely surprised."

He checked his notes. "This was Friday before Christina's death?"

"Yes. He told me to go to bed." Talia threw out her skinny arms. "I told him to take his worthless gift and either sleep on the couch or leave. He promised to make it right."

Travis underlined her last remark. "Did you hear him leave?"

"No, but I heard the garage door go up about four in the morning. He doesn't like parking his car on the street. I thought he was leaving, but he came into my room and told me to say I spent all night with him, and he'd do my accounting for free for three months." Talia hugged herself. "If I'd known it was to avoid a murder rap, I wouldn't have agreed."

They thanked Talia for cooperating and went to the squad car.

"We have motive and opportunity," Travis said. "He found out his wife replaced an expensive necklace and earrings for cheap fakes when Talia confronted him. He drove home and demanded Christina return the real stuff. When she refused, he killed her."

"He had to know the jewelry was fake at the funeral," Emily said. "But when Roger stepped on it, he appeared surprised."

"If he was planning to collect the insurance on the fakes, he needed to act surprised."

"It took months for Amanda to create replacement pieces," Emily said. "But she probably had all the real jewelry replaced by the time Ken gave Talia her gift."

"I agree," he said. "Christina may have gotten away with the switch if Talia hadn't checked to see how much it was worth."

Travis contacted Crane on the police radio and updated him on the interview with Talia.

By the time he was done, he arrived at Emily's apartment.

"I hope you didn't have any plans. I need those reports written up tonight," Crane said.

"Yes, sir. Any word on Lucy Vance?"

"She's in ICU and unconscious. I hope to talk to her tomorrow. You'll need to come in for a few hours so we can review the case."

Travis made sure the radio was off. "I'm sorry, but that means we'll have to cancel our date for tonight."

"I don't think we could have enjoyed it after everything that has happened." Emily's face was pale.

"Would you like me to come up?" He took her hand. "We haven't talked about the attack on Lucy. I had a hard time handling it. I can't imagine how it affected you."

A tear fell down her cheek. "I can't believe someone would do that to another human being. It was barbaric."

He wanted to reassure her. "Crane sounded like he expects her to be able to talk tomorrow."

"I work Saturday. I can stop by during my shift and check on her."

Color had returned to her cheeks. He kissed her hand. "You just met her, but you genuinely care about others and want to help."

"Not always successfully. I know it's selfish, but I wish Roger had been guilty. Now I have to convince Doreen not to take him back. You would think with the evidence of his cheating, she would know he'd do it again. Besides, Lucy and Sue said he was in love with Christina. Why else would he ask for a divorce?"

"I understand why he wanted a divorce," he said. "What I don't understand is why he went back to Doreen. I don't believe it was for love."

"Doreen will do anything for him, and Roger knows that."

He walked her up the steps and lingered long enough for a deep kiss. "We'll catch the play next Friday."

"I look forward to it."

He kissed her again, caressing every inch of her body and memorizing the spots that made her groan in pleasure. "I can't wait a week to spend time with you. I'll have Monday off. Think of something you'd like to do."

"I have some ideas already."

Chapter Twenty-Nine

Travis had spent hours Saturday afternoon finishing up reports on his interviews and notes about Christina Porter's murder. He had talked briefly with Emily before she reported for her shift and was looking forward to closing the case and spending time with her.

Crane called for him to join him in his office. He had the case folder on Christina Porter sitting on his desk.

"Did you receive my reports?"

Crane patted the thick folder. "Everything is in here. Ken and his lawyer want to talk. I thought you might want to be in on the interview."

"Is Adam joining us?"

"No. I made my decision about recommending a new detective, and the chief agreed. You're good at interviewing witnesses, and you have a knack for putting the pieces together. I think you'll be an asset to the force. Congratulations, O'Toole." Crane extended his hand.

Travis was stunned but shook his hand. "Thank you, sir." He wanted to call Emily, but it had to wait. Besides, she hadn't received word on how her interview went with the medical examiner's office. He didn't want to gloat if she hadn't gotten her dream job.

Crane gathered his folders and notepad. "Talia provided the motive for the murder and assault. Ken wanted the jewelry Christina had taken from his safe."

"Did you recover the real stuff?"

"Not yet." Crane opened the door. "Come on. Let's see if Ken is ready to confess and tell us where the jewelry is. Then we can tie the case up with a neat bow."

Ken had made bail and was dressed casually but looked haggard. His lawyer wore a suit. He looked confident.

Crane opened his folder. "Your girlfriend had some interesting things to tell Officer O'Toole yesterday."

Ken leaned forward, a scared look on his face. "Talia knows nothing about this."

"Detective O'Toole can explain what we know."

Travis looked at Crane. The new title would take time to get used to. He took a deep breath. "Talia confronted you about the jewelry you had given her. She had the necklace and earrings appraised. That's when you found out they were worthless imitations."

Ken wiped sweat from his forehead with a handkerchief he'd taken from his pants pocket.

"You did a pretty good job convincing everyone you didn't know the jewelry was fake at the funeral," Travis said. "But you knew Friday night. You took Talia's car and drove it to your home where you waited for Christina to arrive. You took your wife to the Hair-em, killed her, and dumped her body in the canal before returning to Talia's place."

"That's not what happened."

Ken's lawyer placed a restraining hand on his arm to keep him from saying anything more.

"Must have been a big shock to discover your wife wasn't as meek and mild as you thought." Travis leaned forward. "Talia said you were angry."

"Of course, I was angry." Ken shrugged off his lawyer's hand. "I took that white trash out of the gutter and gave her a life most women could only dream about. Christina was stealing a fortune from me and leaving worthless trinkets in my safe." He looked startled. "How did she know the combination?"

"Somehow she obtained the numbers," Crane said.

"I never saw her open it."

Crane flipped through his folder. "You worked nine to ten hours a day. Do you think she sat around watching television? According to Detective O'Toole, she took out the jewelry in the morning, gave it to Amanda Wright to duplicate, and returned it after bringing the children home from school. She only put the fakes in the original boxes and returned them to the safe when they were completed. We found a copy of your inventory in her gym bag from the Hair-em. She was as meticulous as you. Is this the combination to the safe?" He pointed to the top of the list.

"Yes. How did she get it?" Ken looked up. "She wasn't allowed in my office."

"Just because you treated her like a trained dog doesn't mean she was always obedient." Crane interlaced his long fingers. "Did you keep papers in your safe between you and your lawyer about gaining custody of the children?"

"Yes, but she didn't have access..." Ken leaned back into the chair, a stunned look on his face. "She never said anything."

"She didn't want to tip you off about her plans," Travis said. "She was going to take the children and run, but she needed to duplicate the jewelry first so she'd have enough to start a new life. If Talia hadn't discovered your gift was fake and confronted you, Christina might have pulled it off, and you never would have known you had a safe full of worthless baubles."

Ken slammed his fist against the tabletop. "She knew the jewelry would go to the children when they were grown."

"Minus what you gave to your girlfriends?" Crane asked.

Ken cleaned his glasses. "It was mine to do with as I wished."

"If she hadn't signed a prenup, she would have been entitled to half of your assets." Travis shook his head in disgust. "But you didn't want to share."

"That's why men have to protect themselves." Ken's voice rose in anger. "If a judge awarded her custody, I would have had to pay child support. She would have drained me over the next twelve years. If I had known about Roger Markem earlier, I would have hired a private investigator to get dirt on her."

"But that costs money, and you were tracking her car, so why bother?" Crane asked.

"You and Roger are more alike than you realize." Travis stopped writing in his notebook. "You promised protection and offered gifts but threatened to take it all away. You made her desperate."

"She'd leave better off than when she came to me," Ken argued. "I was planning to give her compensation in exchange for full custody of the children."

Travis doubted Ken would part with much in any settlement. "The children were more important to her."

"When you realized she had plans of her own, you borrowed Talia's car so you could drive home undetected and waited for Roger to drop her off," Crane summarized the case. "She never made it inside. You killed her and dumped her body in the canal. Then you drove back to Talia and told her to lie for you."

"I only confronted Christina." Ken swiped the sweat from his upper lip and put on his glasses. "I didn't kill her. I swear it."

Crane looked from Ken to the lawyer. "If that's true, then tell us what happened."

"Go ahead," the lawyer prompted.

"I was upset about the fake jewelry, but I only wanted the real pieces back," Ken admitted. "I couldn't figure out how the gift I gave Talia had turned into worthless junk. I needed to find out the truth. I took Talia's car so Christina wouldn't recognize it. I parked in the dark across from the house and waited for her to arrive."

Travis leaned forward. "How did you know she was out?"

"The babysitter's car was in the driveway."

"We know Roger brought her home," Crane said. "What happened?"

"He stopped at the end of the driveway and shoved her out of his truck. She stumbled, fell, and stayed on her hands and knees even after he drove off. I thought she was drunk."

"She was alive when you confronted her?" Travis looked at the lawyer. Did he realize his client was now the last one to see the victim alive?

"She was breathing, but her speech was slurred. She'd been crying, and her makeup was smeared. I figured she'd had a fight with Roger. He was taking advantage of Christina, and she didn't even realize it. I put her in the passenger seat of Talia's car and showed her the glass necklace." Ken removed his glasses and set them on the table next to his phone. "I ordered her to hand over the jewelry she was wearing. Her hands shook, and she couldn't work the clasp. I removed her jewelry but realized they were fakes."

Travis interrupted. "How did you know?"

"I scraped off some paint with my key. Talia had done the same thing." Ken stared at the wall. "I didn't realize she had duplicated all of the jewelry until after the funeral."

"Where are the fakes you took off Christina's body?"

Ken chuckled, but his lawyer touched his arm to silence him. "My daughter has a collection of costume jewelry she wears when she wants to be a princess. I hid it in her jewelry box."

Travis softened his voice. "What happened with Christina in Talia's car?"

"She kept crying and babbling on about how Roger found out. He hit and kicked her to punish her. She said she was dying and asked me to take care of her babies." Ken rubbed his eyes and looked up at the ceiling. "I didn't know she was seriously hurt. I needed to know where she had hidden the real jewelry. I went a little crazy and slapped her face, but that was all. She finally confessed everything was at the Hair-em, so I drove there."

Crane looked at his report. "You were at the salon for forty minutes."

He shook his head. "I couldn't get in. The place was locked up, and the key Christina gave me didn't fit the front or back doors. There was nothing but an old beat-up van parked in the rear. When I returned to the car, Christina was dead."

"Dead?" Crane asked. "How did you know?"

"I thought she was passed out at first. I shook her, and she was limp as a rag. I felt for a pulse. There was none. I turned on the light and saw bruises on her face and neck. When I examined her more, I found bruises on her arms and marks on her stomach where Roger must have kicked her with his cowboy boots."

Travis searched for the medical examiner's photos. The marks on Christina's belly matched the shape of a pointed boot. He shared with Crane. "Roger's boots have steel tips."

"Maybe Roger hurt Christina, but you can't blame him for your crimes," Crane said. "He didn't even know about the fake jewelry."

"I don't know why he beat her that night, but he knows about the jewelry. Maybe Lucy told him when he beat her. Maybe he guessed at the funeral." Ken's voice deepened. "You heard how he talked. Taunting me about ripping off the insurance company. He was trying to make me look guilty."

Crane pointed to a picture of Christina's battered body. "Why didn't you take your wife to the hospital?"

"How was I going to explain her death?" Ken glanced at the photo and turned away. "When they saw the bruises, they would assume I beat her."

Travis thought of her body bobbing up in the water. "But you dumped your wife in the canal."

Ken's hands shook as he picked up his glasses. Tears streamed down his face. "I didn't know what to do. I headed back to Talia's and had to drive through the park. It was raining, and the parking lot was empty. I left her body in the water and left."

Crane leaned in. "Where is the jewelry? We searched the Hair-em from top to bottom."

"I swear I don't know." Ken mopped his face with his handkerchief. "Christina said it was at the Hair-em. She went there every day. I tracked her GPS signal. She never left."

"Yes, she did," Travis said. "Roger gave her Doreen's wrecked van to drive. The one you saw behind the Hair-em."

"Why? She had a car."

Travis pointed to his phone resting on the table. "One you could track."

Ken put his glasses on. "Is that why she spent so much time at the Hair-em? I kept wondering why her car was parked there most of the day."

Travis watched his expression. "She was driving the van to other locations."

Ken's brow furrowed. "Do you know where?"

Travis pointed at him. "The question is do you know where your wife was going?"

"How could I?" Ken's voice rose in anger. "I didn't even know she had a second vehicle."

Crane slid a business card across the table. "She went to the Tally-Ho."

Ken stared at the card. "I've heard of it. Nothing good." He slid the card back at Crane. "Only someone like Roger would take Christina to a place like that."

"Roger took her there the Friday night she died." Crane leaned forward and lowered his voice. "You don't know why she went there during the day without Roger?"

Ken looked confused. "No."

"She needed money to pay Amanda Wright to create the costume jewelry that replaced the real items in your safe," Travis said. "Your wife worked as a prostitute."

"What?" Ken's shock was real. "Christina would never do that. She was a lady."

"She loved her children enough to do anything necessary to keep them," Travis said. "She needed quick cash and the jewelry to escape with them. She sold the only thing she still possessed, her body."

Ken smacked his fist on the table. "I'd kill the woman I loved before I'd let her do that."

Crane closed his folder. "Is that a confession?"

"No." Ken went pale. "I did love her. Once. She was beautiful, and others admired her. She was a prize. But trophies gather dust."

"You were tired of her?" Crane asked.

"She was more interested in the children than me. They were her whole world." Ken gasped and grasped his hands as if in prayer. "The children can't know. They loved their mother. You can't make what she did public."

"She was discreet." Crane wrote something on his notepad. "Nobody knew about the van she drove to the hotel."

"Except for Roger. He recognized the van at the Tally-Ho." Travis jumped to his feet. "He didn't make reservations for romance. He wanted to teach her a lesson. A violent one."

Crane gathered his folder and signaled Travis to step outside before he spoke. "Do you think Ken is innocent?"

"No," Travis said. "He let Christina die instead of taking her to the hospital, but Roger was the one who killed her by beating and kicking her. The steel toes on his cowboy boots could inflict a lot of damage."

"But why? You made it clear he didn't know about the jewelry Friday night."

"Ken gave us the answer," Travis said. "Roger loved Christina according to Lucy and Sue. He *punished* the woman he loved because he found out from Debrowsky she was selling her body and lying to him. He made a big deal about all women being liars. Everyone said he was angry Friday night at the Boot N Scoot. He was plotting his retribution."

"He didn't want anyone to know he took her to the Tally-Ho, so he left at eleven and came back later," Crane said.

Travis paced a few steps in the hallway and turned. "We've been looking at this crime as if one person committed it. Christina had the misfortune of two men seeking revenge on her on the same night. Roger beat her for working at the Tally-Ho while keeping him at arm's length. He dumped her on her lawn barely alive. She could have sought medical help, but Ken showed up and took her to the Hair-em to retrieve the jewelry. While he's trying to get in, she dies from her injuries. He panics and dumps her body in the canal."

"But we found Ken over Lucy's beaten body."

"What if Ken told us the truth?" Travis looked toward the closed door. "Lucy called him, and he arrived just before the police received the 911 call."

"Dispatch documented two calls." Crane considered his theory. "But why would Roger beat Lucy?"

"He wanted the real jewelry. Christina told the truth when she told her friends her jewelry was costume, but at the funeral, Ken said it was real. After Roger beat Christina, he had to wonder about the cash she was earning at the Tally-Ho. He may have figured if the jewelry in Ken's safe was fake, then Christina had the real stuff. The logical place to hide it was at the Hair-em, and the person who would know its location would be Lucy. Roger beat her for the information."

"I'll put an APB out for Roger's truck."

Travis snapped his fingers. "Ken said his wife gave him a key when they arrived at the Hair-em, but it didn't fit the door locks. Do you have any keys in evidence?"

"In my office."

Travis followed Crane who dumped the contents in the evidence box onto his desk.

Travis picked up a single key attached to a miniature soccer ball. "This is a vehicle key. Could it go to Doreen's van?"

"We searched it. There was no jewelry inside."

"Doreen had a spare key and time to move the van," Travis said. "What if she cleaned it out before we searched it?"

"Do you think she's hiding the jewelry?"

"Emily had a box of unopened condoms in her backpack. The same brand as the ones found in Christina's locker and in the room she used at the Tally-Ho." Travis looked through the evidence box. "What was in the box of condoms we took from the Hair-em?"

"I never opened it." Crane found the evidence bag and removed a box of condoms. He slid his finger under the top flap and removed a new roll. "Condoms. What did you think was in the box?"

Travis examined the empty box. "I was convinced she hid the jewelry in here. Who would look in a condom package?"

"According to Ken's inventory, she would need a number of boxes to store all his jewelry."

"Emily only had one, but she said they found a pink backpack full of condom boxes in the van." Travis took out his phone. "Let me call her."

"Where is Emily?"

"She's working at the hospital." Travis looked at his phone. "It went to voice." He left a message. "I need to talk to you immediately. It's urgent."

"How much do you trust your girlfriend?" Crane repacked the box. "What if she found the jewelry and has been stringing you along?"

"She's a straight arrow, but Doreen is as crooked as a boomerang." Travis felt his heart flip. "Emily told her to report the van, but she moved it. I mentioned the backpack to you but didn't think it was important. Why would we need more condoms for the case?"

"But if that's where Christina hid the jewelry, then the backpack is key," Crane said.

"She gave Ken the key to the van, but he didn't look inside." Travis clenched the soccer ball key ring. "I wondered why Roger went back to Doreen. What if he suspects her of knowing about the jewelry?"

"If he didn't find the jewelry inside the Hair-em, then Roger is still looking for it," Crane said. "We need to find him."

Travis looked at his watch. "I'm going to the hospital. Doreen will be going in soon, and if Roger is looking for her, Emily could be in danger."

Chapter Thirty

Emily received a message from the medical examiner that the job of forensic investigator was hers. After accepting, she called Travis to tell him the good news. She wanted to tell him in person and left a short message when her call was sent to his voice mail.

Work was busy for a Saturday night, but after delivering her printed reports, she checked on Lucy. The intensive care unit was on the first floor near the emergency room. Beds and all the equipment necessary for critical patients were enclosed in glass rooms. Nurses could see everything going on from their central location, and monitors at the desk relayed information for each of the patients.

Emily barely recognized Lucy. Her eyes were swollen shut. A thick bandage covered her forehead and wrapped around her head, nose, and jaw like a mask. Her fingers were wrapped in gauze.

Sue sat in a chair near the bed, flipping through a magazine. Dark circles shadowed her eyes, but she smiled when she looked up. "I'm glad you came."

Emily stood by the bed. She had grown up comforting the mourning relatives and friends of the deceased during countless funerals. "I'm so sorry this happened. How long have you been here?"

"A few hours. They wouldn't let me visit yesterday."

A nurse entered and attached a fresh IV bag of saline solution on a hanger on a metal pole by the bed.

Emily studied the monitor displaying the rhythm of Lucy's heartbeat, pulse numbers, and other information. "How is she doing?"

"Better. We have her on morphine for the pain, so she's in and out."

Sue waited for the nurse to leave. "The police wouldn't tell me much. What do you know?"

Crane had made his arrest. "Ken Porter tortured poor Lucy and tore the Hair-em apart looking for Christina's jewelry. The police are charging him with attacking Lucy and murdering Christina."

Sue touched the top of Lucy's head, the only place not swathed in bandages. "I'm glad the police caught Ken. I hope they give him life in prison."

"And the stupid police thought I was a suspect." Roger stood in the doorway, his hand on Doreen's shoulder. "I knew it was that pencil pusher! It's always the quiet ones that go insane when they don't get what they want."

Doreen remained near the door, a shocked expression on her face.

Emily stepped toward her. "Are you all right, Doreen?"

"She's fine." Roger moved to the end of the bed and stared at Lucy. "Is she awake?"

"No," Sue said. "They have her on pain medicines."

"I told you it was too soon to visit," Doreen said.

Roger turned and gave her a look, the sort men give to women as a silent command. Doreen either ignored it or didn't see it.

"I had to see how my darlin' friend, Lucy, was

doin'," Roger said.

Lucy's body shook beneath the blanket. She raised a bandaged hand, and Sue leaned in close.

"What is it, Lucy?" Sue asked.

Roger gripped the bed frame. "What did she say?"

Lucy groaned but fell quiet as sleep returned.

Sue shrugged. "Nothing I could understand."

The nurse entered and frowned as she studied the monitors. "She needs to rest. You'll have to leave. You can visit tomorrow, but only two at a time."

They exited the ICU and paused in the hallway.

Sue removed a tissue from her purse and blew her nose. "The police said I could go to the salon today, but it was such a mess all I did was cancel appointments."

Emily patted her back. "I can come in the morning and give you a hand cleaning."

"I'd be happy to help," Roger said.

Roger? Help? Two words that didn't go together.

"You can't help," Doreen said. "I have to work all night, and you're supposed to take the children tomorrow so I can sleep."

"The children can help," Roger said.

He'd offered twice. Doreen had complained how Roger never did anything at home but drink beer and watch television. Why would he volunteer to clean a beauty salon? Did he think the jewelry was still there? "Sue, did the police find the missing jewelry?"

"No. They asked me if I knew where Christina could have hidden it, but the safe was empty. What if nobody finds it?"

"Finders keepers for the lucky person who does," Roger said.

"That's not how it works," Emily said. "The jewelry

belongs to Ken. Although I don't think he can benefit from a crime."

She reviewed what she knew. Ken had found out Friday night from Talia that Christina was switching costume trinkets for the genuine jewelry. He'd driven home and confronted her, but why kill her? Especially if she hadn't told him where to find the real stuff. "I don't understand why Ken would kill Christina. Once he discovered her scheme to switch the real for fake, all he had to do was notify the police about her deception and theft. It would have doomed her chances for custody of the children."

"Ken is a violent man," Roger said. "He killed his wife for stealing from him, and look what he did to Lucy for hiding the jewelry."

"But he claimed Lucy called to tell him she had found the jewelry. Why didn't she hand it over?"

"She changed her mind," Roger said.

"No one would keep a secret under torture." Emily waved back toward the ICU. "Lucy didn't know. So why call Ken?"

"I never saw any jewelry," Sue said. "Are you sure Tina had it?"

"She kept the jewelry in the Wright Stuff safe until Friday," Emily said. "The owner said she took all of the real pieces with her in a gym bag. She saw her go into the salon before picking her children up from school. What do you remember about that day, Sue?"

"She came in and went to the office with Lucy. That's where the safe is. Then Tina went back where her locker was located. I remember Lucy reminding her it was time for her to pick up her kids because she was taking so long. She left with a backpack. It must have been her daughter's. It was pink."

Doreen gasped. "With a kitty on it?"

Roger studied Doreen before he stepped toward Sue. "What did she do with the backpack?"

Sue yawned. "She took it with her when she went out the back door."

"The back door where the van was parked?" Roger spoke so fast spit splattered from his mouth.

Sue wiped her cheek. "The police took the van."

"Go home and rest," Emily said. "You'll have plenty to do tomorrow. I'll be by to help."

As soon as Sue was gone, Roger grabbed Doreen's arm. "You knew about the van parked behind the Hair-em."

Doreen yanked her arm free and rubbed it. "What if I did? It was my van."

"Was there a backpack inside?"

Doreen threw back her head and laughed. "All it had inside were boxes of condoms and a bunch of business cards for the Tally-Ho."

What did Christina need them for? If Friday was her last day working at the Tally-Ho, why did she have so many condoms in her backpack? Unless something else was in the boxes. Emily looked at Roger.

His face was distorted with rage. "Where is the backpack?"

She'd had a hard time imagining Ken beating and torturing a woman, but Roger was easily capable of violence. But when had he realized Christina was hiding the jewelry? Even Ken hadn't known until Friday when Talia showed him the fake necklace. "When did you figure out the jewelry was real, Roger?"

He turned, his eyes wide with anger. "I got

suspicious when the detective showed me a picture of the necklace Tina wore Friday night. Why were they so interested in costume junk? Then at the funeral when I stepped on the necklace, Ken insisted the jewelry was real, but the broken pieces proved he was wrong. Tina replaced all his valuable inventory with fakes. She had played him for a fool just like me. Only I outsmarted him. If Tina wanted to hide something, it would be in the safe at the Hair-em. I waited for Lucy to arrive at the salon and forced her to open the safe. Except for the register cash, it was empty. It took some persuading, but Lucy said Tina had put the money and jewelry in a pink backpack."

"When did you talk to Lucy?" Doreen asked.

Emily stared at the villain. "Yesterday morning when he tortured her."

Doreen gasped. "But the police said Ken did that."

"No. He only went there because Lucy said she found the jewelry." She turned from Doreen to Roger. "How did you make her lie to Ken?"

"Curling irons are hotter than they look." Roger shoved his hands into the pockets of his leather jacket and rocked on his heels. "Then I called 911 on her landline so the police would catch Ken with Lucy."

"You tortured that poor woman?" There was just enough outrage in Doreen's voice to give Emily hope she was beginning to understand the truth. "But it was your idea to visit Lucy tonight."

"Why?" Emily asked. "Why did you want to visit Lucy?"

"I wanted to make sure Lucy wasn't awake to talk to the police so they wouldn't figure out my role in all this. I needed time to find Tina's stash, and then Sue mentioned the backpack." He saluted Doreen. "Thanks for asking about the kitty. I knew you had it. I appreciate the fact you removed it from the van before the cops could find it."

Emily had told Travis about the backpack, but he thought only condoms were in it. Would he figure out the truth in time?

Roger stared at them. "Where is the backpack?"

"The police have it," Emily said.

His open hand flew across her face so fast she had no time to react. The blow was hard, sending a shock of pain through her body and to her brain. She stumbled and went down on one knee.

"If the cops had it, they wouldn't have searched the Hair-em yesterday." He removed a revolver from his pocket and pointed it at Doreen. "You lied to the police when you said you didn't find anything in the van. Don't lie to me."

Doreen helped Emily rise to her feet. "Don't hurt us. I put it in my locker in the computer room."

"Why?" Emily asked.

"I was going to confront Roger with the condoms and the cards we found, but then he wanted to reconcile." Doreen shook her head. "I forgot about it until Sue said something."

He waved the gun at them. "Let's go get it."

Emily stood her ground. "It doesn't belong to you."

"Do you want to give it to a murderer? He won't need it in jail."

"The jewelry belongs to Christina's children if Ken goes to jail," Emily said.

"I don't care about my own kids. Why would I care about hers? I'm taking the jewelry and money and getting out of this town."

"What about me and the children?" Doreen asked.

"Do you think I want to be married to a nagging shrew? I'm tired of women taking me for all I have. You kept badgering me for child support, and Tina wanted a van. The whole time she's stealing from her husband. No wonder he killed her."

"But Ken didn't kill Christina," Emily said. "You did."

Roger laughed, the sound echoing in the empty hallway. "She was alive when I dumped her on her lawn."

"After you beat her. She died from internal injuries."

"I kicked her a few times to teach her a lesson," Roger admitted. "Ken finished her off and dumped her body in the canal."

"Ken was angry about the jewelry, but you didn't know about it Friday night," Emily said. "Why did you beat her?"

His eyes narrowed, and he spat the words, "She was a lyin' whore."

"You found out about the Tally-Ho," Emily whispered. "You saw the van there."

"A job on Friday afternoon was canceled, and my boss sent me home. I was going through the restaurant's drive-through next door and saw the van I gave Tina. I drove over and talked to the man at the desk."

"You saw my van parked there?" Doreen screeched. "She went to the Tally-Ho without you? Didn't I tell you she was a whore!"

"For once in your stupid life, you were right, Doreen," Roger said. "The owner showed me a picture of Tina and told me I could make an appointment. I was too shocked to react. She always told me she was too much of a lady to do anything perverted. I thought about all those men and her laughing at me for being in love with her."

"What do you mean love?" Doreen demanded. "You said you were never in love with her and loved me!"

"I lied," he admitted. "Everyone does it, Doreen."

Roger had a motive. "You were angry because Christina lied and used your love to help escape her husband," Emily said. "She needed the van and a way to raise quick cash to pay Amanda Wright so she would have a fortune in jewelry to start a new life with her children."

"Don't defend her. The lyin' slut suckered me out of money, drinks, and my van. She owed me." Roger's voice echoed down the deserted hallway. "Now I'm getting what is rightfully mine."

Chapter Thirty-One

Emily glanced around as they walked from the ICU unit along the corridor, hoping they would run into someone who could help, but most employees had gone home, and fewer employees worked the late shifts.

A man with a mop and bucket was cleaning a spill on the cafeteria floor but didn't look up as Roger hurried them to the elevators. The basement wasn't a good place to go with Roger. It was secluded, and the security doors would keep others locked out.

He had a smug expression on his face. "I have to thank you ladies for helping me."

She had never helped Roger. "What do you mean?"

"I stayed one step ahead of the police through Doreen and you." Roger put his arm around his wife's shoulders. "Why do you think I wanted to reconcile with her?"

Doreen shook off his embrace. "Emily told me you were in love with Tina, but I thought she was wrong because I still loved you. Doesn't eighteen years of marriage mean anything to you?"

"It means I know your weakness, Doreen. When you told me the police had questioned you, I wanted to find out more." Roger looked at Emily. "Then you introduced Emily and her police officer boyfriend. I had an inside line into the investigation. That's why I knew they hadn't found Tina's stash."

Emily had unwittingly helped Roger. Travis had warned her about telling Doreen too much, but she hadn't listened. She'd been determined to keep Doreen from going back to Roger and had missed his connection to the crimes.

Roger brushed the gun barrel against Doreen's cheek. "A few words of love, and you told me everything you knew."

They were nearing the elevators and running out of time to escape. Emily glanced around. Maybe if she pushed him, they could reach the elevator and close the door before he reacted. Once safely inside the computer room, they could lock the door and call for help.

"Emily!" a familiar voice called from the other direction in the hall.

Travis. Emily needed to warn him. "Roger has a gun!"

Travis picked up his pace as he drew his pistol. His voice had a dark, dangerous tone. "Surrender, Roger. We know you beat Lucy and killed Christina."

The police had figured out the truth, too.

The elevator doors opened.

Roger waved the gun at them. "Get inside."

Emily didn't move.

"Do it, or I'll kill your boyfriend cop."

All thoughts of her own safety vanished as she realized Travis was in danger. "Look out!" Emily tried to grab the gun from Roger's hand.

He gave Emily a straight-arm shove that knocked her to the ground. She slid across the polished linoleum and crashed into the concrete wall.

Roger squeezed the trigger of his gun.

Emily, still sprawled on the floor, watched the

smoke shoot out of the barrel. A deafening roar camouflaged her scream.

Travis raised his gun as his body flew up and back from the impact of the bullet striking him. He crashed to the hard floor, his gun clenched in his fingertips. He didn't move.

"Travis!" Emily scrambled to her feet and bolted toward him.

Roger grabbed her sweatshirt from behind. The fleece tore at the seam as he yanked her back and shoved her into the open elevator. She crashed into the back wall. Doreen rushed in and helped Emily to her feet. Roger closed the door and pushed the button for the basement.

Hot tears rolled down Emily's face as she replayed the shooting. Where had the bullet struck him? "I never told him I loved him," she confessed to Doreen, who was stroking her hair. "What if he's dead?"

"What the hell is going on, Roger?" Doreen demanded. "You just shot a cop."

"Shut up!" he screamed. "Just because you castrated me for eighteen years doesn't mean I haven't grown some new balls." He kept hitting the button for the basement. "I finally have an opportunity to be rich, but I've got to hurry now."

"Turn yourself in," Doreen urged him.

"No way," he argued. "I've got you two to help me."

"I'm not going to help you!" Emily shouted in defiance.

"I don't need two hostages." He waved the revolver at each of them. "Who wants to die?"

The ride down the elevator seemed to take an eternity. Doreen and Emily looked at each other in terror.

"This is not the Roger I know," Doreen whispered. "He scares me."

"We'll cooperate," Emily agreed. For now.

The elevator door opened, and Roger ushered them out. They walked the short distance to the information services department. Doreen entered the code, and everyone went inside.

He followed them to the common area. "Which locker has the backpack?"

Doreen pointed at hers.

Emily stared at it. "What if the boxes only contain condoms?"

He pointed the gun at her. "For your sake, they better contain the jewelry."

He would never get away with his crimes. If Travis knew, then Crane knew Roger was guilty. They needed to cooperate until help arrived. She nodded to Doreen. "Open it."

Doreen's hands shook. She worked the combination several times, but the lock wouldn't open.

"Tell me the combination," Emily said. She turned the dial until the lock clicked. She removed the backpack and realized it was too heavy to hold just condoms. She unzipped it.

Roger waved the gun. "Dump it on the table." A shower of condom boxes fell out along with bundles of money hidden in the bottom. He grabbed a wad of bills and flipped through the different denominations. "Pay dirt." He waved his gun at Emily. "Open a box."

She grabbed the nearest box and opened the sealed edge. A few packaged condoms fell on the table along with several plastic bags lined with cloth.

"Remove the contents."

She removed the soft cloth and unfolded it to reveal a pair of emerald earrings. They glittered in the fluorescent lights with an eerie green cast.

"I always thought of myself as a pirate. This is a huge haul."

Emily's voice was filled with rage. "They hanged pirates for their crimes."

Roger shook the boxes. "There's something inside all of them." He laughed. "I'm rich." He waved his gun. "Repack it."

Emily packed the money and the boxes inside and zipped the bag closed. "Now what?"

He grabbed the backpack and pointed his gun at them. "Let's make our escape, ladies."

Chapter Thirty-Two

Travis heard someone calling his name in the distance as if through a tunnel. His head throbbed from smacking against the hard floor, but luckily, his back and shoulders had hit first. He felt for blood but found none. When he inhaled, a pain radiated in his chest. He'd been shot.

He rolled to his side to rise and groaned as he fought to catch his breath.

"Stay down," Crane ordered. He examined the hole in his shirt. "Thank God, you wore your vest."

Travis ignored Crane. He retrieved his gun from the floor, holstered it, and rose on unsteady legs.

"You better go to the ER," Crane said.

"No, Roger has Emily. He took her and Doreen down to the computer room. We'll need a code to get in." He assessed any damage as the pain subsided. "I'm fine."

Crane called dispatch and relayed for help. "Security is on its way, but we'll have to wait for a rescue team."

Travis shook his head. A headache throbbed behind his eyes, but he ignored it. "They may not have time. You saw what he did to Christina and Lucy. I won't risk Emily's life with that monster. Once he has the jewelry, he has no reason to keep the women alive."

"Promise you'll do exactly as I say," Crane said.

"I will." It was an empty promise. He'd do whatever

necessary to save Emily.

He turned at the sound of footsteps. Two security guards were running down the hall, followed by two police officers who had responded to the call.

"How many ways into the computer room?" Crane asked.

"Two. The elevator and a staircase."

"Can you lock the elevators down?"

The older security guard lifted a ring of keys on his belt. "Yes."

Crane pointed at him. "You wait here for the others and bring them down the elevator. The rest of you follow me down the stairs. We know he has a gun and two female hostages. The safety of the women is our priority."

The younger security guard led them down the stairs and unlocked the door. Crane motioned him to move to the rear as he led the way into a dark room filled with cubicles. They moved into the work space nearest the hall that extended into the common area and led to the computer room.

The main door opened. They were hidden, but a gap in the cubicle frame allowed Travis to see what was going on. Doreen and Emily entered the hallway with Roger behind them. He had a gun in his hand.

"Who would lock the elevator?" Roger demanded.

"Security," Doreen said. "Do you think no one heard the gunshot?"

"We're in lockdown. You won't be able to escape," Emily said. "You should surrender."

"The hell I will."

"You shot a police officer. They'll shoot first and ask questions later," Emily said. "And I'll be the first to testify they had no choice."

"Not if you're dead."

Emily's eyes narrowed. His brave girl might cause more problems by antagonizing Roger. They needed to eliminate him, but the women were between them. Crane had his hand raised to keep them quiet and in place.

Emily's sweatshirt was torn, but she appeared calm.

Roger acted like a trapped animal, searching his surroundings. He turned toward the door. A pink backpack was draped over one shoulder. He turned and pulled on Doreen's arm. "How many people know the code to this room?"

"Only the people in this department," Emily said.

"I don't believe you." Roger waved his gun to motion them up the ramp to the computer room. "Unlock the door. I know that room is secure." The women disappeared from view.

Crane bolted down the hallway, and Travis followed. Roger saw them and dashed up the ramp. By the time they reached the computer room, the door clicked closed. Travis yanked on the metal handle, but it was locked.

Emily saw him and ran forward. "Travis!"

Roger shoved her toward the three printers lined up to his left. He pointed his gun at the glass door and fired. Travis jumped to the hallway and crashed into metal shelving where reports slid off onto the floor. He looked up. The bullets were embedded in the thick layer of glass that protected the computer room.

"The glass is bulletproof." Crane turned toward the security guard. "What's the code for the door?"

He shook his head. "I'll have to call the supervisor."

"Do it."

Travis walked to the front hallway where he stared at Emily peering through the glass. He offered a smile.

Chapter Thirty-Three

Emily stepped to the front wall of windows and pressed her hands against the thick glass. Travis reached up and placed his hand against hers. He was alive and well. His shirt was torn, and the bullet must have hit his vest. His blue eyes searched hers, and she gave him a reassuring nod. She was terrified but couldn't die now. She wanted to live a lifetime with the man before her.

"Sit down," Roger ordered. "I may not be able to shoot him again, but I can shoot you."

Emily touched her fingertips to her lips and placed them on the glass. Travis nodded and turned his attention to Roger. If looks could kill, her captor would have been dead.

She took a seat near the window, and Doreen sat next to her in front of the computer monitors. Doreen's skin was pale, and her hands shook. They needed something to take their minds off the shock and danger. She gave Doreen the hospital pager just like she always did for shift change. Doreen grabbed her notebook and pens from the shelf above the monitors to begin her normal routine.

Roger turned and waved his gun toward them. "What are you doing?"

"Midnight processing." Doreen glanced in his direction, turned back to her job, and marked off her run sheets.

Emily stood. "I need to load the printers." She opened the door to the large printer between them and Roger. Nearly four feet high, it was a metal box that held a box of paper used for printing reports. The green-and-white-striped paper was nearly gone. She looked around the room. "Do you have a full box in here?"

"It's by the door." Doreen turned to Roger. "Would you mind carrying that box over here?"

His voice dripped with sarcasm. "I suppose you want me to load the paper, too?"

"If it isn't too much trouble," Doreen said.

"The hell I will!" He kicked the box of paper, but it barely budged.

Doreen wouldn't detour from her usual routine. She walked past him, picked up the box, and placed it on top of the printer.

Her bravado inspired Emily who removed the nearly empty box from inside the printer. "You've got the jewelry and money. Why don't you just run along and let us do our job?"

"I need one of you to be my hostage so I can get past the cops." He pointed his gun at Emily.

She dropped the box on the floor, closed her eyes, and prayed dying would be over quickly.

"Not you, darlin'."

Emily opened her eyes.

Roger had his gun pointed at Doreen. "You won't have to sign those divorce papers after all."

"What the heck do you mean?"

"It's a long ride to Canada, and I might get lonely."

Emily stepped back against the monitor table. He wanted to take her hostage. "Doreen is your wife."

He sneered, his yellow teeth bared. "And after

eighteen years, she ain't got no surprises."

Doreen stepped around the printer between Roger and Emily. "She doesn't want you touching her!"

Doreen was right, but he had murdered one woman and sent another to the hospital. He wasn't likely to take no for an answer.

As if to prove her point, he swung his arm up and knocked his wife on the side of her head with the barrel of his revolver. Blood spurted from the wound, and Doreen stumbled backward and fell to an open area on the floor between the printers and mainframes. Emily knelt beside her co-worker and felt for a pulse.

Doreen grunted.

"Keep quiet," Emily whispered.

Roger grabbed the back of Emily's torn sweatshirt and yanked her to her feet. The fleece shredded beneath his rough hands. "I better show you who's boss."

The images of Christina's and Lucy's beaten bodies reminded her Roger would show no mercy. At one time experts cautioned women to comply with attackers in the hope they would not be killed, but Emily preferred to fight. After being attacked by the man three years ago, she'd taken self-defense classes. She thrust her fingers straight at his throat with the momentum to drive them through his spine.

His eyes widened as he gasped for breath. The surprise attack gave her a brief chance to escape. She was inches from the handle on the door when he tackled her and slammed her into the glass and metal frame. Travis ran up the ramp and yanked at the locked door. Roger grabbed her shirt and shoved her toward the center printer.

If it hadn't been on wheels and moved with the

impact, she would have collided with the hard steel. She grabbed on to the top to keep from falling. He snatched her arm and twisted it behind her back. She bit down to keep from crying out as a pain shot through her shoulder.

"I won't make the same mistake twice." One of his hands clamped her wrists while his legs pressed tightly against hers. "I need to take some of the fight out of you so you'll be a good hostage."

She turned her head away from him to escape his stale breath and slobbering mouth. A shudder of revulsion shook her as she attempted to concentrate on something other than his excitement-filled body behind her.

"Oh, you've got one tight ass." He humped her through their clothes.

His words angered her. She flung her head back and hit him with a head butt.

"Hell!" he cried.

She felt dizzy. The defensive move had hurt her just as much as him. Only he was madder. He shoved her face down on the printer lid. Luckily, she turned her face just in time to take most of the impact on her cheekbone instead of on her nose.

He gripped his gun in his right hand as he wrapped his left arm around her throat, cutting off her air supply. With her hands free, she clawed to loosen his grip, but he held firm. What self-defense she knew was useless in the tight quarters.

The door clicked open.

"Let her go!" Crane ordered.

Roger spun, positioning her like a shield between him and the police, his arm still wrapped around her neck. He pointed the gun at Crane and then Travis who blocked his escape. "All I'm asking for is an hour head start. I'll let her go once I'm in the clear."

"You're not taking Emily anywhere!" Travis promised.

Emily heard something strange in the tone of his voice that frightened her. Travis was tense, ready to pounce. His sky-blue eyes had turned to cold steel as he stared into Roger's. He was no longer the cool, in-control cop but an angry animal, barely containing his fury.

"I'll kill her!"

Her sweatshirt was bunched around her neck, but Roger's forearm tightened. She gulped for air.

Roger stepped sideways into the open area where Doreen had fallen. "Move out of the way."

Crane stepped back toward the mainframe computers to allow a path to the door and ramp. "Let him leave."

Travis didn't budge.

"Move!" Roger dragged his hostage closer, his arm tightening on her neck.

Emily was dizzy and fought to stay conscious. She didn't want to faint. Then an idea burst into her oxygen-deprived brain. Why not pass out? She went limp, hoping her body weight would take her captor down with her. Only his grip tightened.

A dull thud echoed in her thundering brain, and she fell to the floor. Roger's arm loosened, and she gulped mouthfuls of air as she stared up at ceiling tile and fluorescent lights. The shadow of someone stood over her.

"Travis?"

"Just me." Doreen leaned against the back of a chair, blood matted in her short hair. She panted to catch her breath.

Travis tore the printers from their assigned positions to reach Emily. She grabbed his arm as he lifted her off the floor and pulled her tight. She glanced down at Roger's unconscious body and kicked him just to make sure he stayed down.

"I've got Roger," Crane commanded as he blocked Travis from reaching him.

"He's mine," Travis growled.

"You take care of the women," Crane ordered.

"Help me," Emily pleaded to draw his attention away. She put her arms around his neck and kissed him. "You don't have to turn into the monster to fight the monsters."

His eyes widened. He understood. He needed to stay true to his honorable beliefs, and she didn't have to lose parts of herself to fall in love and be loved. He kissed her between examining her for injuries.

"I'm all right," she told him but winced when he found the bruise on her cheekbone. He helped her untangle what was left of her sweatshirt. A twisted clump was around her neck and had probably saved her from Roger's crushing grip. "I'm glad you wore your vest." She patted his chest. "But what happened?"

Travis led her to one of the chairs in front of the monitors and nodded at Doreen who had sat in the other chair. "She saved you."

Emily turned to her co-worker. "What did you do?"

"I slammed the box of computer paper on his head to knock him out." The full box of printer paper was next to Roger's sprawled body. "I never should have taken that worthless shit pile back. Are you all right, honey?"

Emily hugged Doreen. "Thank you."

Crane placed Roger's gun and backpack on top of the printer and handcuffed him. The movement woke him, and Crane pulled him to his feet. Travis stood between Roger and the women, his hand resting on his gun.

Roger glared at them, settling on his wife. "What happened, bitch?"

"Consider the divorce final." Doreen gave him the finger. "I'm sure you'll meet someone sweet and loving in prison." She touched her bleeding head. "Do you think we can find a doctor in this place?"

"Paramedics are on their way in." Crane waited until two officers escorted Roger out of the room before unzipping the backpack. He dumped the contents on the printer top. Condom boxes spilled out along with bundles of bills wrapped with rubber bands. "Did you open them?"

"Only one. It contained sparkling gems, and I expect the rest do, too," Emily said.

"Roger killed that woman for her jewelry?" Doreen asked.

"No, he didn't know about the jewelry until later," Emily said. "Don't you remember what he said in the hall? When he saw your van parked at the Tally-Ho, he discovered Christina was earning money doing tricks and wanted to teach her a lesson."

Doreen winced as she touched her head. "But why would he care what that woman did?"

"He loved her," Emily said. "Only, Christina didn't recognize Roger's feelings had turned from love to hate until it was too late."

"Roger dumped her battered body in her front yard where Ken picked her up," Travis said. "She must have given up any dreams of escaping because she told him the jewelry was at the Hair-em. She gave him a key, but he didn't realize it was to the van parked in the back."

"How did Roger find out about the condom boxes?" Crane opened a box. "The one we took from Christina's locker had real condoms."

"When he tortured Lucy, she told him about the backpack. Sue was visiting Lucy, and I asked her about Friday's events," Emily said. "She saw Christina leaving with a pink backpack out the back door where the van was parked."

"I gave it away." Doreen tapped her pen on the desk. "I asked if it had a kitty, and Roger realized I had it. He was using me to find out what the police knew. I was a fool to think he loved me." She smothered a sob.

"We were looking at Ken as the only suspect." Crane examined a bracelet and put it back in the box. "You helped us figure out Roger had a role in Christina's death."

Emily didn't see the two men as partners. "They worked together?"

"No," Travis said. "They didn't know what the other was planning. Unfortunately for Christina, they both attacked her on the same night for different reasons. She didn't have a chance."

"Is Ken innocent of killing her?" Emily asked.

"He didn't take Christina to the hospital and instead dumped her body in the canal. He won't go away as long as Roger, but he'll serve time." Crane repacked the backpack. "It's late. I'll lock this in the precinct vault and check it against Ken's inventory in the morning."

As Crane left, a paramedic came in. "Who needs help?"

Travis pointed at Doreen and Emily seated at the monitors. "I can wait."

Doreen looked at the clock. "I need to start midnight processing."

"You can't work," Emily said.

"We called your supervisor," Travis said. "He'll be coming in."

Doreen touched Emily's hand. "Help me start."

"You let the paramedic bandage your head, and I'll start the program," Emily said. "Once the reports start printing, you're going home. Your children will need you."

She didn't argue. The paramedic wrapped Doreen's bloody head and checked her for a concussion. They recommended she spend the night in a room for observation, but she refused. He examined Emily's face and neck while Travis removed his shirt and bulletproof vest. When he lifted his T-shirt, a circle of bruising revealed where Roger had shot him. The paramedic gave them ice packs and recommended pain medicine.

When the supervisor arrived, he took over midnight processing and told them to go home. Emily said good night to Doreen and headed for her car.

"I drove my personal car to the hospital," Travis said. "Why don't I follow you home and make sure you make it all right?"

"If you're not tired, you can rub lotion on my bruises." She purred the words. "And I'll return the favor."

His blue eyes widened. "You've had a rough night. Are you sure?"

"I caught my second wind. I had good news today and feel like celebrating." She did a little dance across the parking lot.

He caught up to her. "What good news?"

"The medical examiner hired me."

"Congratulations." He pulled her into his arms and kissed her.

"And was Crane impressed by your good work apprehending Roger?"

He nodded. "I made detective."

"I think we both need to celebrate."

Travis couldn't misunderstand her innuendo. She was planning to score a ten between the sheets even if there wasn't a scorecard in the morning.

They drove in tandem to her apartment. She waited for him to lock his vest and gun belt in the trunk of his car and follow her up the stairs. Emily tossed her purse in a chair. "I miss my backpack."

"Christina was clever hiding the jewelry in condom boxes in a kid's backpack in an old van," he said. "If only Ken hadn't given Talia that phony necklace."

"I sure would like to see all that jewelry," she said. "Amanda does beautiful work. Do you think Crane needs help inventorying his haul?"

He took a seat on the couch. "Crane is going to want every piece accounted for. The real and the fake pieces."

She removed her shoes and socks. "What will happen to the fake pieces?"

"I don't know." He watched as she wiggled out of her jeans.

"I can afford those." She was going to show him how happy she was he had survived Roger's gunshot. "I can't believe Doreen had a fortune in jewelry stashed in her locker all week." She pulled her tee off over her head.

"No one thought to look inside the condom boxes."

He stood. "Should I be getting undressed?"

She gasped. "My backpack." She grabbed her old bag, dumped the contents on the table, and snatched up the box of condoms.

He pulled his T-shirt off. "I was sincere about taking you on a date and properly courting you, but we have spent a lot of time together. If you don't think we're rushing things, I won't disagree."

She shook the box at him. "Do you know what's inside?"

He kicked off his shoes and unzipped his pants. "I'm ready if you are."

She tore open the lid, pulled out a few condom packages, and dumped the plastic bags on the table. She unwrapped the cloth and waved the emerald and diamond necklace in the air. "Isn't it beautiful?" The other bags contained a bracelet and two rings. "How much do you think they're worth?"

He picked up a ring. "You can't keep these. They're the real ones."

He was nearly naked. "Why are you wearing nothing but boxer shorts?"

"I thought you wanted me to wear one of these." He grabbed a condom package. "To celebrate being alive."

"You wear that, and I'll wear this." She fastened the necklace around her neck. "And nothing else."

His fingers traced the jewels on the necklace. "I have to take these trinkets to the police station."

She snuggled close, rubbing against his bare chest. "You're such a cop."

He snapped the hooks on her bra. "In the morning."

A word about the author...

Laura Freeman was a reporter for sixteen years for local papers and the Gannett national papers in Northeast Ohio. She won the Press Club of Cleveland's Ohio Excellence in Journalism award twice and the Ohio Newspaper Association award several times. Her novels include historical romances "Impending Love and War," "Impending Love and Death," Impending Love and Lies," "Impending Love and Capture," "Impending Love and Madness," "Impending Love and Promise," a holiday novella "Tackling Molasses Crinkles," and crime mystery "Raining Tears."

Thank you for purchasing
this publication of The Wild Rose Press, Inc.

For questions or more information
contact us at
info@thewildrosepress.com.

The Wild Rose Press, Inc.
www.thewildrosepress.com